MYTHUMBRA

MYTHUMBRA
A COLLECTION OF STORIES

Storm Constantine

IMMANION
PRESS
Stafford England

Mythumbra: A Collection of Stories
By Storm Constantine
© 2018

http://www.stormconstantine.co.uk

Cover by Danielle Lainton
Interior layout and illustrations by Storm Constantine, except for illustration on page 120 by Danielle Lainton

Set in Palatino Linotype

IP0138
ISBN 978-1-907737-87-9

An Immanion Press Edition
http://www.immanion-press.com
info@immanion-press.com

CONTENTS

THE DRAKE LORDS OF KYLA

First published in NewCon Press's Legends, *edited by Ian Whates, this story was inspired by the landscapes of Pandaria, an imaginary country in the online role-playing game, World of Warcraft, which I've played and travelled in for over a decade. WoW's landscapes have often given me ideas for stories, and Pandaria in particular felt vibrant and steeped in ancient history – even though it's only a virtual world. The Lighurd people in this story are very loosely based on WoW's Saurok race, in that both are akin to lizards, but the similarities end with appearances.*

The City in the Mists is reached via ten thousand shallow steps, which rise from the verdant farming valleys of the province of Tusk, up into the clouds and the land beyond. It is like venturing into the afterlife, or the secret country at the top of an enchanted ladder of vines: Kyla.

Halfway up the steps, where by now your lungs are hot with pain from trying to breathe the rarefied air and your limbs like the jelly-stars that cluster in the warm waters of the distant south coast, you will see a fairytale edifice looming out of the mists, taking on form, with its many floors, wooden struts and protective serpent carvings. Clouds of incense hang around it, unable to rise or fall in the thick air. This is *The Last Inn Before the Mountains*, the name of which is not entirely accurate, but for travellers conjures a delicious frisson of inevitability and danger. Beyond here – nothing of the world you know.

The mists of this land are clouds because here the land

touches the sky. The clouds are not always there and when they are absent you might feel that the aching blue you gaze upon is truly Paradise. You will see things in the sky you have never seen before; creatures that fly without wings, daytime stars and birds the size of lions.

There is no entry into Kyla but for this one path. To the north it faces the cold ocean with cliffs thousands of feet high. The Black Mountains surround it on all other sides, but for this narrow passageway, the steps and then, beyond the inn, the throat through the mountains by water, the Old Path.

At the *Last Inn,* and the small village of Semum that straggles around it, you will first encounter the Lighurd. You will no doubt have been greatly anticipating this meeting, and your mind will be full of fancies about it. Then you will see your first two or three, squatting in the frozen dust outside the inn, the ground imprinted with the pattern of their hot, webbed feet. They might be playing knuckle-bone dice with a gang of guides, flaring their quills at one another, uttering the strange yet surprisingly lively croak that is their laughter. They were once dragons, this race. This is why you're here; you want to listen to them hiss of greater times.

It is not far to the ruins of Gyth, the City in the Mists, from the Last Inn; just a boat ride through the mountain tunnel and then on foot for less than two days. Guides there are aplenty, all eager for you to fill their purses – and they are not difficult to fill, this being a poor land, and you, of course, rich. Swarthy Sarks, black-and-yellow-skinned Meronnes, fey Fards; each of these native races are exotic and intriguing to travel with. But there are Lighurds too for hire, and who better to lead you into the whispering mists than the most ancient inhabitants of this lost realm? No, it was never really lost, merely forgotten, neglected. But that aside, your eyes might light upon a lone Lighurd, squatting apart from his companions, quills lowered and hanging long down his back, snake visage tattooed with mystic curls. You will glance at the gracefully long-fingered, clawed hands, the muscled thighs that might be scaled in turquoise, cobalt or deepest emerald. Never will you have seen a creature at once so primitive yet so magnificent. He might sense your interest and turn his long face towards you, gaze back with those golden snake eyes, nod once to indicate 'yes, I am for hire'. Your heart might pause then, as if you have won a great and unimaginable prize; a treasure from the past.

Despite what you might see, close up, of this incredible creature – the length and sharpness of his claws, the wide maw that might contain too many teeth – there is no need to be afraid. Lighurd guides – all male, for their females are rarely seen – will neither rob nor damage you. To the very few, for some unfathomed reason, they might even sell one of their whelps to take home with you. The stories of these young ones sickening and pining away from the Black Mountains are untrue. They will outlive you and have to be bequeathed to your descendants or gifted to someone who might fancy such an ornament in their home. Lighurdkind can never be servants – *quite* – and no, I have not heard of them being taken as lovers. There is no such familiarity between our species.

So then, through me you know something of this land, its people, and you want to know what happened when I went to Kyla, how I came to acquire my companion.

I had been advised to travel there in the month of Pearly Rains, this being the most clement time to broach the ten thousand steps. I wanted to see Gyth, as every young historian does; it is an initiation into the mysteries of our calling, this distant, haunted tumble of stones. Not many can make the journey, its prime obstacle being the cost of the expedition rather than any physical difficulty. Kyla lies at the centre of the distant continent of Oort. Merchant ships from Tasmagore will offer accommodation for passengers, but not cheaply. The way is hard, the ocean tumultuous. My Order had paid for my journey, and also for me to be instructed in the language of Oort for a year before I left the University at Tasmagore. My tutors had given me certain tasks to complete, such as people to meet and ingratiate myself with, relics to secure, stories to record. My itinerary was full, and I'd been four months in Oort before I even had the time to turn my thoughts towards the Black Mountains. By then, I had made my way slowly to Tusk and the lush Valley Below the Steps. Here I had been greeted by the mayor of Valley's Heart, become a guest in his sprawling wooden house. Foreigners visited these parts for only one reason; the desire to ascend. The inhabitants appeared amused by this.

The mayor said to me, 'Kyla lies upon our dreams. Yes, we go up there, but the Lighurd never come down *here*. The climb is long, the air thin, and there is not much left other than memories. If you seek memories, naturally the land will call to you.'

I dreamed of it every night before I finally made my climb; my sleep buffeted by the scream of gigantic birds and oppressed by images of cyclopean remains that were stone, that were flesh, that were stone.

The journey too started like a dream. I was given a guide from Valley's Heart who would take me to Semum, since she had business there at the Inn. In fact, most transactions between the Valley and Kyla took place at this inn, Heartfolk not having much desire to travel further than that. The trade was mainly in relics; the Heartfolk would buy them with their own produce, and then sell them on to merchants travelling to the coast and beyond, to lands where the antiquities of Kyla were much prized.

My guide, Zharn, was a grand-daughter of the mayor. We set out just before dawn: Zharn, two grey goats with yard-long horns who would carry our belongings, and me. Zharn was short and stout; at sixteen years old a veteran of this journey. We were both dressed in the heavy, cream woollen tunic and trousers favoured by the Oorts, embellished with rich coloured scarves at the waist and with ornate embroidery at cuffs and hems. Our boots were of toughened goat leather, scored with spiritual symbols.

The climb began at a huge stone archway cut into the cliffs, and the first few miles were completed in shadow. There were no mists yet, just the murk cast by the overhanging rocks and the grey predawn light that didn't illuminate much at all. Zharn lit a torch, which she placed in a sconce conveniently attached to a horn of one of the goats.

After only an hour my thighs were hurting greatly, although we had now emerged from the tunnel of rock and the steps were far wider. We no longer needed a torch. Zharn grinned at my weakness but let us pause while she made a fire to brew us breakfast tea. The goats, hung with bells, tinkled as they chewed the tough, yellow grasses beside the path. As I sat, gratefully, and sipped the scalding sweet tea, I gazed at my surroundings: this wide and shallow stair, worn by many feet; how ancient it was. I could feel history around me, as if time was but an illusion. The era of the dragons is long gone; it has become merely legend. Few people really believe the Lighurd are the debased descendants of dragons, but rather that the stories of a dragon race grew up around the lizard people, who had perhaps once been a greater civilisation and had somehow lost it all. I had then no idea if this was true, but what was undeniable was that Kyla was full of mighty ruins. Whoever had lived there had been a great and powerful race and they had been physically huge, if the size of the ruins was anything to go by.

After the tea was finished, Zharn put out her fire and we set off once more. 'Mistress Marala, we climb for nearly a day,' said Zharn. 'Don't expect tea every hour.'

I managed a laugh. 'I have travelled to many far lands and have climbed mountains before. My legs will become accustomed to the ascent.'

Zharn smirked; she did not believe me.

Strangely, the steps were busier than I thought they'd be. We came across merchant camps at corners in the path, where there were wide verges fragrant with herbs, and space for tents to be erected and rugs to be spread out in order to display wares. We passed other travellers, again predominantly traders, descending the path. Zharn swapped produce with just about everyone we met. She was particularly taken with a charming little black goat a Meronne boy wanted to sell her, but then hardened her heart because it was too expensive.

We did have to pause our journey a lot, because no matter how hardy I'd considered myself to be, the climb punished my body. By midday I could barely breathe. Happily, Zharn wanted to linger at every camp we encountered and examine the wares arrayed on the rugs. I bought a small serpent head fashioned in soapy, dark green stone; an unbelievably ancient relic. Zharn was scornful. 'Mistress, you can pick those up by the dozen in Gyth. Why pay?'

But to me it seemed part of the adventure.

By late afternoon, having made good time, (so perhaps I wasn't as feeble as Zharn had feared), we reached *The Last Inn Before the Mountains*. I shall never forget the thrill of turning that final corner of the path, going beyond the last step and seeing the high, peaked roofs of the immense building rearing before us. It was surrounded by a wide veranda, crowded with chairs and tables, none of which matched. Here, guides, merchants, brigands and perhaps even slavers, sat together talking and laughing loudly, making flamboyant gestures, and clearly getting greatly drunk. The air was thick with the intoxicating perfume of incense and the fume of *makh*, which many of the company were smoking. Three musicians were making a racket upon strange stringed instruments I'd not seen before, comprising complicated webs of strings and delicate wooden struts. Another hammered upon a hand drum and yodelled. Altogether it was a scene of chaos. I didn't even think of Lighurds at that moment, let alone see one.

'It's not usually this busy,' Zharn told me. 'There was a fair held at Yee-Anan, the first town beyond the Old Path.

It finished today.' She grinned greedily. 'They will have much to sell, and they are nearly all drunk. Why don't you get us a room for the night? I won't go home until tomorrow and I believe my lodgings were part of the fee.'

'Of course.'

I sidled up the crowded inn steps and between the haphazardly-placed chairs on the veranda, but no one gave me a second glance. Inside, I found myself in an immense, high-ceilinged room fashioned entirely from pale wood and again crowded with tables and chairs, most of which were occupied. The air was far muggier and hotter than on the veranda outside and the din even louder. A grill was set up in one corner, smoking voluminously, but issuing wonderful aromas of cooking spiced meat and root vegetables. Saffron rice steamed in great pans, smelling like incense. I realised how hungry I was.

Owing to the amount of guests in the establishment, I feared I'd have difficulty securing us a room, but the woman in black silk, who stood behind a high desk near the door, dealing with reservations, made no protest. I took one room with two beds to save money.

'Trading here?' the woman asked. Her long, pointed fingernails were lacquered a very shiny obsidian hue. A band of black cosmetic was painted across her face, from which her eyes peered, shockingly white with inky irises.

'I'm a Historian from Tasmagore,' I said. 'I've come to view the ruins and... whatever else is found beyond the Black Mountains.'

The woman grinned. Several of her teeth were studded with gemstones – blue and white crystal. 'Need a guide, then. Or join a caravan.'

'Yes, I will attend to this in the morning.'

'Will keep my ears open for you,' said the woman. 'Here's your key. Room 38. Third floor.' The key was small and black and seemed hardly a key at all, as if it would fit any lock in the building.

Zharn had been seeing to stabling the goats, and now shouldered her way into the inn. She grabbed my arm. 'Let's go back out.'

'Food,' I said plaintively, pointing at the grill.

'There's better outside,' Zharn insisted, 'by the hot spring.'

The atmosphere was quieter round the back of the inn. A dozen roaring braziers warmed the air. Some patrons, of both genders, were sitting naked in the heated waters of a bubbling pool in the rock, lit by a multitude of tiny firefly lamps that had been hung in the trees around them. Those languishing in the waters seemed faintly drugged; they spoke in low voices and their laughter was gentle. Nearby was another grill, and here a pretty boy was also cooking. Watching his careful, graceful movements was like observing a ritual being enacted; he clearly took his job seriously.

Carrying wooden trays crowded with dishes of beautifully-scented food, Zharn and I sat down at a table beneath a tree blazing with red and blue points of light. The subtle radiance dyed the girl's skin; she looked half supernatural. She smiled at me, uttered 'welcome to the door step of Kyla,' and then spooned a vast quantity of pale yellow rice into her mouth.

'It's wonderful,' I said, gazing beyond her.

Ahead of us, to the north, against the star-sequinned sky, reared the mountain barrier that shut Kyla off from the rest of the country, but for the tunnel that pierced it.

The Black Mountains were unthinkably old, the realm of gods long lost to human imagination, but not perhaps to the minds of Lighurds.

'I need to find a guide,' I said.

Zharn nodded. 'One will find *you*, don't worry. The inn hostess will have passed the word about you. Already they will be debating which one of them will slim your purse.'

'Tell me of Lighurds,' I said. 'I didn't notice any here. I'd like a Lighurd guide.'

Zharn wiped a long grain of rice from the corner of her mouth. 'You foreigners are obsessed with them.'

'Well, we've nothing like them at home. Tell me now, are they fierce, cruel, mindless, what?'

'They are men in serpent skins,' said Zharn, 'to be feared no more than any other man, and yet... They are different too, owing to the age of their race. There is no older species on this Earth, or so my grandmother told me. It weighs heavily upon them sometimes.'

'What of their women? Do they look different to the males?'

Zharn nodded, took another mouthful of food and spoke through it. 'If you are lucky, you might see one. They do not interact with humans greatly.'

'And yet a man told me back in the Valley they will sometimes sell their children to foreigners...'

'That is true, though rare. Just because they are old and primitive does not mean they have no desire for their young to see the world. The humans who come here are rich and offer good opportunities for the youngsters of any race or species. That much you must concede.'

'A good point,' I said, although really it didn't ring true with me. The explanation was too mundane.

'But then,' Zharn continued, suddenly appearing

wistful, 'I've heard there are people who can't bear the company of Lighurdkind in their homes, because some nights they keen for the vanished glory of their people, and the song is beautiful and terrible, capable of driving the most sensitive of listeners into the deepest melancholy. They are reminded of the futility of greatness, how glory is fleeting, and nobility may be lost. Those long, scaled throats that hold no fire may burn a person with song.'

'That is beautiful, Zharn,' I said, somewhat aghast at her sudden eloquence.

She shrugged. 'My grandmother says it to people.'

Later in the evening, I was approached several times by individuals claiming they would be my best guide into Kyla. All of them, to my eyes, offered the promise of an intriguing journey, but I was waiting for something. You, of course, may have guessed what. He came to me as midnight drew near and a group of Roosha priests began to chant to the Goddess of Turning Days. Drunken inn patrons took up the song, as did the half dozen in the pool nearby.

'None of the cackwits here have my sense of the road,' my latest applicant, a great bear of a Sark with a huge yet silky black beard, was saying to me. 'I can take you to places few travellers see.'

All of them had said that. Perhaps they did not all speak of the same places.

I nodded slowly at his words, somewhat intoxicated by the saffron-infused wine Zharn had fetched for us. 'What is your price?' I asked.

'Too much,' said an extremely sibilant, whispery voice behind me. At first, I could not distinguish if it issued from a male or female throat.

The guide before me laughed good-naturedly. Whoever stood at my back was a friend of his. I could smell this person: dry, musky, hot.

'It is me she wants,' they said.

The man narrowed his eyes. 'And what interests you so much about her?' He glanced at me, pointing over my shoulder with a stiff finger. 'I warn you. Don't be misled. He sees some profit in this.'

I turned round, because not to do so would have seemed odd by now. He towered over me; seven feet of Lighurd. His emerald and black striped quills were very long and reached to his waist, many decorated with silver rings. On either side of his nostril slits, delicate tendrils drooped, rather like the whiskers of a cat fish. He spoke like a man, yet was not a man. It seemed preposterous he could speak the language of Oort, albeit in a struggling manner, because his jaw was not fashioned to utter it. He had no soft lips to form the words yet, even so, he spoke clearly. That always puzzled me.

'What is your price?' I asked him. Whatever it was I would afford it.

They called him Agouzi; this was not his real name. He came from a Lighurd settlement this side of the mountains; trader people, naturally. Zharn and I sat with the guide and his Lighurd friend, plus a few others who ambled over to join us, until at least two in the morning. Once our business arrangement had been finalised, Agouzi said nothing more to me, but I was aware of him constantly, also aware it was a feeling very similar to being near a person to whom you are greatly attracted, yet it was not that with him.

Zharn and I rose later than usual the following day, both of us bearing the ill-effects of drinking too much alcohol at such a high altitude, after a long day's climb. As we ate breakfast in the vast room downstairs in the inn, I began to wish Zharn would continue the journey with me and even suggested carefully she might consider it.

'I can't,' Zharn replied. 'I have to go to the market in the Jade Hills tomorrow. Don't worry. You'll be quite safe. The Lighurd will look after you.'

'They are... *trustworthy*, then?'

'Like all the people in this place, they know where their money comes from. Only a fool would hurt a traveller; they are walking purses, every one.'

'So not even robbery?'

'A robbed person doesn't recommend a place to their friends,' Zharn said. 'Even less so if they are dead.'

'I will bring you something back,' I said. 'From the ruins. You have been good to me, Zharn. I appreciate it.'

Zharn shrugged. 'We will hold a party on your return.' She stood up. 'Ah, here is your guide. Travel well, friend Marala.' She bowed to me and departed.

And there stood Agouzi, regarding me inscrutably. His long black tongue slid out and licked the air.

'Would you take tea before we set off?' I asked, gesturing at the cups and pot on my table.

He shook his head, making his quills rattle. 'We should begin,' he said, 'or we will miss the next raft to Yee-Anan.'

I had already settled my account with the inn, so I only had to pick up my travel-bag to be ready. Zharn had instructed me not to buy pack goats before Yee-Anan, since it would be cheaper there; I intended to return with them laden.

Two dozen people crowded onto the raft that would carry us through the rock. A girl lit torches at each corner of the vessel even before we entered the dark. I sat next to Agouzi on a bench, pressed against him owing to the crowd. His body felt unnaturally hot. He seemed barely aware of me and did not speak. I found it hard to believe he was there beside me, like a myth come to life. I wondered what thoughts he had, or *how* he thought.

The tunnel beneath the mountains took two hours to traverse. There was quite a jolly atmosphere aboard the raft as the pilot's assistant, who had lit the torches, dispensed refreshments and then began to regale her water-bound audience with various recitals and songs. Lulled back into a half-doze by her lilting voice, I gazed dreamily at the tunnel walls; black rock occasionally starred with crystal veins.

When we emerged at Yee-Anan, and the pilot swung the raft up against the wide but sagging jetty, Agouzi politely suggested we might hire our goats and then continue our journey immediately. Perhaps he sensed I would be seduced by all the merchant stalls scattered about the town, which was really little more than a village. The buildings were old and low, sway-backed like geriatric horses. I pressed paper money into Agouzi's hot, clawed hands. 'Buy us goats,' I said, 'and anything else we might need.'

He bowed his head and loped off, switching his long tail in a manner that to me suggested faint irritation. But perhaps Lighurds don't express themselves with their tails in the same way cats do.

While I waited, I sat upon a tree stump near the jetty and shrouded my eyes with one hand to look around. The thin air sparkled with clarity and the smudge of a few clouds was high, high above me. I felt chilly, but not cold. The sun blazed without impediment. Beyond the flag-hung northern gateway to the town, I glimpsed a spreading vista of hilly plains, covered in gold and green lichens or grasses. Immense carrion birds sailed upon the air currents, uttering mournful cries.

Presently, Agouzi returned leading two black goats, each hung with four capacious panniers. Two of these baskets appeared to be full of supplies and camping equipment. I didn't expect any change from my money and didn't receive any. It was of no consequence.

'If the goats aren't enough, you may hire an Egni carrier later,' Agouzi said. 'The people of Kyla are used to transporting heavy loads.'

'That depends on how successful my foraging is,' I said, in what I wincingly realised was rather a flirtatious tone. 'I hope you will guide me to places of wonder where I may plunder the past fantastically.'

I realised then that when you are faced with a being who cannot physically smile or frown, lacking the fleshy facial tissue to do so, it is difficult to judge reactions and moods. Agouzi just stared at me. Perhaps he didn't have a sense of humour. I got to my feet. 'Well, lead on!'

A rutted road led north, with thin straw-like grass growing like a stiff mane along its centre. People riding goats, slightly larger than our pack animals, trotted past us, waving hello. I wondered whether riding-goats might also have been a luxury I could have afforded. The natives of the area seemed to comprise mainly a short-statured, dark-skinned race, whose faces were almost invisible owing to the large hats, helmets and complicated veils and turbans they favoured. I had yet seen no Lighurds other than Agouzi.

'Where are your people?' I asked him as we walked, each on one side of the centre tuft of the road. 'I thought Kyla was your land, yet all I see are these quaint little people, who are indisputably human.' I smiled at him.

Agouzi cast me a sidelong glance. 'It is the time of year,' he said, as if that meant anything to me.'

'I see... religious festivals, something like that?'

'Something like that,' he replied. 'Once we leave the main road, you might see more of my kind. We might need to buy supplies from them, in between the Egni settlements.'

'Egni being the... little people.'

'Yes.'

'People never speak of them when discussing Kyla; it is always Lighurds who are the topic of conversation.'

'And you know little of either of our races,' Agouzi observed, but not in a sharp tone.

'I'm surprised more people don't come here,' I said. 'It's so beautiful, so... unspoilt.'

'They will stop altogether when the plunder is finished and everything is gone,' Agouzi said.

'It's important to preserve the past.' I was aware I sounded too defensive. 'We learn much from it that helps us understand how we are now.'

'This land is not your past,' Agouzi said, without inflection.

I fell silent after that, sensing whatever I said would provoke similar answers that would, from any other mouth, sound sour and criticising. From Agouzi's mouth, it was difficult to divine his thoughts on the matter.

Conversation discouraged between us by my companion, we travelled on for the rest of the day in near silence. Occasionally, Agouzi would direct my attention to particular landmarks and tell me something of their history. Always ruins – sometimes just humps on the ground covered in lichen. My spirits fell, despite the clear, heady air; this land felt like the graveyard of all the species of the world. I felt too listless to reply to Agouzi's remarks or question him for further details.

We paused once to refresh ourselves in the afternoon, but after building a small fire and preparing us tea and hot spiced rice, Agouzi wandered off by himself. He took his bowl of rice to a clump of rocks some distance away and there squatted to consume his meal, his back to me.

At sunfall, we came upon an Egni settlement and Agouzi suggested I take a room with one of the local families. This I did, and was somewhat revived by the cheerful tribe who offered me accommodation almost as soon as we stepped beyond the gate of their village. These people spoke a dialect I could barely comprehend, but they seemed happy simply to talk *at* me, and did not appear to expect responses. Chattering, they dragged me to their home and offered me vast amounts to eat and drink. I was very tired, and after eating collapsed upon the mattress in the attic to which they directed me and fell into the deepest of slumbers. Where Agouzi slept I had no idea.

In the morning, I was awoken by the family and given more food. Agouzi presented himself at their door minutes after I'd finished eating. I paid my hosts and we set out once more. Today we would reach Gyth.

Now the air was colder, and once a flurry of snow passed before my eyes, vanishing almost in an instant, as if the gods of the weather were teasing me. There was no one else upon the road now, which surprised me. I'd expected a steady stream of plunderers, whose motivations would not be quite as noble as mine. The wind wove a lonely song, which was quite beautiful. Snow leopards, who appeared almost tame, lay, sat or stalked among the high rocks beside the road, observing us mildly. Sticks of incense the thickness of my wrist burned at intervals along the path, releasing a heavy perfume. I wondered if it was this that lulled the leopards.

Midmorning, Agouzi led us off the main track onto a tiny, twisting goat path between sharp black rocks. Here, tufts of a heavily-scented herb grew in the deep fissures, making the air almost narcotic. I could hear the bells of goats but could see none nearby. And now the mists came to claim us, stealing in like prowling cats, wisps that might be soft paws and tails, or hot carnivore breath. I mentioned none of these fancies to Agouzi, but even so he said to me, 'The servants of Shah Mahra, the Great Snow Leopard, travel in the mists. They observe the hearts of those who come here.'

'And do they judge?' My question came out sharp.

Agouzi laughed softly. 'That is not their function. Look up there.'

I raised my head and saw enormous dark shapes motionless in the dancing tendrils of mist. As I stared, these shapes resolved into the forms of two black granite leopards sitting erect, yet with their heads lowered; a watchful stance.

'We approach Tin gurra Lath, the gateway to Gyth,'

Agouzi said, 'and here are its guardians. In years gone by, this was a city of towers so high their crowns brushed the realms of the sky. Its people rarely ventured into the lower areas and the towers were connected by bridges of golden ropes. It was called the City Above the Birds in the modern tongue.'

In the silence that followed these words, I peered through the dance of the mist, and tried to imagine the ghosts of these towers around me, but all that remained were stumps; I could see that now. A graveyard of tumbled masonry stretched into the distance. Agouzi led the way over and through it, nimble on his long feet. I came more unsteadily behind, still giddy from the gift of the rock herbs. Occasionally, I would spy a face in the stones, the ripped visage of a tumbled statue, blind in surprise. But these were too big to pick up. Everything was. The fallen stones were mountains in themselves and cast thick dark shadows. I found the atmosphere oppressive.

'How far to Gyth now?' I asked, my voice unnervingly muffled.

'Beyond the gateway,' Agouzi said, pausing ahead of me. He allowed me to catch up. 'At the north gate of Tin gurra Lath lies the Queen's Step, or the wide road to Gyth. The two cities were almost one, except Gyth was on the ground.'

Perhaps it was simply the combined effects of the rarefied air and the scented herbs that made me so dizzy, but I was finding it increasingly difficult to keep walking. Agouzi, now quite a distance ahead of me, again paused to wait. He appraised my condition and then, stooping down upon one knee, said, 'climb upon my back.'

And so I entered the city of Gyth like a child, riding

upon the back of an adult.

The Queen's Step was not a long road and, once we emerged from the depressing stones of fallen Tin gurra Lath, the path swept down gracefully into a valley of golden grasses. Amid the mist, I saw trees with white bark and golden leaves, as if it were autumn, but the season was young. Nervous white deer grazed upon the grasses, pausing skittishly to observe our descent before bounding away, becoming one with the clouds around us. The Queen's Step was remarkably well preserved, each slab of its surface carved with different pictures. The images themselves were somewhat worn down but I was sure I could discern depictions of Lighurdkind upon them. As we drew nearer to the city, the mist rolled itself up, drawing back to reveal the mysteries of Gyth to me. 'Set me down,' I said to Agouzi.

It is difficult to describe what I saw. My first thought was that the city had been *scythed*, in that its buildings had been sheered away at the same height, as if with an immense blade. Even so, they remained gigantic, constructed from pale stone that now glistened in sunlight. This was a city of columns and turrets, of hidden walkways, narrow streets and wide plazas. Ceremonial ways – or roads I took to be as such – radiated from the centre to each point of the compass. Everything about the place seemed to whisper, 'come, I am waiting to be explored. Look upon me. See my many ways, my empty palaces that are perhaps not quite empty, my temples blistered with the jewels of gods. Come to me now; immerse yourself within me.'

Gyth was, without doubt, a goddess of cities. And I was compelled to run, again like a child, into the goddess's waiting arms. As I ran, the years seemed to peel back, and both Gyth and I became younger; the buildings became bigger around me. And my legs were pumping so fast I could barely keep up with myself; I would tumble into the city. And tumble I did, down the last stretch of the Queen's Step, over and over and over, as if I were trapped in a kaleidoscope, colours of sky and city and landscape blurring into one.

The sky is a queen's gown of stars, encrusted so thickly it is a blanket of light. I am lying on my back upon stone. I can hear myself panting and the beat of blood in my head. No, I am not lying, I am sitting. Images around me are shadows yet becoming more distinct with every moment. Am I dreaming? I'm unsure, but I'm not afraid. I am where I'm supposed to be. I hear the tumult of many voices raised in excitement. From the ground beneath me comes a sensation of throbbing that is not quite a sound, but as I fix my attention upon it, so it becomes louder, more recognisable as sound; a deep and immeasurable moan. I'm reminded of whale song, but it is not that. Now, I see I am sitting with many others within a stone amphitheatre that is the size of a small town. My companions are Lighurds, all of them, who are far taller than Agouzi; they are true giants. They are dressed in garments of metal scales that emulate the gleam of their natural scales. Some have decorated their quills most fancifully with streaming or spiky ornaments. I am looking for females, but they all appear the same to me. How would it be possible to tell? I can perceive now, upon the cliff-like walls of the structure, great pipes or horns from which the immense moaning notes are emanating. This strange music stirs my blood, for I can tell it heralds an approach of some kind. Then, wooden gates at either end of the amphitheatre swing open in a slow, ponderous fashion. There is only darkness beyond them. The horns issue their notes a final time – a blast that shakes my very fibres – and then *shapes* lumber forth from the darkness.

These are creatures the size of cathedrals, taking careful steps with their surprisingly graceful webbed feet. I wonder if they are dragons, but then I'd always believed dragons to be beautiful, attenuated beings, at one with the air. These before me are incontrovertibly creatures of earth. Their hides are the colour of clay, although one is lighter in tone than the other. Their immense heads are reptilian but blunted, and have no quills like the Lighurds'. They are bipedal with legs proportionately larger than their arms, and long thick tails culminating in what appear to be natural spiked clubs. They face each other, clapping their clawed hands, shaking their heads, switching their tails. Above them, the horns boom once more, and around me the crowd rises to their feet, uttering cries. I expect the beasts to fight to the death, conjuring a greedy blood-lust from the spectators. No doubt they have placed bets upon the combat.

And then a lone Lighurd steps into the arena. He must be around eleven or twelve feet tall, yet is an insect in comparison to the snorting giants. They turn their heads sideways to regard him. Their mobile toes flex in the dirt of the arena floor. Is he a sacrifice? I don't want to see, convinced something terrible and sickening is about to happen. The Lighurd has copper and emerald scales, and is draped in a garment that appears to be fashioned of metal disks, yet it moves around his body like linen. He raises his arms and throws back his head, striding slowly towards the gigantic beasts. When he stands between them, he raises his quills, which surround him like a starburst. Crystal ornaments upon them capture the light of the sky and he becomes a being of starlight.

The beasts begin to circle around the Lighurd, very slowly. And now the crowd is uttering a crooning song, their lean bodies swaying as one in a sinuous dance. Someone next to me reaches for my hand and I see for the first time that I am Lighurd too; my hand is long and clawed and I am wearing a ring with an immense jewel, perhaps a topaz, on one of the fingers. I am singing too. I know the song. We are calling to the stars, to our ancestors. We are calling upon the wisdom of the Ahn Toth, these two immense beings before us. We have called them down from the Holy Peak to work their magic for us. They have travelled for over a week to reach us. They are the last of their kind.

The Lighurd in the arena is Kurra'Koor, the chosen one of our season. The Ahn Toth loom over him, weaving the air with their claws, drawing substance from it that I cannot see, cannot understand. They sing, too, and the sounds they make are tools to change reality. The starlight becomes an inferno around the body of Kurra'Koor. He can barely be perceived within it, and then it somehow falls and folds around him like a garment. A deity stands before us, clothed in light. Kurra'Koor's scales are of luminous pearl. Where once were quills are now spreading vanes or fins that gently float upon the air; unutterably beautiful. The crowd falls to their knees before this vision, myself among them. I feel a stirring deep within my being that is at once holy and lustful. I am also aware of a feeling of relief, as if some part of me feared this ritual might not work.

The paler of the Ahn Toth gently lifts Kurra'Koor with

one hand as if he were a doll, only now he is no longer he but she, as is the being who holds her. She places Kurra'Koor upon her shoulder, where there is a convenient seat between knobs of bone-like protuberances. We will follow Kurra'Koor to the White Temple of Spring Flowers, and there our next generation will be created. For some time thereafter Kurra'Koor will bear eggs within the sanctum of the temple. Each one of us will have a son and we will know our own by sight. There is never any mistake over that.

I am given no more than this.

When I came back to true consciousness Agouzi was cradling me in his lap. One hot hand was on my brow. I felt the tips of his claws against my left temple. He was not looking at me but out across the city.

'Does it still happen that way?' I asked him.

He tilted his head to regard me, in the way the great Ahn Toth had done with Kurra'Koor.

'I *saw*,' I said. 'Kurra'Koor... the Ahn Toth...'

'They were the last of their kind,' Agouzi replied at last. 'We had to learn what they knew.'

'Were they... your ancestors?'

'In some ways,' Agouzi replied. 'We were certainly connected. Once the Ahn Toth ruled this land you call Kyla. They made us to survive them, but before they left the land there was much they had to teach us.'

I struggled away from him, still awkward in my movements, disorientated. I was surprised he did not question me about what I'd seen, or *how* I'd seen, but then I was not surprised at all. 'It was so unthinkably long ago. Your people... what happened?' I gestured at the ruins around me.

'Others came who coveted our land. They flew in above the mountains. There were wars. There always are. But as you said, that was long ago, and even the conquerors are dust.' He stood up. 'You must drink.'

Agouzi fetched me water from our supplies, which I drank greedily, while Agouzi squatted before me, observing me, perhaps concerned my experience had made me ill. The sky seemed to be ringing like a vast bell, but perhaps that was in my head.

He did not owe me explanations. What I'd seen had been private, a racial memory of his kind. Why it had been shown to me particularly, I did not know. Yet still I had to ask. 'You are all male until a certain season, then one becomes your queen?'

'We came down the Queen's Step,' he said, as if this explained everything. Getting to his feet, he offered to me a hand. 'Come.'

By the time we reached the arena, or what was left of it, the moon had risen, blue in the velvet sky, surrounded by her starry court. The place was just a jumble of pale stones that dreamed of starlight. The Lighurd of the past were gone, aeons ago. Those who lived in Kyla now were very different. Did they still build? Were there fabulous academies hidden away somewhere, full of arcane astronomical equipment? Were the bones of the last of the Ahn Toth enshrined in some immense underground chamber, locked in by secrets and labyrinths, and guardians not of this world? I wanted to believe these things.

'Were you dragons?' I asked wistfully.

Agouzi squeezed my hand. 'If that is what you wish.' He threw back his head and uttered an ululating sound. For a while this echoed around the immense silent ruins, then other songs rose in response. My skin prickled.

'It is our *choice* now,' Agouzi said.

And then they came over the broken stones, Lighurd maidens with their floating hair that was not hair, their almost feline yet serpent-like faces, their utter grace, their indescribable ancient beauty.

'I will give to you my son,' Agouzi said. 'Take him out into the younger world and tell him stories, show him wonders as is the privilege of your profession. He will tell you stories in return. When you are dead, he will bring your stories back to us.' He opened his mouth, narrowed his eyes: a grin. 'Perhaps even before that.'

I managed a shaky laugh. 'The children you give us, they are chroniclers.'

Agouzi again narrowed his eyes in a smile. 'We are intrigued by the follies of youth.'

The ethereal Lighurd women had formed a circle around us now. Their light was not supernatural; their fish-fin hair merely snared the starlight and stored it.

One reached out to me and I took her pearly hand. She had chosen me in some way, and so had chosen Agouzi. 'Can you be like her?' I asked Agouzi softly, 'if you wish?'

'I *am* like her,' he said. 'Let the others take you, they will feed you. At dawn I will return to you.'

The women took me to a bower among the golden-leafed trees. Here they bid me recline upon a bed of flowers and grasses and gave to me delicacies enjoyed by their people. The nervous deer were drawn to investigate and some of the women fed them. I lay back and gazed up at the firmament. Across it flowed an attenuated, graceful shape – a serpent of the sky that flew without wings. Or perhaps it was simply a flight of night-singing birds, like lace against the stars.

In the morning, Agouzi returned to me, as he'd promised, and I woke from perhaps the most refreshing sleep I'd ever experienced. The Lighurd women had gone, but they had left me gifts; a delicate stole of silver disks, a collection of tiny statuettes depicting goddesses and spirits of the land, four nets of fruit, two cooked birds, some steaks of a meat I took to be goat, spiced potatoes wrapped in muslin, and a flagon of golden liquor. Agouzi too seemed pleased with the food and drink they'd left behind.

We set out again, leaving Gyth behind, seeking out further remains even more ancient. You can see what I brought back with me – all these treasures. I travelled for three months with Agouzi among the vast ruins of Kyla. I found so many wonders, great and small, I had to buy another goat and hire two Egni as well. We climbed the highest mountain in the world, and at the top I shouted out my wishes for the future, since that peak is closest to the gods and they can hear you clearly there. We visited the vast catacombs that wormed through the mountain, filled with the tombs and creations of monstrous beings, the like of which I'd never seen before. Lighurds were more human in comparison. We visited a secret province few outsiders have ever been shown that is like the Garden of Creation, populated by a race of people so fair they must have been hidden away by the gods for their own protection. I have many stories to tell, but the one you really want me to finish telling is about the gift Agouzi gave to me, isn't it?

He was waiting for us as we returned to the ruins of Gyth. Poor child, he might have already been there for days before he spied us. He and Agouzi called to one another, long before I could see him with my physical eyes. He was like a smaller version of Agouzi rather than having the proportions of a human child. His quills were pale and soft and did not quite reach his shoulders.

'Leshi will have told him he is to go with you,' Agouzi said to me as we approached his son. Leshi must be the Lighurd with whom he'd... well I suppose the word is 'mated'.

'Aren't you afraid for him?' I asked.

'No,' Agouzi replied, again with his usual lack of inflection. His confidence could mean many things: he felt I was trustworthy, or the child was capable of looking after himself, or Agouzi could already see his son's future. I still don't know which of those it was. The young Lighurd's name is Ran'zar and I brought him home with me.

My employers were very interested in him, of course, and he was – and is – very interested in them. He has a great curiosity for the world and is less concerned about our past than how we are now. Sights and experiences are like food to him. He knows the past of his kind – all of it, because I believe it is handed down as clear memories from one generation to another – but he will not speak of it to me. Not yet. As a child, he is more interested in his own desires and that is knowledge of us and our world.

Does he sing? Yes, all Lighurds sing, but I have yet to be driven to despair by the sound. He makes up songs in the evening about what he's seen during the day. But he is young, and for now I am happy he has innocence and a sense of wonder at the world. Only with the passing of time does history have more relevance to us.

Ran'zar will be less changed by his life here among us

than I was from the brief time I spent in Kyla. I *will* go back. It's as if I have no choice in the matter. There is a secret life to Kyla that I am compelled to discover. No, not yet, but in some years' time. And I will see again the pale ruins of Gyth, the golden orchards around her and the white deer who graze there. I will take rarer paths into the mists, amid the shadows of great leopards and the creatures that swim in the sky. Led by ghostly bells, I will discover the most ancient of tombs and palaces, and the knowledge of who subjugated the Lighurd, who razed their cities, but did not quell them, who are now only dust.

Yes, the land has crept into my blood and the songs still call to me from there, at night, in my sleep. I believe Agouzi knew how my vision in Gyth would affect me, and that was why he entrusted Ran'zar to my care. In truth, the child is *my guardian*, rather than the other way around. He will stay with me until death, as was promised. And when the time comes he will lead me home to whatever waits for me there.

LONG INDEED DO WE LIVE...

Ian Whates asked me to submit a story for an anthology he was editing for his NewCon Press, called 'Looking Landwards'. The stories must involve how agriculture might develop, with a science fiction theme. I loathe what humankind is doing to the earth, and my visions of the future are mostly bleak. I wanted to write about this, but also with hope – the possibility the earth itself could clean up after its thankless children have made such a mess of their home. I found quotes from Homeric hymns to include in this tale – the voices of the ancient goddesses themselves.

> But at our birth,
> pines or high-topped oaks sprang up with us
> upon the fruitful earth.
> Beautiful flourishing trees,
> towering high upon the lofty mountains,
> (and men called them holy places of the immortals,
> and never did a mortal lop them with an axe).
> But when the fate of death was near at hand,
> first our lovely trees withered where they stood,
> and the bark shrivelled away about us,
> and the twigs fell down,
> and at last our life, and of the tree,
> left the light of the sun together.[1]

She opened her eyes upon the mealy darkness and wanted to breathe. That was how she knew it was time.

In Ampelus Arbour, Leo stands beneath a mist mouth, ghost moisture teasing his uptilted face. The greens in t corner of the arbour are dark, almost black in the shadows, with occasional acidic bursts of moss between the immense glossy leaves, upon the furred trunks of the trees. While some of the wardens prefer the soaring domes and stunning vistas of Suke Arbour and Arbour Thetis, Leo is most at home in this humid, rustling jungle; his child. He has reared it, nurtured it, shaped it. This is his work of art, nestling beneath more sparkling splendours.

Leo was born in an arbour, raised in several. He has never seen the world that lies beyond the great arbourtropolis of Olympus Peak, other than through the lenses of mirrors and cameras. He imagines it has no smell, or if there should be an aroma of any kind, lurking in some shadowed place, it will be of burning.

There had been a conversation with his friend Jade, here in this spot, some weeks ago. She had been talking about how she was seeking a commission outside in a survey team, analysing grit samples, fossils, the air. He didn't really believe her, not least because she was prone to fantasising. Also, very few people were allowed outside, because there was little to go for, and it was dangerous. If the past that lived there was resentful and armed with fangs, why prod it?

'You're so narrow-sighted,' Jade said to him. 'The Wasteland has its own beauty; you just refuse to see it.'

Leo made a scoffing sound. 'How can a corpse be beautiful?'

Jade took an apple from one of his trees, bit hard into the ivory flesh. He noticed her teeth were exactly the same colour. 'Embalming.' She grinned, juice on her lips.

Leo didn't find it funny, still doesn't. He aches for the

world that was, even though he's never seen it, or walked its paths or smelled its aromas. He reveres the mote of Paradise, this *replica*, he nurtures and protects.

He designed the arbour very carefully; his especial love is trees. Not only jungles can be found along its winding paths, but mini-forests and orchards. The trees are lush, and the leaves press against the plexi-plates, basking in the sun. The plates let in sunlight yet are dark. You cannot see anything beyond them, outside. High mirrors bring the light to arbour low, the ground. Hidden systems deliver puffs of air or moisture at different temperatures; invisible boundaries allow diverse conditions to be present within one arbour. You can walk from an autumn orchard into a seasonless breathing cloud forest. Everywhere a reckless glut of scents. It is misleading to call the arbour a dome since it resembles more a jumble of polygons thrown together by a child at play, beautiful in its chaotic and accidental design. Not that anything about Ampelus Arbour is unintentional, although Leo often strives, as he extends it, to make it appear as such. Nature, when she'd ruled the world, had been a seething, endlessly moving wave of life, patterns forming haphazardly, then breaking up, decaying, followed by new patterns. Leo is intrigued by these spontaneous motifs; he wants not just to mimic them but create them, give them life of their own.

But the arbour does not exist solely for Leo's pleasure. Its bounties are harvested – fruit, wood, essences, pharmaceuticals. It is serviced by insects and nematodes that are robotic. No stings, no bites, no parasites, just artificial members of staff. Leo can communicate with and control them all via his mind-pad. Some of them he has given names.

It might be better if the world was completely dead out there, but it's not. Life is tenacious; it clings against all odds, even in an ice-sculpted wilderness, or a fevered desert. Creatures are mainly small, or those that burrow. The surface strips life when it can. Leo doesn't want to believe there are still people out there, or what is left of them, perhaps not quite human now. He wants to believe they have all died off, but occasionally there are sensationalist reports of sightings: blackened creatures, or creatures of ice.

The moisture on Leo's cheek is a caress. He can almost sense a soft murmuring that accompanies it, the voice of some invented nature spirit, a dryad, a nymph. Sometimes, breezes rustle through the arbour; the weather is programmed. Now a perfumed tide of air washes over him, carrying within it the essence of every tree within this section. Eyes closed, his mind is filled with the image of a cornucopia spilling produce, spilling right over him, although without weight or substance.

Leo is stimulated by this image, his body vibrating with energy. Yet at the same time he feels languorous. It is strange. Perhaps some system or another is malfunctioning. He had better run a check.

In the early evening, Leo visits a recreational arbour named Thebes where many of his profession choose to gather for meals. He sees Sorsha, an angular, occasionally aloof woman he particularly likes, and goes to join her, where she sits beside a wall vista that is a particular favourite of his. Sorsha's speciality is birds; visits to her arbours can be alarming for the faint of heart. Leo isn't fond of creatures that make so much discordant noise and that drop faeces everywhere. His trees are more domesticated and calming for the spirit; neither can they tear at flesh and eyes with beaks and claws. The robotic fauna that flourish alongside them are well-behaved and predictable.

As Leo sits down across from Sorsha, a menu pod is already gliding to his side. It knows him, so he can say, 'Just the usual please, Hortense.' All the menus have been given names. Leo has always thought it a shame they weren't given personalities too – that little extra work would have been a nice touch. But the management does like to save costs where it can; such embellishments for an employee recreational area no doubt come under unnecessary expenses.

Sorsha appears preoccupied and doesn't notice she now has company at her table beneath the palm trees. Beside her, filling the wall, the simulated prospect of a lazy lagoon embraces its sunset. Sorsha's examining a tablet of her mind pad, frowning slightly, a tendril of greying pale hair falling over her strong, angular face.

Leo knows better than to interrupt her reverie. He imagines Sorsha as a priestess of the arbours. When she is in trance, woe betide a lesser minion who sullies her meditative silence.

Leo gazes at the vista, content, while he waits for his food. He knows that eventually Sorsha will become aware of him; he's in no rush. The sky in the vista is purple, already blooming with stars above the sunset. At the horizon, the heavens are a scarlet cradle for the sun. Wide-winged birds, mere silhouettes, swoop against the encroaching night. Beneath them, foamy breakers pounce upon startlingly white sand. Occasionally, in the distance, creatures large, dark and sinuous might raise their ophidian necks above the restless waves. There are no people visible, but Leo is always conscious of them, whenever he sits in this spot. People like himself. He can feel them watching, as he does; millions of them, shoulder to shoulder.

'Leo!' Sorsha's voice pulls him from his reverie. 'Sneaking up on me again?' There is a tone in her voice suggesting she's glad he has. He is cautious around her, but occasionally she allows him to spend the night with her. He never takes this privilege for granted, however, and is under no illusion about her feelings for him.

'I was admiring the sunset,' Leo says, smiling.

Sorsha returns his smile warmly. 'This is one of my favourite spots too. Perhaps that's why we meet here so often.'

They both turn their heads to the scenery. Perhaps in another world, another time, they are standing on the beach, their toes digging into the sand, holding hands as the night comes down.

The moon lifts from the ocean, full and waxen. The waters offer a road of light from her to the land. Leo never fails to be affected by this sight. Could it ever have happened like that? It seems too perfect to be true. And then...

A figure is emerging from the sea, stumbling a little: a lithe female figure, small and slight. He can make out no more details than that. 'Sorsha...'

He glances at her. She is staring dreamily at the stars that have opened their shutters to the approaching night. 'What...?'

'Someone's coming out of the sea.'

Sorsha extends her neck a little, peers. 'Where?'

Leo points, although now he's not sure what it is he's seeing. 'There. Looked like a girl.' He indicates to where a series of tall, barnacled wooden posts throw their moon shadows across the sand. Is it a girl there, standing very still? Or just another post? 'Perhaps I was mistaken,' he says.

Sorsha shrugs. 'Difficult to tell. They don't normally include people in this vista. I've never seen one before.' She grimaces. 'It's supposed to be peaceful. People aren't that peaceful.'

That night Leo dreams of the ancient world coming back to the land. He stands in his arbour and the plates that form it are now transparent and he can see outside. He sees the green coming down, over the mountains, across the scorched fields, the cracked river beds. It is a tide of life and he is afraid. He turns in his dream and sees about him that his arbour is arid and parched. The boughs of the trees are withered, the leaves have come down. He is surrounded by death, yet outside life surges forward, relentless and without sentiment. It will splash against the plates of his arbour and splinter them. It will consume him and all his works, and they will be forgotten.

> 'When the earth blooms
> with every sweet-scented flower of spring,
> Then from the murky gloom we will once more ascend,
> And will be a mighty wonder for gods and mortal men.'[2]

Leo wakes feeling anxious. He goes for his breakfast to Thebes Arbour and sits beside the vista of the beach. Few others are present at this hour. Before the vista, the observer has little option other than to stare out to sea, but swathes of beach sweep off to either side, down which it is possible to peer. In the distance, half hidden by a mantle of cloud, are the peaks of mountains, where birds hang like black rags. Are they, in fact, carrion birds? Leo wonders. They drift on currents of air but are circling.

I did not kill the earth, he thinks, *but in Her mind is not all humankind equally responsible?*

Perhaps, it is also possible the earth simply shut down, gave up, ravaged as she was, violated and broken. Natural disasters once conspired with the depradations of humankind to scour the world of life in some areas, inimical to it in others, except for the hardiest and most adaptible of creatures and plants. But humankind, like the most efficient of diseases, lived on, adapted, created a host for itself. The arbours.

Leo rubs his face with his hands, concerned about the strange thoughts that are coming to him. If they continue, he must visit the medical arbour, seek advice. It's not unknown for arbour engineers to succumb to melancholy. For some it is all too keen a knowledge that they may not create, only *re*create, perhaps with no more depth than a vista in a wall, merely giving the semblance of life and space. In reality, it is flat, a fake, and what humanity has become must live upon its produce.

Leo lowers his hands from his eyes, where they have pressed too hard. What he sees beside him makes him jerk back in his chair, cry out.

A face is pressed against the surface of the vista from the other side, as if it were a plate of glass. It is the face of a girl, a naked girl, whose pale hair hangs wet across her features. Her eyes are closed, gummed with sand. Her hands too are pressed against the membrane that separates them, the fingers slightly moving, tapping.

There is a rustle, a crack, surely the glass must break

and *she* will come through. Leo knows true fear. There is a rushing feeling. He throws his arms across his face with another cry, and then it seems as if the world falls upon him; bristly, reeking of green, engulfing. He is aware, amid his high screams, of the sound of other voices, of running feet. And then they are upon him, his colleagues, pulling him free.

A palm tree, inexplicably, has fallen, right onto him. Not a large palm, not too heavy, but thick with fronds. His face has been scratched by them, and his hands. Now the broken limbs loll against the vista, reflecting its daytime fake light. There is no girl there. Perhaps there never was. Just a shadow conjured by the falling fronds that looked like hair and hands pressed against a pane of glass.

The robotic medics are soothing. Their slim appendages are a feather caress against the skin of Leo's throat, his bare arms. Some sealing has been done to wounds. Bruises have been purged. Evidence of attack by tree removed. What had made it fall? They said the soil had dried out in its trough. But none have fallen before.

The underwater light of the sanatorium arbour is soothing also; water tumbles from tiers of ornamental rocks. The air is damp and fragrant.

The medic still examining Leo makes a mild sound, nothing too alarming. 'I've picked up an emotional anomaly,' it sighs. 'What are you afraid of, Leo?'

'Nothing.' He is reluctant to confess, even though he knows the medic will be aware he's lying. 'I'm just tired. Been overworking.'

'Report to Arbour Eos for therapy,' murmurs the medic, retracting some of its limbs into its carapace neatly. One delicate frond of metal still rests against his brow.

'All I need is a sedative,' Leo says limply. He knows it is pointless to argue with a machine whose opinions can rarely be changed.

'I will prescribe one for you,' says the medic, 'but even so you must report to Arbour Eos. You will feel better for it.'

Therapy involves light and massage in the arbour of the dawn. Leo cannot help but be relaxed by it. The therapists resemble attenuated women, machines without angles. This too is soothing; the suggestion of breasts in a soft thoracic swell. They are swathed in cream linen robes and exude odours of fresh bread, of vanilla milk. Beneath their touch and their gentle, bee-like humming, Leo drifts into sleep.

He stands at the top of a slope in one of the grain arbours. Before him, an ocean of wheat sways in an endless breeze. The roof is a vista of the sky, deep blue with small clouds. He sees in the distance a dark shape in the gold, moving towards him. He has to shade his eyes to see. As it approaches, he perceives that the gold is withering behind it. His sight zooms in. He sees a woman dressed in dusty brown rags, her long dark hair hanging down about her body in tangles. Her eyes are black and mad. She brings death with her. The wheat shrivels in her wake. But then the dome of the sky opens wide, to reality, and the glare of the real sun pours in, stark and merciless.

Leo wakes with a start. The therapist at his head murmurs, 'Tell me of your dream.' Her name is Clio.

'A woman walked in the grain and killed it,' he says. 'Then the sun came inside the arbours.'

'No one would ever let that happen,' hums Clio.

'There are systems within systems within systems to keep us all safe. It is impossible for them all to fail together. Remember that, when a dream such as this may come.'

'Do many have these dreams?' Leo asks.

'It is not uncommon,' the therapist replies. 'Your people have had to adapt to survive, but within you lives the root of all humanity.'

'Lucky for you that you don't have it,' Leo says.

'We all share that root,' Clio says, 'in one way or another.' She is the root of all mothers, all lovers, brilliantly made, perhaps by a poet. The therapists are more gifted with the art of conversation than the medics, and certainly more pleasing to the eye.

'We have made you better than us,' Leo says. Despite the dream, he is still languorous from the gentle caresses, the warm light. 'You could even survive outside, I expect.'

Clio utters a tinkle of laughter, like a waterfall. 'And who would look after you then?'

Leo stems the remark, 'perhaps no one should.' It would only invite the therapist's concern. He's already said too much. 'I'm not suggesting you *should* go outside,' he says, in a flirtatious tone, 'but only that you *could*. I would prefer it if you didn't.'

'You mustn't be afraid,' says Clio. 'Nothing is going to change.'

Leo visits his arbour, strolling along the winding paths, stroking the leaves that stray across them. He senses an atmosphere there; is it excitement? The leaves seem to tremble beneath his touch. He remembers the dreams he's had, the visions. This could mean anything – wishful thinking, dread, desire. A girl emerging blind from a virtual sea. A woman bringing death to an ocean of wheat. Symbols. He is not ignorant of the implications. The arbours are all named for Classical deities and creatures of Myth. The arbours of wheat are called Demeter for a reason; she was in the ancient world a goddess of the corn. And once, so the tales go, she turned on humanity and withered the land, because her daughter Persephone, embodiment of spring and growth, was stolen from her by the Lord of the Underworld. Persephone is long gone from the world out there. But she lives in the arbours, doesn't she?

The call rings from mountain top to mountain top in the sparkling air. She stands upon the bare rock, her long toes gripping jagged ridges. She sings to her sisters: 'come forth from your eyries and lairs. Come up from the dark places of stone, of deep earth and the lightless reaches. Come up from the grottoes of the deeps, where hot jets make blood of the seas. Come sisters, rise and wake, for we are Immanent'.

Here first she arrived from the murmuring air.

Leo sits for a long time beneath the apple trees in his orchard sector. The air smells strangely of honey, and he feels drowsy. Sunlight comes down through the branches, filtered but undeniably real, and manufactured breezes, soft as breath, enliven the leaves.

He hears a rustle and a crack, almost as if a heavy object has fallen from a tree and brought a branch down with it, but then he sees Jade sauntering towards him, inevitably chomping on another of his fruits.

'You are a little thief,' he says to her, though smiling.

'Merely sampling the goods,' she replies, 'Anyway, you have more than enough.'

She throws herself down beside him, squinting up through the branches, as if staring at the real sky.

'Imagine a time when you could not say 'What a glorious day', Leo. How dull that must've been.'

He sighs. 'What have you been reading?'

She pouts at him. 'Don't use that tone. I'm merely investigating the past. I have to show an interest if they're ever to let me join a study team.'

'You're too small for that,' he says, and ducks away from her predictable punch, laughing.

'Size is irrelevant. What would I need it for? You can be so rude, Leo. Sometimes I wonder why we're friends.' She pantomimes sorrow.

He pauses a moment, considering, before asking her. 'It's only recently you've had this urge to go outside, isn't it? I mean, with this seriousness of... intent.'

She peers at him through her thick fringe. 'Why? What do you care?'

'Just wondered what brought it on, that's all.'

'Well at the risk of invoking your inevitable scorn, it's like an itch. I just feel there's something I have to see or discover or learn.'

'Do you get dreams?'

Jade looks suspicious now. 'What is this? Are you a therapist now?'

'No, but I had to see one today.'

Jade stares at him for a moment. 'Why?'

'Well, it began with a tree falling on me.' He relates the story to Jade, downplaying what he saw in the vista as an illusion. He does not mention what he glimpsed when he sat there with Sorsha the evening before.

'That's weird,' Jade declares, clearly delighted. 'A tree *and* a vista malfunctioning. The caretakers must've been swarming.'

Leo shrugs. 'They said it was the soil, too dry.'

Jade narrows her eyes. 'Right. In an environment monitored within an inch of its life. Yeah, that's very possible. And what about the girl you saw?'

'I don't think she was real.'

Jade makes a scoffing sound. 'Well of course not. Vistas aren't real. But neither is that one supposed to have people in. Especially creepy ones like that. Aren't you curious about it?'

Leo stares at Jade's face; her expression so open, without censure. He has known her all his life. They were born within months of each other, he slightly the elder. Yet does he really know her at all? Where has this issue of trust come from? What does he fear? 'I think something is happening,' he says quickly, before some part of himself seals the words inside. 'Perhaps outside.'

Jade's eyes widen. 'What do you mean?'

'I don't even know,' he says. 'What I do know is that I have a compulsion to keep it to myself. And now I have told you.'

She reaches out to touch his hands where they lie folded in his lap. 'And that is as good as keeping it to yourself.' She pauses, wrinkles her nose in thought. 'You're not a *fanciful* person, Leo. Not like me. If you're having thoughts like this, they must mean something.'

'I'd rather you told me I'm overworking, need rest, and it's all in my mind.'

'Well, sorry, but I don't think it is. I get the *essence* of what you're feeling. I've always felt like that. You asked if I've had dreams. Now tell me yours, because clearly *you* have.'

While Jade listens to him, Leo is aware of her increasing excitement. It's as if he's an oracle, giving to her pronouncements she has long awaited.

When he's finished speaking, she says at once, 'Leo, can you uncloud the domes?'

'What do you mean?'

'I mean, could we look outside, if you changed them?'

'I wouldn't know how to do that.'

'But the light gets in, so it must be the material of the plates...' She shakes her head. 'It's so frustrating. I need to see what's outside.'

'Aren't you going to, anyway? With your study team?'

Jade utters a sound of annoyance and impatience. 'It could be ten years, for all I know. I want to see *now*. Don't you?'

'I don't know. I think that once you see something you can't unsee it. I'm still hoping I'm going faintly mad, rather than that something real is going on.' He pauses. 'So, what do you dream of, Jade?'

'That I can fly,' she answers simply, and bites once more into the stolen fruit, staring at the ground.

Later that day, back in his Arbour Atlas apartment, Leo beeps Sorsha from his mind pad. She's surprised to hear from him, because he doesn't contact her very often. Their liaisons, such as they are and infrequent, are usually arranged in Arbour Thebes, an afterthought to eating. 'What is it, Leo?' she asks, not allowing him visuals. 'Is everything all right?'

'A tree fell on me today by the vista, and I saw the figure of a girl again.'

Sorsha utters a peal of laughter, delightful and free in tone, so different from her general rather squeezed composure. 'A tree fell on you.' Again, she laughs.

'In case you were worried, I wasn't hurt,' Leo says, rather peevishly.

'Were you hurt?' Sorsha asks, clearly still trying to suppress amusement.

'Very funny.' He tells her what happened, his visits to the medics, the therapists. 'Don't you think it's odd, though? Have you noticed anything... unusual... recently about your birds?'

'Why, are all your trees starting to gang up on you? Do you think they asked the one by the vista to beat you up?'

'Sorsha, I wish you'd take this seriously, like you do just about everything else in life. I'm concerned.'

'Well...' Sorsha pauses for just a fraction too long. 'There have been some anomalies, now you mention it. Something spooked my owls the other night, and several of them flew into the plates. Some were concussed, but could be saved. Two died. They left images of themselves – it was grotesque. Scared owls burned against the plates. The images won't be removed, no matter how many times the plates run their cleaning routines. I've also noticed that the birds will start up a racket for no obvious reason and not at obvious times of day, such as dawn or dusk. So yes, in answer to your question.'

'What do you think is going on?'

'Nothing. Animals will just do unpredictable things at times.'

'Do you think they sense things we don't?'

'That's possible, perhaps even likely. What are you implying?'

'I don't even know.' Now it is his turn to pause. He's not sure whether to be honest or not. But as with Jade, he's compelled to speak. 'I've been having disturbing dreams recently. Even the medics picked up on it. I can't get rid of the feeling that something's – you really don't know how much I hate saying this to you – but that something's happening outside.'

'Why do you hate saying that to me?' Sorsha demands, rather sharply.

'Because you'll think it's ridiculous, put me down with condescending remarks, and then offer a scientific explanation.'

'Isn't that why you've mentioned it to me, though? Or do you want me to say "the sky is falling"?'

'It's because you'd never say such a thing that I'm talking to you now,' Leo says. 'You have more influence than me and I'd like you to use it. Who would know what's happening outside? Can you do any digging?'

'Leo, why don't you just go and see? None of us are prisoners here.'

'But how can I? I'd need a survival suit, a medical pass. I don't think my troubling dreams would provide a good enough reason for me to secure things like that.'

'Who's your therapist?' Sorsha asks abruptly.

'Er... Clio. Why?'

'That's good. Ask her. She has the authority to take you outside for therapeutic reasons, if it's deemed appropriate.'

'Why do you know that and I don't? And what's so good about Clio?'

'I know lots of things you don't because I've made sure I've acquired a reputation that encourages it. And Clio's good because she'll be more accommodating of such an idea.'

'How can you possibly know that? She's a machine.'

'Ten years ago, I was on the committee that formulated the AIs for the therapists and medics. It's an important part of their function. A long long time ago, people had doctors who were in a way like priests. They offered comfort, made people feel safe. It was considered desirable our machines provided the same things. It was me who suggested the personalities, so people would feel more as if they were interacting with a real being.'

'So they have opinions, can make personal decisions? Is that what you're saying?'

Sorsha sighs. 'The machines are all different, Leo. Honestly, have you never noticed that? Surely even your worms have different personalities.'

'I've not had debates with them, so can't really say.' He laughs. 'Strangely enough, I was only thinking the other day it would be good if the menus had personalities. I know most service machines do, to a degree, but I thought it was just a... I don't know... cosmetic thing, like having a piece of furniture that looks good.'

'So today you have learned something,' Sorsha says, but she doesn't sound sharp. 'Go see Clio tomorrow and tell her about the dreams, your anxiety about the outside.'

'I'm concerned I'll be somehow judged for this. Clio will share the information, surely.'

'She'll file it, of course. But like I said Leo, don't get so paranoid you think you're a prisoner here. None of us are. It's just that very few actually want to go outside. Perhaps it's too depressing.'

That night, Leo dreams again. He is walking again amid the limitless fields of wheat in Arbour Demeter. Now, when he sees the dark stain approaching in the distance, he walks towards it. Then he is running. He runs to confront the ragged hag, who trails her hands across the heads of wheat and blackens them. Standing before her, he sees in her face past beauty, a sadness, but also fierceness.

'Why are you doing this?' he asks her.

'They put my only daughter in the cold earth,' she replies.

'Is this to come?' he asks her urgently. 'Will you bring this decay to the arbours in revenge?'

'Unless she stops me, well I might,' utters the crone. She slaps Leo across the face and he is quite sure the mark it leaves will be black, his flesh rotted away.

He awakes with a gasp, as if he's been holding his breath, and for a moment is utterly disorientated. He's not in his bed but is surrounded by rustling darkness, the smell of green. It takes a moment for him to realise he's in his abour, lying beneath a cedar tree. The bark of it looks strange. It's moving. And then a figure emerges from it, slender and green, with leafy hair.

'Look for where she first arrived in the murmuring air,' says this figure. And then she is gone.

He knows he has no choice to but to heed Sorsha's advice.

Three days later.

In the extreme east of Arbourtropolis, at the end of a long tunnel of what looks like obsidian, the exit plates slide up. White dust puffs away from the air that coughs out. Three figures are shown in silhouette at the entrance. Elegant security drones of lilac and silver metal, hovering on the air, are drawn to the disturbance. They glide around the heads of the figures, uttering shrill alarms, until Clio speaks to them in their own language, and they lower their graceful vanes.

'Like birds,' Jade says in wonder. 'They're like birds without wings.' She takes hold of Leo's hand.

The reason Jade is with him is because, rather like a small boy coyly asking his mother for a favour, Leo asked Clio if he could take a friend along on the outside trip. This was mainly at Jade's insistence. All Clio could do was say yes or not, so what was the problem with asking? While Leo agreed with this, he'd also felt weirdly ashamed while asking it and had even blushed, although Clio hadn't commented and told him that yes, that would be fine. Now, here they are.

The suits Jade and Leo wear are mainly to protect them from UV. Clio tells them the air isn't toxic around the tropolis but it's better to be safe than sorry. The therapist is not wearing her flowing robe and has altered her scent. She's dressed in a silvery overall, cinched tightly at the waist with a knotted belt, and smells now of citrus, a more adventurous aroma than vanilla or milk.

'Have you been out here before, Clio?' Jade asks.

'Yes, a long time ago, when I was new,' Clio replies, a certain wistfulness in her tone. 'I wanted to so that I could answer questions about it, if I was ever asked.'

'Were you made with curiosity?' Jade persists, Leo now rather embarrassed by her questions, 'or did it just grow of its own accord in you?'

'Something of both,' Clio says. 'Come now. Let's walk.'

Jade soon lets go of Leo's hand and goes to investigate their surroundings. She picks up rocks from the floor, smells them. To Leo, it is all an arid oneness; the almost white stone and dust. Yet the sky above is achingly lovely, empty of birds but glittering here and there with security drones. He wishes he could have one for his arbour. They are so delicate and pretty, rather like humming-birds in their quick movements, their arcs across the blue.

Clio comes silently to Leo's side. She can move so adeptly without sound, so gracefully, like a wild creature. 'How do you feel here?' she murmurs, her silver optical orbs staring into him, perhaps reading his soul.

'Just... overawed at present,' Leo says. 'But no sense of unease, exactly. I can't believe I'm here, that it was so simple to come.'

'There has to be some procedure in place,' Clio says, 'otherwise people would be wandering out here all the time, falling into chasms, getting sun-stroke, becoming disorientated, lost...' Her lips do not move, those perfectly sculpted shapes, yet Leo feels a smile.

'Did that happen at one time, at the start of the tropolis?'

'No, they were too afraid to come out for some time, but that was before I was new.' She strides a few steps away, swivels her head on its long neck. 'There were toxins out here then. It was a long time ago.'

'The air smells less than inside.'

Clio makes no comment.

'Can we go to Arbour Demeter, see it from the outside?' The exit Leo had specified was as close to this arbour as an exit could be.

'Of course,' Clio responds, then calls, 'Jade!'

Jade comes running back, like a child to her mother. 'Look, I found fossils,' she says, holding out her hands.

The skulls of mice, perhaps, something that once scurried.

'They are just weathered bones, Jade,' Clio says, as she scans them. 'Not that old, not fossils.'

'Oh well.' Jade puts them into a pocket.

The shadow of the arbours looms over them. From outside, it's possible to see just how immense they are.

They look impossible, as if someone could poke them and the entire lot would tumble down.

'The first arbour was built over a well,' Jade says, as they walk in the blue shadow. 'It was just like it was when people were first settling a country, way back in history. First they would find water for their animals and crops, and to keep them alive. Did you know about the well, Leo?'

'I was probably told at one time,' he says.

'You can still visit it underground. I went there once but it's not very impressive. Just a metal cover in the floor of one of the lowest levels. You'd think they'd have done more with it. It was the most important thing.'

Jade seems almost drunk with this excursion. She chatters like a girl ten years younger, full of facts that have to keep spilling out.

Soon they reach the enormous construct of Arbour Demeter, which is actually a series of domes, reaching out across the landscape. Leo wishes he had some inkling of what he was looking for, what good this will do. He walks right up to the nearest dome, places a hand against the warm plates. Clio moves to his side. 'You see, nothing can get in. Those plates are thick and strong.'

'I'd like to walk alone for a while, if that's ok,' Leo says.

Clio doesn't hesitate. She has no need to worry. Her senses would find him wherever he roams. 'Of course.'

There's nothing here, Leo thinks as he walks. The white dust extends to all horizons with occasional outcroppings of bleached stone. Here had once been fields and forests, all gone. He emerges from the shadow of Demeter and the sunlight hits him strongly. A quick movement at ground level reveals a tiny grey lizard running through the dust. He can hear Jade's voice telling Clio about some other treasures she has found. The sound is echoing, as if from far away. He is moving away from the world, he realises, drawn into the wilderness. It occurs to him now there might be no going back.

Leo climbs a slope of white shale; his feet slip, and he has almost to crawl. He has the idea that if he reaches the crest of the ridge beyond it he will see something wondrous – perhaps an ocean or a verdant valley. He can no longer sense how much time has passed. It can't be long, because Clio would have come for him otherwise. He glances up, but there are no humming-bird security drones in the sky. Yet surely they could find him quickly if instructed to do so.

Now he reaches the top of ridge and shades his eyes to look across. There is a wide basin below, perhaps a meteor impact site, which is seamed by a silver thread, glistering in the harsh light. Water? Or just silver?

He raises his eyes to the opposite lip of the basin and someone is standing there. He isn't surprised by this. He raises his hand and the figure stares back motionless. At this distance, he can tell it is a person of slight build, but is not for sure if it is male or female. He thinks it must be female. It must be the avatar of the past he has sensed and seen. He waves his hand vigorously. No response.

Now he is running down the side of the basin, sure the figure above him will disappear. It is watching him, somewhat impassively, he feels.

The silver is in fact a narrow stream, just a quick lick of liquid, yet bright and clear. Small hardy plants grow alongside it, the first mist of green, yet not much of it. He does not pause to touch the water, simply steps over it.

He runs up the slope before him and can see now that the figure is not slight at all, but rather tall. She is dressed in a russet robe, with a fringed brown shawl around her head and shoulders, and before he reaches her she turns and strides away.

He does not call to her, simply follows. She takes him into a petrified forest. The trees stretch for miles, like spikes of white bone. His guide walks faster and faster and he can't keep up. His heart is pounding, his chest painful.

'Wait!' he calls to her. 'Wait.'

He stops and leans down, hands braced on thighs to catch his breath. His vision sparkles with dark motes. He's quite sure the strange woman will have marched onwards, disappearing into a heat haze, a ghost, a vision. But when he straightens up, she is standing right in front of him. She is middle-aged, weathered, but handsome – not the woman of his dreams, yet similar in some ways.

'What do you want of me?' he asks. 'You must tell me. I can't go too far. They will come for me.'

The woman indicates the parched relics around her. 'Take them inside. Take their sleeping spirits. It is time.'

Leo regards the trees. He is to take these into his arbour? What good would that do? They are long dead, probably calcified.

'She has come,' says the woman. 'Times are not the same, but she has come.'

'Who?'

'The daughter of the earth, but her minions have shrivelled and parched. They are like seeds. They can be revived. If she is to bring springtime across the mountains and valleys once more, she will need them.'

'How can I do this?'

'Break off twenty small pieces from different trees and take these with you. When you return across the pale stream, gather water from it. In your tree temple, bury the fragments, water them with what you gather from the new flow. That is all it will take. They will find their own way out.'

Leo stares at the woman. 'Who *are* you? How do you live out here?'

She smiles grimly. 'You are not the only ones,' she says. 'Not everyone was invited into your temples. Some fended for themselves, and waited. Some of us are adapted to it, and continued our duty, as we always have. We have felt you, Leo of the Arbours. Hurry. Do as you are instructed. The first who quicken will see to the rest.'

From the distance an echoing call: 'Leeeee-ooooh.' He turns instinctively to the sound, even though he has so many questions, wants so many answers. But there is no time. When he turns back, mere seconds later, the woman has already gone, faded into the white forest.

His fingers shaking, Leo breaks off twenty small twigs, each causing a sound like gunfire. He hurries then back the way he came. The only container for fluid he has with him is the small water flask Clio provided as part of his survival kit. This he now drains: a drink for himself, the rest into the dry ground. Then he is running back towards the crater. The stream there is so narrow, even if it is bright, it's difficult to gather water from it, especially as his hands are still shaking. *People living out here. Something happening. The return. They believe in a return and see it in the form of a woman...*

He shakes his head to clear it, and then Jade is bounding down the slope towards him, stones flying from beneath her feet, with Clio following behind with her gliding walk.

'Where did you go?' Jade demands. 'It was like you vanished for a moment.'

'Nowhere,' Leo says, smiling. He conceals the flask within his garments. 'Are you happy with what you've seen?'

Jade regards him curiously, aware of his secrets and no doubt eager to hear them. 'I haven't really... seen anything. But I'm glad I came outside. There's a feeling in the air, isn't there?'

Leo nods. 'Look at the water.'

Jade hunkers down, runs the tips of her fingers over the soft green sprouts growing alongside it. 'I want to believe this is new,' she says, and smiles up at Leo. 'Now, I think I want to sit in your orchard and eat stolen fruit, hear what you have to say.'

Leo grins. 'Ok. Let's go home.' Inside, hidden beneath his smile, there is a worm of fear. Should he take the tree fragments into the arbours? Might they not be contaminated in some way and bring the blight of his nightmares?

And yet, part of him feels he should not question, just do as he's been asked, let the process unfold.

Once they are back in Arbour Ampelus, and have escaped Clio's protective presence, Jade says, 'Did you see her, Leo? The woman, or the girl...?'

'I saw a woman, but it seems so... unlikely now,' Leo replies. 'She implied people live outside the arbours, but it wasn't that far away, so surely we'd know about it if they did. I don't know.' He sighs and pulls the crumbling tree fragments from his pockets, puts them on the lawn of his orchard. Such frail remnants. Can anything at all live within them? What if they are blighted? But then his clever insects would detect that, come buzzing over to disinfect. So far none of them have been alerted.

Leo digs a hole in the moist earth and lays the fragments in it, as if it were a grave. Over them, he pours the trickle of silver water from the stream. The fragments go grey with the moisture, but that is all. Leo covers them with the soil, smoothes the skin of turf back over the ground. A ritual act. Perhaps that's all it is. Everyone yearns for the goddess to return, to bring life back to the corn, to cease mourning for her daughter lost to the underworld. *This is what we crave*, he thinks. *And the nymphs will be her vanguard, lifting her once more into the bright air, free of her imprisonment in the dark. This is the cycle of life.*

> 'We rank neither with mortals nor with immortals:
> long indeed do we live,
> eating heavenly food and treading the lovely dance
> among the immortals,
> and with us the Sileni
> and the sharp-eyed Slayer of Argus
> mate in the depths of pleasant caves...' [3]

1. From Hymn 5 to Aphrodite, Homer
2. From Hymn 2 to Demeter, Homer
3. From Hymn to Aphrodite, Homer

A Winter Bewitchment

This story was written for the anthology Femme, *another NewCon Press publication. The editor, Ian Whates, was looking for stories about* femmes *fatales, but with a difference or a new twist. As I've grown older, I've naturally become interested in how we change as we age. We lose the gilded bloom of youthful bodies but gain objectivity and wisdom. These don't cancel each other out – and the state of heartbroken youth and mournful maturity both have their tragedies. The mood I wanted to invoke must be wistful and magical. It must involve an ageing, wise woman, but with a swift-beating heart. Then Areta and Mimosa introduced themselves to me, like archetypes of maturity and youth, and the story unfolded from there.*

Areta, the countess of Graserve, sat upon her morning terrace; the breakfast things had been cleared away. A clean perfume of star pine and doebloom wafted down from the hills behind the villa, warmed by the late summer air. The countess sat at a table of iron, forged carefully to appear delicate, which was covered in packages of letters and other papers. She wore a saffron morning robe and her luxuriant moss-blonde hair, thinly streaked with silver strands, was bound up on her head in a tousled pile. She was frowning a little. Her graceful left hand rested upon a stack of letters on her knee; these had been bound with a faded red ribbon, which now lay about them in a tangle. The lady's companion, a young, dark-skinned woman named Mimosa, sat on a stool beside her, helping to sort out the papers. The countess made a small sound.

'What is it, my lady?' Mimosa asked.

The countess smiled ruefully, her mouth turning down at the corners. 'Ah well, I was only thinking.' She tapped the letters. 'Some of these are from my husband when we first met. He knew poetry then, of course.' She laughed tightly. Her free hand indicated the letters on the table. 'Some are from other men, dated both before and after the day of my marriage. Now they are no more than fading ink upon paper. I think I must burn them all.'

The young companion stirred. She was from the far south, her dark skin tinted a curious shade of green that was so subtle you might think you imagined it, or it was a caprice of the light. 'They are more than paper, my lady.'

The countess smiled down at her companion, rested her right hand upon the unruly tumble of inky curls that seemed to burst from Mimosa's dark green head scarf. 'I have no man to say sweet words of love to me. I have no man eagerly awaiting clandestine meetings, his heart full of poetry and beating fast in his hunger. I have no man to make exquisite love to me; I only have men who want sex, which is meaningless.' She tapped the letters again and then shuffled them into a neater pile with both hands. 'That is what I mean.'

She referred to her husband and her lover, both of whom had come to disappoint her. She thought upon how time had faded the splendour of first love, of excitement. All that was left was passionless domesticity in the marriage, and a kind of dull routine in the affair. She and her lover met for coffee, discussed books and plays, occasionally went to a hotel room, but there was no fire in their eyes, no fervour in their hearts. Hardly a point even for secrecy anymore. Perhaps this was just an inevitable part of growing older.

The countess was quite sure she had said none of this aloud, yet Mimosa appeared to have heard every word. 'Perhaps all this is true, but if you'll forgive my importunity, it is the love affairs that have aged. Your own ageing is irrelevant.'

The countess raised her brows. 'What are you saying?'

'You talk as if all is lost, but it is not.'

'I'm not sure what is lost would be welcome back, in all truth.'

Mimosa grinned. 'If you could have any man in the city, who would it be?'

'Well, the obvious answer would be one, if not all, of the beautiful young things who strut about the stages of our world, or who paint, or who write books. There are many beautiful ones of those, aren't there?'

'There are,' said Mimosa, but she too sounded unconvinced.

'But really...' The countess closed her eyes for a moment. 'If it were to be any man, I would like it to be a man of character, of... power... perhaps someone of whom I might be slightly afraid. By that, I do not mean a bad or violent man, but something of a mystery.'

'That too would be my choice,' said Mimosa. 'This is partly why my family sent me north, ostensibly to discover and learn about different cultures, but really to separate me from home. My choices were not universally approved among my people.'

The countess laughed. 'Were you sent away in disgrace?'

Mimosa sighed. 'I wish that were the case. I simply kept a journal.'

'Ah.'

'It is no easy thing to have your dreams laid bare to the light of day, then mocked and criticised. I burned the journal as you are thinking of burning your letters, but if anyone is to destroy such precious memories it should *not* be the dreamer herself.' For a moment Mimosa's face wore an expression of heart-breaking wistfulness, then she made a visible effort to pull herself together. 'But that is not our subject on this beautiful morning. Come, my lady, think of the man you want.'

'I think, dear Mimosa, there must be an archetypal man, who is the ultimate desire of all intelligent women. We could list all his traits, but is there such a man within the city?'

Both women were silent for a few moments, then: 'Zachary Wilde,' said Mimosa.

The countess considered. 'He is handsome, true, rich beyond imagination, and overlord – for there is no other word – of one of the most successful businesses of our time. But he is also *very* married, and happy with it, by all accounts. His public image is of the contented family man, always seen with dogs and children.' She grimaced. 'I fear he is beyond temptation.'

'Show me a human being beyond temptation, and I will show you a changeling,' Mimosa declared, a trifle bitterly.

'I don't want another affair,' said the countess. 'It's far too demanding. What would be preferable is admiration, some fluttering of the heart, some excitement... Perhaps no more than that.'

The conversation was cut short by the arrival of the count on the terrace. He was a tall, lean man, who like his wife had aged well. He was still what was called "darkly handsome", and no doubt desired by many women who didn't know him, but he had a tendency to obsess over petty things nowadays, and had also taken to whistling in a warbling way, or humming tunelessly, both of which the countess remembered her grandfather doing.

The count sat down, lifting a sheaf of papers from his chair. He seemed not to notice the contents of the table but nodded at Mimosa. 'How's your father, my dear?' he asked. This question emerged every time he saw Mimosa.

The countess sighed inwardly.

Mimosa inclined her head politely. 'He is very well, thank you, my lord. In his last letter he enquired about your new horse.'

'When you next write to him, tell him I will be sending him a shipment of vine seeds, which I believe grow very well in southern soil. They don't do badly here, but from what I've heard wine made from these vines when grown in the south is like a catsup of the gods. In fact...'

'Well, let's clear away these things,' said the countess to Mimosa, gathering up the letters and papers strewn around her.

The count began to hum beneath his breath, staring out over the terrace at the perfect sea.

The Wildes had come from the ocean, the family and their entourage arriving two centuries before on three stout ships. The Graservites had been puzzled why this obviously monied clan had decided to uproot themselves from their estates in the western land of Saravey and sail *en masse* to Graserve. They had brought cobblers and farriers with them, bakers, farmers, sock-menders, jewellers, perfumiers and doctors. In fact, the entourage could well have comprised the stock of a small town.

Before bringing any of his tribe ashore, the patriarch of the Wildes, Jebariah Amos, had requested an audience with the mayor of the city. The meeting had been private, but afterwards the mayor had appeared convinced the Wildes, though numerous, would be a worthy addition to the population of Graserve. The reason given for the mass emigration was that the Wildes were uncomfortable with the politics of their native land, where wealth and success were frowned upon as being the fruits of demon worship. Saravey was notoriously puritan, but it seemed conditions were worsening. In comparison to the average Graservite, the Wildes were to a man and woman far primmer and more conservative in outlook. Only the fact that Jebariah Amos requested permission to build an estate some miles from the city convinced the mayor their rather alien ways wouldn't upset any of the natives. And he'd made clear to Jebariah Amos that he would countenance no subtle attempts at religious conversion.

The Wilde patriarch had agreed to this. Subtly, and miraculously without causing insult, he implied it was the wish of he and his wife to keep their people separate from the Graservites. As they'd sailed the coast looking for a home, it was the land that had called to them from the sea, not the people of the city. The mayor approved a parcel of land for the Wildes, and tax arrangements were made to mutual satisfaction.

The Wildes flourished, and over the centuries mingled more with the people of Graserve. They always retained a certain aloofness, but on the whole were absorbed into the populace. As in Saravey, they became immensely successful in business.

Such was the heritage of Zachary Wilde.

Mimosa and the countess walked that afternoon in the Raven Park that overlooked the hills behind the city rather than the sea. They fed the ravens, paused by the fish pond to watch the lightning glimmers beneath the smooth surface, and finally sat down upon Lady Miranda Terrace, where they purchased tea and saffron buns, and here observed other walkers who came to refresh themselves.

'Have you thought more upon our plan?' Mimosa enquired.

The countess turned her eyes to the girl. 'What plan?'

'Of seducing Zachary Wilde.'

The countess laughed. 'Dear Mimosa, I thought that was a game. I don't have the energy to make it a reality, even if I could.' She reached out with a cool hand and touched Mimosa's cheek. 'You, my dear, would stand far more chance of such a victory than I.'

'I don't think you realise how beautiful you are,' said Mimosa.

The countess was flustered by the compliment, also a little unnerved. 'Well...' she began, touching her throat.

'It's a plain truth,' Mimosa continued, 'and it saddens me to think you've lost sight of that.'

'I've not lost sight of reality,' the countess said. 'You are kind to flatter me, but the truth remains I am not a frothing girl with all the attributes of youth. Men, on the whole, like women young.'

'Nonsense,' said Mimosa. 'I dare you to say that to my grandmother, who even to this day has men dying for love of her.'

'Perhaps maturity is viewed differently among your people.'

'It is, but mainly is this not down to how you view it yourself?'

The countess considered. 'I see the wisdom in your words. Even as a girl, I believed in what my mother told me: that I should *think* myself wondrous at every social event I attended.' She sighed. 'Somehow, over the years, that conviction slipped away, and now it is more difficult to put on the mask than it was.'

'What if I could help you put on that mask once more?'

The countess narrowed her eyes at Mimosa, but she was smiling gently. 'I think you have a streak of wickedness in you, my dear.'

'*That* is something I do not intend to let slip over the years,' Mimosa said dryly. 'Well, my lady?'

'Supposing... supposing you *could* do such a thing, how would it happen?'

'Slowly,' Mimosa replied.

Zachary Wilde first saw her reflected in a tall silver vase. He was arrested by the sight of the slim figure that filled the gently swelling shape as if it had been painted there. He raised his eyes and saw a woman inspecting an array of candelabra on a merchandise table nearby. She wore a long dark coat cinched tightly at the waist and a wide, night-blue hat adorned with trailing black feathers. He could tell she wasn't young but on the other hand she appeared *ageless*.

This was the night of the grand opening of the new Wilde Emporium: a gargantuan indoor market that offered the produce of many distant lands; its food hall was a delight to all senses, oozing unidentifiable perfumes from dozens of unimaginable types of fruit and vegetable. In its cosmetics department were the same pigments and unguents that adorned the faultless faces of exotic foreign queens. Gowns and gentlemen's suits of curious cut were displayed on the clothing floor, if anyone could actually see them through the pressing throng of inquisitive customers.

Zachary Wilde was pleased with the launch, but then it was no less than he expected. Now he was watching a woman in a vase, a somehow mysterious addition to his triumphant night. She did not appear to be reflected elsewhere, and yet a mass of receptacles of different shapes and sizes, fashioned from different materials, were arranged together – some with shining surfaces.

Wilde approached his customer. 'Might I be of assistance, madam?'

The woman raised her head somewhat slowly from the item she was inspecting and regarded him. She did not appear to know who he was. She smiled. 'I'm just looking, thank you.'

He lifted a matte black, three-pronged candelabrum, turned it in his hands. 'This was found in the catacombs of the city of Parnella.'

'I am *not* anticipating a funeral.' Her voice was low, humorous.

Wilde replaced the item on the table and laughed. 'Yes, perhaps its origins should remain a secret.'

Again she smiled. 'I imagine your employer would prefer that.'

'Well, if you need any help, please ask.'

'I will.'

Wilde was about to move away when an impulse seized him. He removed a calling card from the inner pocket of his suit. 'Perhaps you would care to join us for a small reception once the emporium has closed. You would be most welcome.' He offered the card.

The woman took the card and inspected it, holding it from her as if she was long-sighted. 'Why is this?' she enquired. 'I don't believe we've met before.'

'I don't believe we have either, but my wife and I are inviting people who we feel will be... interesting.'

The woman laughed. 'I'm gratified to give this impression upon such short acquaintance.'

He held out his hand. 'Zachary Wilde,' he said.

'Areta Winward,' she replied, offering her own hand in return.

Countess Areta did not attend the Wilde reception but left the store discreetly once Zachary Wilde had moved on to talk to other customers. She felt rather dazed. Two days before, Mimosa had quietly informed her she must attend the launch of the emporium. The girl had been working on their project, she said, employing the ancient arts of her grandmother. The countess need do nothing but be present at the event. Zachary Wilde would notice her there, and in this way the scheme would begin. The countess must not pursue the acquaintance beyond the first meeting, whatever was offered to her.

Areta had to concede that all had gone as Mimosa had predicted, yet was there really magic at work here? Could it not be simple coincidence that Zachary Wilde had spoken to her? He was making his rounds of the floors after all, talking to everyone, hoping they would buy. He most likely told many of them they were "interesting" and asked them to attend his reception. He could smell influence and money and no doubt scented it on her. This trait must be essential in his kind. And yet, the countess could not help but think of the fact that despite his groomed, affluent appearance, and the strong mien he wore that adorned all men of power, he had the most remarkable eyes. If anything, there was a deep sadness in them. This in itself was more attractive to an intelligent woman than gruff bravado, swaggering self-love or the blithe assumption than any woman would fall before him. These were not the beliefs of Zachary Wilde, she could tell. *Something* had influenced him. But no... It must have been coincidence.

As for Zachary Wilde, he found himself scanning the room throughout the sumptuous reception, seeking the tall, slender woman he had seen reflected in the vase. He remembered the exaggerated, attenuated shape of her. She had been somehow different to all he knew, gliding in a world that seemed removed from his. He found this extraordinary because he wasn't given to noticing women in that way. But he wasn't surprised she didn't appear. As time separated him from the meeting, she no longer seemed real.

Something can be made extraordinary by a single change to its being: a blue swan, a swan with human eyes, a swan with the voice of a woman. Or a small green cat. When Areta stepped out into the crisp autumnal air, with the blazing radiance of the Wilde Emporium behind her, she saw such an animal trotting up to her, tail held high, its great yellow eyes staring right at her.

No, she thought to herself. *No. Do not speak. Do not drive me from my mind.*

The way the animal was looking at her, she was truly afraid it might speak. How could she have such a notion? Before she'd left the villa, Mimosa had given her a calming elixir to drink, which must have affected her in an unexpected way. A cat could not be green, could it? Unless some rich woman had dyed her pet. People did that, didn't they? Areta turned away. She was rarely out alone, especially at night, and felt unsettled. The cat followed her, twined around her legs, mewing. When the countess glanced down, it raised itself to its hind legs, butted her coat with its head. She needed a carriage. This was a silly venture. Why had she agreed to go along with it? Briefly, she pressed both hands to her face. When she lowered them, the cat had vanished, and a carriage was approaching, which halted before her. She saw Mimosa inside it, beckoning, and then the door was open, and she was stepping within. She lay half swooning on the plush upholstery as the carriage took her home.

The Emporium was dark and still, although occasionally the ponderous chandeliers would tinkle as if a breeze stirred their crystal drops and beads. Zachary Wilde had sent his family home. For now, he wanted to walk in his property, absorb the feeling of it, the sense of all those who had been there before. He was drawn inevitably to the second floor, where household accessories were displayed. Moonlight came in through the vast windows, conjuring gleams and stars in the cut glass, the polished surfaces, the silken drapes. Wilde's steps were almost silent upon the thick carpet. He smiled, thinking of how one day his ghost might haunt these halls and people would whisper of it. In that instant, the past, present and future seemed to converge, and he felt disorientated. Was he already dead? Or was he visualising the emporium as he hoped to build it? No, he was walking within it, flesh and blood; his store existed, and he was alive.

He came to the display of vases, which were gleaming in the moonlight. As he approached, he saw within the tall silver object that dominated the display the attenuated shape of a woman. Impossible. He glanced to the candelabra table, but no one was standing before it. Was this the answer? Her reflection had never been in the vase at all; it had been and *was* something else, a collection of objects around the room that mimicked the shape of a woman.

And yet, even as these thoughts formed in his mind, the woman reflected in the vase began to walk away, recede into the swollen image of the store. She rippled like ink until she was no more than a distant dark thread.

Wilde continued to stare at the vase without blinking for several long seconds. Was he going mad or simply overtired? He worked too long and too hard and perhaps this incredible *vision* was a symptom of that.

Over the following weeks, Mimosa arranged for the countess to be present in places where Zachary Wilde might be. She must not speak to him at all, and if possible not even catch his eye. She must merely hover at the edge of his vision, then disappear. Carriages were placed carefully to expedite this. The countess must seem to be a part supernatural creature, appearing and disappearing like a phantom. Mimosa had requested from her grandmother a particular perfume that was made on the family estate by female servants, who were tied intimately to the grandmother through a lifetime of witcheries and schemes. The countess must adorn herself with this scent whenever in the presence of Zachary Wilde, for it would linger on the air, long after she had departed the scene, and make him think of her. The countess was disturbed the girl might have revealed everything to her grandmother, but Mimosa stressed this was not the case. She liked to wear that scent herself sometimes, so it was not unusual to ask for it. When the green crystal bottle arrived, astonishingly quickly, it held within it all the spicy nights of the south, a breath of heavy lilies, a touch of earth.

The countess began to enjoy her little excursions; a visit to a theatre, an open-air concert, a charity event held by the Wildes. She realised that she often passed by people she knew but they never acknowledged her, as if she was invisible to them or somehow changed beyond recognition. She did not, however, attempt to speak to them, in case this shattered the magic. She was content to be the ghost, gliding among the people, taller than most. She did not know exactly what Mimosa was doing, for the girl never included her in any of the procedures she undertook. She had no idea if the plan was working.

Zachary Wilde became a haunted man. Surely it could not be possible that the woman he was beginning to see more and more often at public events wasn't real? And yet he could never get close to her; she was always some yards ahead of him. Then she wasn't there at all. She left behind a lingering scent that somehow transported him, made him think not only of her but fantastic landscapes, exotic creatures, magic. He felt she must have a message for him, or was important in some other way, but how? If he could not speak to her, he could never find out. He shrank from confiding in anyone else about these *visitations*, as he chose to think of them. People would think him mad or else put some prurient slant upon the situation, which would demean what he was experiencing, and anyway was far from the truth. He dreamed of her, and when he awoke, her scent was in his bedroom, eclipsing the scent worn by his wife who slept beside him. The woman had told him her name but now he couldn't remember it, only that it began with an A: Aria, Arianna, Ava? The information had slipped from his mind. He had men who did clandestine *tasks* for him sometimes, but he shrank from asking any of them to search for a tall woman whose name began with the letter A. He could visualise their bemused expressions vividly, and even if they were the sort of men who would not talk, they would *know*.

Often, Wilde went to his emporium at night, hoping to glimpse the woman's form in the silver vase, but it was never there again. He realised upon one of these starlit excursions that he must arrange another event, because she was sure to be there, and this time he would be as tricky as she was. He would be invisible in the crowd, creep up on her and take hold of her arm. He would root her in this world with him and then... then something could be said or done.

The year was fading fast. Wilde felt he had to act before it ended. He would host another charity event in two weeks' time, just as the first festival decorations began to appear in houses, streets and stores. He would hold the event at the Glass Fortress, a building popular for such occasions, in the sprawling Raven Park to the north of the city. He would invite everyone of importance: landowners, rich merchants, doctors, scholars, lawyers, artists, actors... anyone of note. Surely his fascinating ghost would not be able to resist such a sweetly-baited trap?

'I hope you are ready,' Mimosa said to the countess, one morning at breakfast, 'because very soon you must speak again to Zachary Wilde.'

The countess froze in the act of buttering a piece of toast. Her husband had already left the table. 'I'm not sure I want to.'

Mimosa smiled. 'I know how you enjoy teasing him, but you must speak to him.'

The countess was assaulted for a moment by a hideous image of panting breath and grappling bodies, which seemed altogether gross and undignified. 'Why?' she asked feebly.

Mimosa reached out to touch her arm. 'You can have a secret companion, a man in love with you, who will travel with you to marvellous realms. The enchantment must gain strength. You may speak of love with your eyes, with the very images you create before you, and kisses need not venture beyond the eyes. Do you trust me?'

The countess stared hard at the girl. 'I do,' she said, 'whether against my better judgement or not, I do.'

'Good, for I love you as I love my grandmother, and she, as well as I, want wonders to be yours.'

'You *have* written to her about this!'

'No.'

'Then...?'

Mimosa smiled, and all the secrets of women were held in that smile.

'I see... Well, all right, if it must be so. But I have no idea what to say to him.'

'Some things should remain unscripted,' said Mimosa.

'But what about the restrictions you placed before, such as not agreeing to go anywhere with him, or even speak these last dozen times I've seen him?'

'When he makes a certain invitation to you, you must accept,' Mimosa said. 'You will know when this happens. It might not be the first invitation. You must let him catch up with and speak to you, and let him believe he has snared you himself, through his own wiles.'

The Glass Fortress was beautiful, a radiant fairy-tale palace dusted with the lightest touch of fresh snow. As Countess Areta alighted from her carriage some distance from it, the flakes settled softly upon the shoulders of her coat and upon the wide brim of her hat – the same dark garments she had worn the first time she'd spoken to Zachary Wilde. She walked slowly to the gleaming edifice ahead of her, which through the light snow looked as if it were made of ice. A scrum of carriages jostled at the entrance, as guests wished to avoid the snow; when Areta entered the building, she was the only one touched by it.

A man in dark red livery offered a tray to her, on which stood tall glasses filled with sparkling wine. Areta took one and sipped from it. *The Fortress* was filled with people, too many of them. Voices were loud and sounded hysterical to her. Every other woman seemed to be dressed in bright, festive colours, while she was this dark, looming creature; long black feathers trailing from the crown of her head.

Areta walked around the edge of the room. She could not see Zachary Wilde amid the throng but then there were so many people, all pressed together. Still, at previous events she'd been able to spot him straight away. He wasn't tall, certainly not as tall as she was, but he stood out remarkably: a neat man, with a short tidy beard and just the slightest unruliness to his thick, dark hair, which came to his collar. Areta noticed his wife sitting on a plush couch against the far wall, surrounded by friends and accompanied by her eldest daughter. This woman must see Zachary Wilde every day; to her he might be a mundane entity, hardly noticed. They'd been married many years. Areta smiled a little to think that some predatory female might even think that about her own husband. How sad and grim that the familiarity of years erodes the initial wonder of first meetings. In fairy stories, the tales end often with marriage, the princess and her prince. As far as she knew, no one wrote stories about those same characters after twenty or more years had passed. What would there be to say, other than to write about routine and boredom or in lucky cases comfort and companionship? No, it would be the grandchildren of those fairy-tale princesses who would be having the adventures by then, woken with kisses, rescued from peril and carried before brave knights on white chargers with their gowns and hair trailing down.

What am I doing? Areta thought. *What is possibly to be gained from this other than a brief frisson like a firework lighting the sky, its marvels gone in seconds?* She sighed. Mimosa meant well, and clearly enjoyed this little game, perhaps more than Areta did herself. But the time had come to end it. Waiting longingly for a man to appear in a room was a feeling that should remain in memory, for there could be no fairy-tale, no marriage, but possibly a variety of disasters.

Areta put down her empty glass on a spindle-legged table and at that moment, someone took hold of her arm, very firmly. Alarmed, she turned at once and saw she had been apprehended by Zachary Wilde himself. He must have discovered her scheme somehow, learned her purpose. Perhaps she would be asked to leave.

'Forgive me,' said Zachary Wilde. 'I didn't mean to alarm you, but I would very much like to talk to you.' He smiled in a boyish fashion. 'You look so very fierce. Please. Just a few moments of your time.'

'I... I don't mean to look fierce,' Areta said, feeling far from that. 'But everyone is looking at us, Mr Wilde. Perhaps you should let go of my arm.'

'And if I do, you won't vanish?'

'I'll try not to.' She smiled then. He hadn't learned her deceit, after all.

Wilde let go of her and for a moment appeared unsure of what to say. People were so close and because of who he was, and the fact they did not know or recognise Areta, they were curious.

'Mr Wilde, you are on the brink of causing a scandal. What is it?'

He appeared to control himself. 'This might sound uhinged, but you've become rather a mystery to me. Let me explain. I see you so often, at nearly every public event I attend, yet I do not know who you are or why you're here. You don't arrive or leave with any companions. No one talks to you, almost as if they can't see you. And yet – I am happy to say – you are not a ghost. Will you satisfy my curiosity?'

'People can see me now all too well,' Areta said sweetly. 'In fact, soon the whole room will be gossiping about me.'

'Must you always remain a mystery?'

'There's nothing mysterious about me. I visit public events because I like to get out of my house. I enjoy them. But while I like to mingle with people I don't necessarily want to talk to them. What's mysterious about that?'

Wilde pondered her words for a few seconds. 'Yes, I

can see that now it is *me* who is being the mysterious one. But there is...' He narrowed his eyes. 'No, to say more would make me sound even more unhinged. I do apologise. But despite that, I would like to know you better. Would you care to meet my wife and family?' He gestured towards the far wall.

Areta glanced in this direction and noted that Mrs Wilde was not paying attention to her husband's conversation – yet. She wondered if this was the invitation she was supposed to accept, but he'd made no others yet. 'That's kind of you, but... I was just about to go home. I'm sorry. I have guests later.'

Wilde pulled a face of disappointment. 'What a shame. Perhaps you would be free to meet me at the Café in my emporium tomorrow?'

All around Areta, the occupants of the room seemed to be slowing down. Arms rose and fell as if under water. Heads turned languidly, but away from her. Voices became a low murmur. But it was not yet the moment to comply; she was sure of it. 'This sounds as if I'm making excuses, but really I can't meet you tomorrow. I have prior engagements.'

Wilde grimaced, raked a hand through his hair. 'I wouldn't blame you for refusing, excuses or not. The request was perhaps importunate. How about this? Every year, we hold a party at our home just before the Winter Festival. I would very much like you to attend. If you'd give me your address, I could ask my wife to send you an invitation.' His hand went to his jacket pocket, presumably for writing implements.

After a pause of three heartbeats, Areta said, 'Thank you, I would gladly attend.'

Wilde relaxed, as if in great relief. He grinned, again

with that almost heart-breaking boyish air. 'Your address?' He held a pencil, poised, over a small notebook. Around them, the cacophony of voices started up again and people moved swiftly.

'If you will indulge me, I'd rather not give you my address. Might I simply turn up, or will I need the invitation to pass your threshold?'

Wilde considered. 'I can leave your name with the Welcomer at the door.'

'Splendid.'

Wilde sighed, rubbed his face. 'This is going to sound extremely rude, but...'

'But what?'

'What is your name?'

Areta laughed. 'Areta Winward. Perhaps you should write that down.' She held out her hand to him. 'And now, I really must go. Congratulations on a marvellous party, Mr Wilde. I shall look forward to your Festival celebration.'

He took her hand. 'I haven't told you the date...'

She let her fingers lie cool, but not limp, in his own dry palm, resisting an impulse to squeeze him. 'The whole city knows what the date will be. I doubt there's any risk of me missing it.'

'The 18th, at 8 o'clock.'

'Yes. I know.'

She felt him watch her wind her way through the crowd to the entrance. Of course, she must not attend. And yet... She resisted the urge to glance over her shoulder.

'He has my name, Mimosa,' said the countess, 'and this time he wrote it down, so he won't forget. He might try to find out things about me.' She had recently arrived home and Mimosa had been waiting for her in her dimly-lit boudoir. While the countess had yanked off her hat, pins and all, and thrown her coat onto a chair, she still wore her gloves and a vanity purse dangled from her left wrist.

'There will be more than one woman in Graserve named Areta,' Mimosa said, 'and the chance of him discovering the name of your great-grandmother's surname on your mother's side is remote.'

The countess put her hands to her face. 'Oh! I am unnerved.'

'This is plain to see,' said Mimosa. 'You look like a girl – a very excited girl, I might add.' She was sitting on the wide canopied bed with her legs drawn up, her arms clasping her knees.

'Now, stop it, you naughty minx!' the countess declared, making a vague slapping gesture in Mimosa's direction, but she was smiling widely. Then her hands flew to her face again. 'Oh, what am I doing? This is madness, and also dangerous.'

'Isn't that the attraction?'

The countess picked up a cushion from the chair and threw it at the girl, who dodged. Then they were hurtling about the room, laughing, ultimately throwing themselves onto the bed, out of breath. 'You are the first proper witch I have ever met,' said the countess.

'Your mirror might disagree,' said Mimosa.

That night, Zachary Wilde dreamed of Areta Winward. In the dream, he was walking through a garden that was rather complicated with winding paths and too many trees, and shadowy people strolling among them. The shadows did not interest him. He was pursuing Areta

Winward down a narrow walk. She was wearing a cream-coloured summer dress, but did not carry a parasol as the other women did, nor wear a hat. *This must be her garden*, he thought and called out her name. She turned, put a finger to her lips and then gestured for him to come to her. He saw there was a fountain of stone fish beside her, which had created silvery rippling patterns on her skin.

'Come with me, Zachary,' she said. 'I would like you to see the real garden.'

She held out her hand and he took it.

Areta led him between high hedges of boxwood, and then they were in a maze, the hedges towering over them, closing in. The woman increased her pace and eventually they were running, along narrow pathways, round corners, again and again. He supposed she was taking him to the heart of the maze, which would be magical, but then they turned another corner and were beyond the hedges. A landscape of extraordinary wonder and beauty spread down before him, as if an enchanted carpet was being shaken and unrolled before his eyes. He stood hand in hand with Areta Winward gazing over this sparkling vista. A white city of spires and turrets and banners reared over a green lake. Beyond was the lilac smudge of high mountains. From where in Graserve could this be seen? Or was it merely an image conjured by the soft sunset light in the peach-coloured sky, the fire-edged wispy clouds, that made it all so lovely?

'Incredible,' he breathed. 'What a view you have.'

Areta's hair was loose about her shoulders now, and her feet were bare beneath the hem of her dress. He drank in the sight of her; her noble height, her sculpted patrician face, her long hands and feet, the wheaten-gold of her hair. He had never beheld a woman so stunning to the senses: a pagan priestess, a witch, an oracle.

'This is my garden,' she said, 'and it extends forever. Fear cannot live her, nor madness, nor despair.'

'This is a dream,' Zachary Wilde said sadly.

'Yes,' Areta said, 'but it is ours, and it exists, here beyond the portals of the mundane world. Inner life can be rich beyond imagination. We need discover only how to meet here, to step beyond.'

And with these words she transferred to him the kiss within her eyes, hardly more than the passing of a breeze and yet so potent. Then she was some distance off, down the hill before him, eventually dwindling to nothing. She had a small green cat by her side.

On the night of the party, the countess dressed in a clinging robe of white silk velvet that had an enormous hood trimmed with snowy marten fur. Over this she flung a white satin cloak that had no hood, but which reached to the floor. Mimosa arranged her hair so that coils of it were wound upon her head, while other locks flowed down over her breast, carefully curled.

The countess felt removed from reality. Over the past weeks, she'd been living two lives, one in the mundane world, the other... the other somehow lost in a dream of impossibilities. She had dined with her husband and had enjoyed his company. She had met her lover twice and had laughed at his wit. But all the while she'd been thinking of Zachary Wilde. Mimosa had done something terrible to her, and part of the countess yearned to undo it before anything else could happen. But at the same time, she could not act.

When Mimosa told her the carriage was waiting for her outside, the countess moved slowly out of her room, down the wide, sweeping staircase to the hallway of her home. Her husband was absent at some men's gathering; he would not be back until dawn. The snow was heavier now than on the night of the *Glass Fortress* party; it came down in flakes the size of florins.

The Wilde manse stood upon a hill, surrounded by farming land and forests. The house shone like a festival tree; every window blazed with golden light. As if in a trance, the countess stepped from her carriage, passed the stamping horses, and climbed the shallow white steps to the main entrance. Here, her name was a charm that allowed entrance, and she became this *other* woman.

'May I take your cloak, madam,' murmured a girl in uniform and Areta surrendered this to her.

She was late, intentionally, so that that Zachary Wilde and his wife would not still be in the hall, greeting the first of the guests. Now, they would be mingling among all these people. Areta knew she did not have to concern herself with speaking to anyone. Unless Zachary anchored her physically, she would remain unnoticed here. Servants, however, were immune to this effect and offered her wine in an indigo glass, and a small dish of delicacies. Areta drank the wine and nibbled on a few of the delicacies before discreetly leaving the dish on a table. She wandered through the radiant salons, looking at all the people. At one time, she'd attended parties like this at least once a week; now they were strange territory to her, no longer compelling.

Presently, a young footman approached her and asked her to accompany him. Languidly, half dazed, Areta complied. She followed the boy through the blazing caves and tunnels of the house, past many doors flung wide, until they came to a region, at the top of several stairways, where all the doors were closed and there was neither light nor noise. They were in a corridor, lit by the moonlight that fell through a tall, arched window at the far side. Here, as far as Areta could see, was a dead end but the page opened a door to the right, which revealed a flight of descending stairs. Alone, Areta walked down them. The footman closed the door behind her.

She came to an oriel hallway, dominated by an immense stained-glass window depicting stylised blooms and peacocks that was circular at the top with a rectangular pane beneath. Two curling flights of stairs led down, one opposite to where she stood, these eventually conjoining into a single flight that led to a bare, dark chamber beneath.

And here Zachary Wilde was waiting for her, sitting on a simple wooden chair, such as you'd find in a kitchen. He did not notice her at first, lost in his own thoughts. He seemed so sad. Was she causing this, bringing a kind of madness into his life? Did he wish he hadn't asked her here, wished desperately he'd never met her so he wouldn't have to feel like this? Resigning oneself to an arid life was one thing, invoking the flaming follies of youth was another.

She could turn now, glide back up the stairs, find her way out. She didn't need to subject them to this; the power was hers. But then he raised his head, and while the sadness remained in his eyes for several long seconds, this was presently replaced by joy. He stood up, held out his hands to her.

Zachary Wilde regarded this creature as she came to him; a snow goddess, an ice nymph, a sorceress of blizzards and storms. How could she possibly be real? Yet here she was. 'I didn't think you'd come,' he said. 'I'm not sure anymore what is a dream and what is reality.'

'I feel, Zachary, that this is both,' Areta said, and took his hands in hers.

'I've realised I have somehow fallen in love with you,' he said, 'and yet I don't know you. What I love is hardly more than a ghost, or the woman I would like you to be. The fact that you are here...' He frowned, shook his head, gazed at her once more. 'Do you feel anything of what I feel? Or are you really a delusion, a vision?' He laughed sadly. 'Can you even answer that?'

'You don't have to worry you are going mad,' said Areta gently. 'I am real enough, and yet perhaps our meeting here like this is not. I think we are perhaps seeking something we have lost – the gardens of our youth. In each other's company, those gates hidden by ivy and cobwebs and years are somehow unlocked. Will you follow me?'

He nodded. 'Yes.'

He went after her out into the silent garden, over the snow-crusted lawn and then onto cold paved pathways. He followed her into the ice-mantled trees at the edge of his estate, and then into the winter fields beyond. White, winged creatures that were not birds flew across the gemmed sky, which looked as hard as frost. If he reached up, perhaps he could pluck the gems right from it. And still he followed her, across frozen rivers, through sleeping hamlets and into the foothills of white mountains. She ascended the snowy slopes with ease, never faltering, while now he was stumbling, the cold biting right into his bones; his shoes and trousers were sodden, his feet numb. But above him, in the mountains, he saw the soaring turrets of a marvellous citadel, golden lights gleaming from all its windows as if in welcome. Near, yet far. He was too weak in body to reach it, the icy frost too severe for his flesh. When he thought he must die of cold and exhaustion, he called to Areta to stop and wait, and she did.

'We have come too far,' he said.

She smiled. 'No, not far at all.'

Then he turned to follow her gaze and saw the lawn of his house, with their prints in the snow – his shoes, the serpent trail of her hem – and beyond this the festive shine of his home. There were no mountains, no shining citadel. He fell to his knees, panting.

'When I first saw you tonight,' said Areta, 'I thought of turning back, for I have no wish to cause you pain. But then I knew how I could show you the truth. Do you see now?'

He shook his head.

She leaned over him, took his face in her hands. 'What are the passions of youth but fantasies, idealised landscapes and blissful dreams? We can *be* this – in some precious moments. I don't know how to explain, nor truly understand it, but perhaps it is a gift we should not question.'

He clasped her legs. 'Is there not a danger we could vanish into that world? It seems...' His gaze shifted to the trees beyond the lawns. Snow had begun to fall again. 'It seemed so real.'

She stroked his hair, which was dappled with snowflakes. 'We all know, Mr Wilde, that dreams – like this festival snow – do not last.'

The countess arrived home in a tranquil yet thoughtful mood. As before, Mimosa was waiting for her in the boudoir. 'Well?' she asked.

'A dream happened in reality,' said the countess, slowly taking off her cloak, her gloves. 'Zachary Wilde and I both saw this; it was quite real. I don't know how I took us there, but I told him I could do so again. Is this true or was I deceiving him?'

'You have the ability now,' Mimosa said.

'Rather more than a mask.'

'Yes. Rather more.'

The countess pinned Mimosa with a stare. 'I noticed you weren't there tonight. I saw no green cat.'

Mimosa smiled and rose from the plump chair where she was sitting. 'What makes you think the cat is me?'

The countess merely laughed.

'Did he declare his love for you?' Mimosa asked.

'I don't think he knows himself what he feels, other than bewitched.' The countess frowned. 'If he does indeed believe he loves me, it is not through my own doing, or the charm of my personality, is it?'

'You're not supposed to care about that,' Mimosa said.

'I care about hurting people, stupid though that may be.' The countess sat down in the chair Mimosa had vacated and rubbed a hand across her brow. 'I know you meant the best for me, my dear, but I can't foresee anything good deriving from this deceit. I am in a superior position to him, having much freedom. He has a large family that demands his time, never mind the work he has to do. He has too much to lose.'

'His wife and family can't follow him into a dream, especially when it isn't his own,' Mimosa said, rather coldly. 'And I don't believe you want it to stop. You would miss him, wouldn't you...?'

The countess held Mimosa's gaze for some moments, as a thread of realisation stitched through her mind.

'What is this to you?'

Mimosa turned away.

The countess got to her feet. 'There *is* some personal reason behind all this, isn't there?' She shook her head. 'Have I been even more foolish than I thought?'

Mimosa wheeled around. 'No, no, I want nothing evil for you, my lady. I care for you very much, but...'

'But?'

The girl took a deep breath. 'There is more than one race whose people are in some sense refugees upon this continent. My family too once came from Saravey. We were... We were driven out.'

The countess gripped Mimosa's shoulders, shook her slightly. 'Mimosa, please tell me this isn't some personal vengeance you're enacting upon Zachary Wilde's people – his *ancestors*, even.'

Mimosa would not meet her eyes. 'The Wildes were part of it, the cabal of men who stole our land, accused us of crimes we didn't commit.'

The countess expelled a small groan. 'You speak of "we" and "us", child, but whatever happened was hundreds of years ago, terrible though it might have been. Your family have lived and prospered in this land for centuries, as have the Wildes. If anything, your father is richer and more powerful than Zachary Wilde. Can't you see that the past is not relevant to you now?' She held Mimosa close. 'My dear child, don't let your young heart be corrupted by these bitter feelings. *Please!*'

Mimosa's voice was muffled, as her face was pressed against the countess's chest. 'I never wished you harm, my lady. Haven't you enjoyed our story? It has brought you happiness, hasn't it?'

The countess held the girl at arm's length. 'Yes, it has;

a pleasant dream, but perhaps not for him. Wasn't that your design?'

'To ruffle his smug existence?' Mimosa smiled wanly. 'A little maybe.'

'A lot, I think!' The countess sighed. 'Now this sport must cease.' She kissed Mimosa's brow. 'Go to your bed, my dear. We have much to plan for the festivities ahead.'

Left alone, the countess allowed a few tears to fall, but only for a short while. After this, she dried her eyes and confronted herself in her mirror. She and her reflection smiled at one another. Then she went to bed.

On the festival day, after a late lunch, Zachary Wilde felt an urge to leave his family and the warmth of the house. He went out onto the terrace beyond the drawing-room. Even so close to his people he felt alone. He found waiting for him a black lioness, seated upright on the cold pink granite that had been swept of snow earlier by servants.

He stared at her and said, 'Is this you, my heart?'

The lioness stirred, and as she rose to her four great paws, obsidian wings unfurled about her. The bright winter sun conjured shades of blue, purple and deepest green in the jetty feathers. She regarded him with snow-blue eyes, and as if dreaming he took a step towards her, with every intention of climbing onto her broad back.

But then it happened that his youngest grand-daughter came out onto the terrace, running and chattering, as a child will. In a moment the lioness spread her wings and then was in the air.

'What are you waving at, Grandpapa?' asked the child.

'A lioness with wings,' he replied.

'I want to see her too.' The child came to stand before him, leaned against his legs. 'But where is she, where?'

'There, my dear.' He pointed.

'Does she want us to go with her?'

'We can go with her if we want to.'

'She's flying away.'

'Yes, she is. This time.' He lifted the girl in his arms and together they gazed at the already distant speck.

THE SAINT'S WELL

This story was written for an anthology called Tales of the Vatican Vaults, *edited by David Barrett. What secrets might be contained within those vaults, perhaps uncovered by agents of the Vatican who investigate claims of miracles? I've always been interested in how Christianity pasted itself over Pagan traditions around the world to help convince people to adhere to the new religion without making too many sweeping – and off-putting – changes. It was common for local goddesses to be 'transformed' into saints, for example, so people might continue in their habitual spiritual practices to a certain degree. When people (often young girls) had visions of the Virgin Mary or female saints, did they represent memories of an older spirit? That is where this story begins.*

On Lammas eve, I walked the path to *The Bwythn*. The day had been hot; the land still baked and shimmered beneath the lowering sun. My path to the cottage was narrow and steep, and it was easier to walk than ride my hired bicycle. The Welsh mountains swept away in all directions, dotted with sheep nearby, melting into the sky in the distance. I had in my pocket the letter from Father Contadino in Rome, validating my authority to investigate this case. Before I visited the local Catholic church, before anyone had wind of my arrival, I wanted to see the cottage, the pool behind it, the girl herself.

The world is full of miracles, or what appear to be, but holy miracles are things apart. They must have the full light of the Church directed upon them. They must be tied down and explored in depth, because a true miracle is the work of God and must therefore be catalogued. Sometimes action should be taken. But the world's fullness of miracles is more often fake – or the consequence of delusion – than genuine. I am sent to find out the truth in such cases.

All I knew of Mai Davies was that she lived in an isolated cottage near the small village of Llanelyn, was twelve years old and had visions, which she claimed to be of a saint. Twice she had apparently effected cures of the afflicted, but the power of the mind is great indeed, and that is a gift from God. He allows people to heal themselves occasionally, but in some cases their faith falters because they are afraid, and they need a hint of theatre to help believe in it. Theatre like Mai Davies.

At the start of an investigation I never know whether what I'll find will be astounding, disturbing or merely disappointing. I have been astounded once.

The Bwythn stood at the top of a hill before a small copse, wherein – so I had read in my brief – lay a deep, narrow pool named Tardell Galar. I understood this meant something like the sorrow well. Here, one summer morning nearly a year before, Mai Davies had been overcome by feelings of ecstatic bliss rather than sorrow. A female figure had appeared to her dressed in blue and white robes and with "a kind face", as she described it.

The cottage was square and straight, with two windows downstairs, two windows upstairs and smoke curling from a chimney. The front door was blue, with two worn steps before it. A ginger cat sat there, washing its face. Music came from a window on the right that sounded like a radio. I heard a female voice singing along, rather tunelessly, to some pop song.

I leaned my bicycle against the wall, alarming the cat so that it scampered off. The front door to the cottage was open, the hall beyond in semi-gloom, although as I stood on the step I could see a grandfather clock beside the stairs and a mirror at the end of the short hallway, strangely bright, that showed me my reflection. I looked odd, as if I were stooping to enter a dangerous place, frozen in time, my hand to my hat, one trousered leg poised above the hall tiles.

'Hello!' a voice called, holding a note of query.

A young woman had emerged from the right-hand room, which I could see now was a kitchen. She wore a full, calf-length skirt decorated with red, orange and yellow flowers, and a pale-yellow jumper and cardigan. She was drying her hands on a brightly-coloured tea-towel that depicted scenes of the mountains. She was pretty and appeared to know it.

'Good day to you, miss,' I began. 'My name is Bartholomew Coombe and I've been sent by the Holy Office in Rome about your...' (my mind scanned the facts for a moment) '... I believe your *sister*, Miss Mai Davies.'

'Oh,' said the girl. 'Mai.' She frowned, taking in my apparel: dark suit, hat, my overcoat over my arm. 'You're not a priest?'

'No, I'm not a priest. My job is to investigate cases of this nature.' I held out my letter to her. She scanned it briefly.

'I see. You'll want to speak to her, then?'

'That would be helpful.'

Another frown, a quick whip of words. 'She's not done anything wrong.'

'I'm not here to judge individuals, only facts.' I attempted a smile, which given what the mirror reflection showed me probably didn't reassure her very much.

'I'm Evelyn,' the girl said, extending a hand. Her nails were well-manicured. I took her fingers, deliberately not strongly, and returned the gesture. Her own grip was firm and swift.

'Well, if you'd wait in the parlour, I'll give Mai a call.' Evelyn gestured at the room on the other side of the hall.

The parlour gave an overall impression of pale blue and lavender, yet dimly, the windows being too small to make it an airy room. There was another large mirror over the mantelpiece, and several religious pictures upon the wall, somewhat faded: a sorrowful head of Jesus, the Virgin with her child. On the heavy sideboard at the back of the room, a plastic crucifixion statuette leaned rather precariously towards a tarnished silver cruet set.

I heard Evelyn shout, 'Mai? Mai, come in, there's a bloke from the Pope here to see you.'

Mai must have dragged her feet or paused before complying, because it took a further two minutes for her to enter the parlour. My first impressions were "dour" and "sour". She did not strike me as the type of person prone to religious rapture. Her face was long and plain of feature, her hair lank and of a nondescript brown. Evelyn bounced in behind her sister, a picture of liveliness, colour and beauty. They were like the Classical theatre masks of tragedy and comedy, so marked were their differences.

I introduced myself and asked if we might sit. I gave Evelyn a long stare so that she would realise I wished her to leave, without me having to ask her to depart a room in her own home. 'I'll make you some tea,' she said and flitted out, closing the door behind her.

'Miss Davies, you'll know why I'm here, of course. Did your priest mention it?'

Mai had perched herself on the edge of an armchair and was now picking at the lace arm covering. 'Yes. Father Brynn said the Holy Father would want to know about me, that he would send someone.'

I then gave her the usual talk about the Holy Office and how it investigated all religious experiences that came to the ears of its officers. I explained that I was based in England but given work of this nature to carry out in the Holy Father's name. I assured the girl I was not there to question her integrity, merely to hear her account and, if possible, be shown any of what she had experienced or continued to experience. I would also want to speak to any other people who might be involved. Mai answered my questions without elaboration or any visible sign of concern or enthusiasm.

'So, tell me in your own words what happened the first time you had a vision,' I said.

Mai shrugged. 'It just came over me at the pool. I felt... very happy, *really* happy, then the light on the water became a... person. She is Saint Galar and God asked her to visit me.'

'Did she tell you this name?'

Mai nodded. 'She said that was her name. She looks like the Holy Mother, all in blue and white. She's pretty with long hair and she smiles.'

'You don't think she could be the Holy Mother?'

'No, I know it isn't. She would have told me if that was who she was. Why would she lie?'

'How often do you see her?'

Again a shrug. 'I don't know. Sometimes.'

'Once a week? Once a month?'

'Maybe once every few weeks. Yes, once a month.' Mai watched me writing my notes.

'And what happens during these visits?'

'Nothing much. I lie by the water and listen to her, but it's not words so much as songs or sounds like birds. I'm so filled with happiness I can barely move. There's light all around me, within everything. It's not ordinary light, but God's.'

'How long do these episodes last?'

Mai's face had taken on some of the light she had reported, transforming her from sour to sweet, then it faded a little as my question brought her back to earth. 'It can't be for that long. I have to do my jobs in the house. I have to go to school.'

'So, what, maybe an hour?'

'I don't know. Maybe.'

'Do these visits leave any physical marks?'

'What do you mean?'

'Well, marks upon your body, in places perhaps where Jesus was nailed to the cross or wounded in the side.'

'No, no. She wouldn't do *that*.'

I smiled. 'I'm sorry. I have to ask these questions.'

Mai shook her head, looked down at her hands. I could tell she thought what I'd asked was crude. 'It's all right.'

'Do you have any physical contact with Saint Galar?'

'No, she stays where she is, although...' Mai looked up, 'it feels like she touches me with her eyes, a touch that can take pain away.'

'Do you have any pain?'

'I had a tummy ache once. She made it go.'

'And not just *your* hurts, I believe. You've been reported as healing people. Can you talk to me about that?'

'First, it was Huw Evans' hand. He'd broken it, mauled it up in a machine at work, and even though it was mended it pained him all the time. The Lady told me to touch it and then it was better. And the Morgans' little girl. She was very sick with the fever.'

'You healed these people by touching them?'

'Yes. Sort of. I can't really describe it.' She wrinkled up her long nose. 'It's sounds again, like birds, or wind rustling in the bushes. And there's a smell too. But it's not like anything I've smelled before so I can't tell you what it is.'

'Can you show me this... *ability*?'

'Have you anything wrong with you?' she asked, rather archly and in a tone beyond her twelve years.

'Fortunately not,' I said. 'So you can't make anything happen unless I'm ill?'

'It's for healing,' Mai replied, as if I were stupid.

Evelyn came into the room carrying a tray, and some minutes were devoted to the consumption of tea and biscuits.

Evelyn threw questions at me. 'You live in England? You don't work for the Church all the time? How far have you travelled? Have you ever met an evil ghost?'

I answered carefully, not wanting to make my job sound too exciting, like that of an adventurer or explorer, although in fact I do love facing the mysteries and in most cases solving them.

'You're a religious detective,' Evelyn decided, and I agreed this was a pertinent term to describe my work.

'Have you ever investigated a murder?' she asked, her eyes alight.

'Not yet,' I replied.

From our conversation, I ascertained that Mai was, of course, still in school and Evelyn was an office junior at the college in the nearest town, there also learning secretarial skills. Their mother, Bronwen, worked as an assistant at the post office in Llanelyn. The father was dead. This being the summer, both girls were on holiday. Evelyn – at sixteen considered old enough to look after her younger sister while their mother was at work – enjoyed the long summer holidays of the educational establishment. I got the impression this was some arrangement that had been made to accommodate her child-minding at home, since the college was mainly her place of work rather than of learning. I was told that Mai liked to go to church every day. Usually, Evelyn went with her, as companion rather than through any religious urges of her own.

What I'd heard so far seemed pretty standard fare to me and was not that uncommon. Many a person – and not always young girls, who are particularly prone to it – claim to encounter holy beings that are arrayed in light and bring with them a feeling of joy and love. Although most of the visions do communicate, often this is not aloud but rather heard within the claimant's head. A proportion of these cases are down to mental illness or some aspect of puberty. Those who are extremely devout and spend much time in meditation and prayer are also more likely to experience visions than others. I believe this is a natural result of an inordinately pious life, where the greater part of a person's time is given over to religious contemplation. I do not regard this as mental illness, but rather a kind of euphoria, an externalising of their intense spiritual feelings. The majority of claimants I have studied believe their visions to be that of the Virgin Mary. Male figures – that of Jesus Christ himself or saints – are not as common now as in earlier times, when the Church was being established. But visions are still occurring and can have a problematic effect upon families and communities. The Church cannot ignore them. My job is to ascertain which of these experiences are *real*. I was chosen for this task perhaps because I am a sceptic. I don't believe any of them are real, but I am good at investigating, enjoy the work, and am able to appear empathetic to the claimants. In their view, after all, what they've experienced is absolutely real. Very few deliberately fabricate these things.

After our refreshments, I asked Mai to show me the place where she'd seen the "saint". I hadn't yet revealed to the girl that there was no "Saint Galar" in any hagiographical list to my knowledge, and after all the years I'd been employed by the Holy Office, I knew the name of just about every canonised individual in history.

A garden containing a chicken run led to a copse beyond a sagging wood and wire fence: beeches and oaks mainly, although I noticed some smaller growths of holly and hawthorn. There was a worn track through the undergrowth, with a tiny stream beside it, and a faint smell in the air of decay or perhaps excrement. The stream looked seasonal to me; it was barely present at this time of the year.

We reached the pool, which was bigger than I had imagined, its waters very dark. There was a rock wall overhung with shrubs on its western side, which was where – so Mai told me – the spring bubbled up from beneath the earth. A larger stream flowed away from the copse across the hills, stronger than the brook through the trees. Mai explained that her saint appeared upon a ledge in the rock above the pool. She did not move from this location, nor speak aloud. 'I hear her inside,' Mai said. She looked at the small-faced watch on her left arm. 'I'm sorry. I have to go. It's nearly time for Mass. It's Saint Galar's day tomorrow. This is her eve.'

'She told you that?'

'Yes.'

There were no saints that resembled Mai's description of Galar who had a feast day on the first of August.

I returned to Llanelyn below the hill and took my evening meal in *The White Dragon*, a small hotel that served also as the local pub, where I had reserved a room. Afterwards, I wrote up my notes neatly. Two things in particular interested me about this case. First, the fact the visions revolved around what appeared to be a fictional saint. "Saint Galar", with her association with sorrow, had correspondences with "Our Lady of Sorrows", an aspect of the Virgin Mary, but Mai Davies had been emphatic Galar was a different person entirely. Second, the healings. I would need to speak to the families concerned. I decided not to visit the parish priest until the following day but would certainly consult with him before calling on the Evans's and Morgans.

The local church was dedicated to St Helen, a Welsh woman of high birth, canonised for founding churches in the country during the 4th century. Her name is an anglicised version of Elen, said by some scholars to be a Christianised reflection of an older, pagan deity. There was both an historical Elen and a literary one – she is mentioned in the book of Welsh folklore, *The Mabinogion*.

But I could make no immediate link between her and Mai's vision of "Saint Galar". Llanelyn translates roughly as "the Parish of Elen".

Father Brynn received me in the parochial house mid-morning, a dark-haired man in his late thirties, who clearly took good care of himself. He appeared sceptical about Mai Davies' visions.

'The Church has taken the place of the dead father for her,' he said ponderously.

We sat drinking tea and smoking cigarettes in the garden of his house, in the shade of a modest orchard because the day was heating up fiercely.

'Mai's always been a serious type of girl,' Brynn said. 'Very devout, even at an early age. Evelyn, on the other hand...' He laughed, flicked ash onto the roughly-mown grass. 'Well, she shows her face in church but only till Mai's old enough to go everywhere by herself. The mother's attendance has always been of the weddings and funerals kind.'

'You think then that Mai's visions are merely hallucinations?'

'Yes, but...' He looked at me warily. 'Nothing too serious. She'll grow out of it. Too much imagination. Children have make-believe friends and such, don't they?'

Not usually saints, I thought.

'What are your thoughts on the healings Mai's supposed to have accomplished?'

'Coincidence,' he answered, shrugging. 'And people wanting to believe. Huw's injury was old, perhaps a memory of pain, and what Mai did helped him believe God had cured it.' He looked faintly embarrassed and added hurriedly, 'God *can* heal, of course, and sometimes through unusual methods, but in this case...' He shrugged. 'I couldn't see it. As for the little girl, she was under the doctor, so who saved her? Mai with a touch, or the doctor with his medicine, or indeed the prayers of her parents?'

'Some might say a combination of all three.'

'Everything is for a reason, as we know,' said Father Brynn. 'I'd very much like to believe that Mai Davies can work miracles, but my instincts say no. She's an odd child, who's always been that way. If I were Bronwen, I'd have her at the doctors now, not... well, I know you have to investigate these things when there's an official report.'

'You didn't report it?'

'I was obliged to report to the Bishop. Someone contacted me anonymously and insisted upon it. Bronwen and I decided we had no alternative.'

'The mother believes, then.'

'It's her daughter. If we *have* to do something, rather than let the poor child grow out of it, we'd be wiser to care for her mind, in my opinion, rather than making a fuss of it or subjecting her to upsetting situations that might make things worse.'

I grinned. 'Mai is *not* being interrogated by the Inquisition, you know.'

Brynn laughed. 'But isn't that what you are?'

I shook my head. 'We are *modern* now. I'm not seeking heresy, if that's what you think. The Office now seeks only to shine the light of truth upon cases like this, where the claims might be dubious. I don't carry thumb screws.'

Again, Brynn laughed. 'In this job, sometimes I wish *I* had them.'

We sipped our tea in silence for some moments, then I put down my cup. 'You must know there is no Saint

Galar. Why would Mai come up with the idea of a saint at that pool? I'd like to hear your thoughts on that.'

'The pool has folklore associated with it,' Brynn said. 'It's said that in centuries past people would take dead children to be blessed there before burial. Perhaps that's why it's a well of sorrows. Many mourned there.'

'And yet Mai sees an entity who makes her feel happy. That's a strange contradiction.'

Brynn shook his head. 'I don't think so. There probably isn't a well or spring in the whole country that isn't regarded as sacred in some way – such things linger from olden times. Mai no doubt heard the stories and she has such a spring in her back garden. Children are imaginative, and why should she invent something frightening? No, to my mind, a girl is more likely to dream up a lady in a long dress who's beautiful and kind.'

'Such as fairy-tale princesses,' I said. 'But this isn't a princess. From the child's description, what she's seen is more like the Virgin Mary, yet she's invented a personality for it.'

Brynn shrugged. 'She probably *has* mixed her invention up with what she knows of the Holy Mother. That's all there is to it. I don't think there's much of a mystery here.'

Father Brynn came with me to visit the recipients of Mai's healing, saying that they would feel more comfortable if he was there. I didn't disagree. Huw Evans was at work, but we were able to interview him in his lunch hour, after Brynn had a word with his supervisor. Huw was a man in his forties, with a wife and three children, and a regular job, who did not appear to be a credulous sort of person. Brynn had told me the Evans's attended church on Sundays but were otherwise not overly devout. We took Huw to a pub where he might get some lunch – a luxury small freedom for him on a working day – and here he showed me his damaged hand. I couldn't stop myself flinching. More accurately, he showed me what was *left* of his hand, this disfigured two-fingered *claw*, far worse than Father Brynn had implied. Turning it before him, Huw said, 'I don't care what others say. When that girl put her light into me, she snuffed out the pain. I'd lived with it for nigh on eight years. Strong medicine could barely touch it. Now it doesn't hurt at all.'

'How did this healing come about?' I enquired. 'Did you ask for it?'

'No, she just passed me in the High Street one Saturday afternoon, and caught hold of my arm to stop me. She said, "Let me see your hand". Well, I thought she was just curious about it, being cheeky even, but for the look on her face... I let her touch me.'

'What did you see or feel?'

'I felt warmth,' Huw said. 'What I saw...?' He stuck out his lower lip and shook his head. 'I thought I saw a radiance like the summer sun. But afterwards, it was like the memory of a memory... Can't explain it.'

'Was there any reason she picked you in particular?' I asked. 'I mean, rather than some other person in pain or who was ill. We can only suppose there were many like that on a Saturday afternoon in town.'

Huw stared at me through the pub's smoky air, skeins of it made almost solid by the sunlight coming through the window behind him. 'I've no idea. I wondered about it, of course I did, but no... I was just there at the right moment, I suppose.'

'What did your doctor say? I assume you went to him.'

'He said I'd got better,' Huw said stonily, and took a long drink of his pint.

The Morgans lived in a newly-converted old cottage on the edge of town. Brynn drove us there in his car, having telephoned Marie Morgan in advance so she expected us. She answered the door quickly, a baby balanced on her hip. After the introductions, she took us to her sitting-room, where we had to wait for the inevitable cup of tea. The house was neat and clean and furnished fairly expensively.

Once we were sitting with our refreshments, Marie told me details of herself: thirty-two, a house-wife. Her husband Joe had a good job as a car salesman in a nearby town. Neither of them was Catholic or even a church-goer. They had lived in the village for three-and-a-half years, so would no doubt be regarded as newcomers for at least another twenty. 'I know you're here about Mai Davies,' she said, 'and I expect you want to prove she's lying or something. But I know what I saw, and I'm not a stupid person.'

'What did you see?' I asked gently. 'And where did this happen?'

Marie directed a misty gaze at her daughter, who was now playing on the floor with coloured bricks. 'Mai just knocked on my door,' she said. 'It was evening, a Wednesday. Lizzie was so ill we thought...' Marie couldn't prevent tears welling at the memory. 'Well, it was perhaps an hour before she would go to hospital. Then there was this skinny girl at the door saying she'd come to see Lizzie, that she could help.' Marie ran her hands through her well-cut, dark hair. 'To this day I don't know why I didn't question it more. I just let her in, like I was half asleep. She walked upstairs, went straight to Lizzie's room. By the time I got there, she had her hands on my baby... The room... I can't describe it, but *something* was there. I just fell to my knees on the floor and put my hands together. All I could say was "thank you, thank you". I wasn't thanking Mai either.' She uttered a shaky laugh. 'Now you'll think I'm crazy.'

I shook my head. 'Not at all. I'm simply here to find out what happened. How long ago was this?'

'Oh, maybe two months now. The doctors were astounded. Lizzie didn't have to go to hospital. Her fever fell... she was just the same as she was before. But they say that can happen with childhood illnesses and that the treatment she was on just took effect. I don't believe that, though. I know what I saw, what I felt.'

'Thank you, Mrs Morgan. I appreciate you giving us your time.'

'Mai's not in trouble over this, is she?' Marie asked, her glance flicking from me to Brynn and back again.

'No, please don't worry about that. It's simply that she claims her *ability* comes from a saint, so the Church has to investigate the matter.'

'It can come from Mickey Mouse for all I care,' Marie retorted. 'She saved Lizzie's life.'

'They sound pretty convincing, don't they,' Father Brynn as said we drove away. We both wound down our windows because the air was so hot; it was difficult to breathe. 'Marie Morgan and Huw Evans believe they experienced miracles.'

'Yet you don't.'

'What do you think about it all?'

I drew in my breath. 'Well, I don't doubt they believe Mai helped them. Coincidence? The doctors would say that. In Marie Morgan's case, she was desperate and, like she said, if Mickey Mouse had turned up saying he could heal Lizzie, she'd have let him in. And maybe Huw Evans was desperate too, in a different way. So therefore they believed, and somehow their minds and bodies used that belief to effect cures, although it's more likely in Huw's case than in a baby's, who lacked the faculties to analyse what was happening around her. Perhaps it was due to a special kind of mother and baby connection, but that's beyond my field.'

'So will you talk to the doctors, or are you ready to write up your conclusions?'

'I will write up what I've witnessed and heard,' I said. 'It's not my job to provide conclusions.'

'Careful answer. Where do you want dropping off?'

'Just at *The Dragon*. I'm going to visit the Davies's again. I'll take a walk up the hill.'

'In this heat?' Brynn laughed. 'Now who sounds mad?'

We drove past the church. Branches from an immense and ancient yew behind the graveyard wall draped as if exhausted from heat over the dedication board, partly obscuring it, so that it appeared the dedication was to Elen not Helen. For some reason, this made me shiver, but what kind of shiver that was I couldn't honestly tell.

By the time I made the climb once more, it was late afternoon. As I followed the path, I considered that Brynn had been right; it was far too hot for such exertions and I should have waited until later when it was cooler. My head began to ache, and it was almost painful to look around the landscape, which seemed to shimmer and undulate as if invisible waves coursed through it. I took off my jacket and rolled up my shirt sleeves. The hills swept away from me, from green at my feet to a lavender haze in the distance. The mournful bleat of sheep echoed about me. There were no other people around. I realised how alone I was. The village far below was a glisten of shining windows, mica gleaming from walls. It seemed unbelievably distant, as if in another, abandoned world.

I am not a fanciful individual, but at that moment I became aware of what I can only describe as a vast *sentience*. I remembered what my mother used to say to me as a child, 'At Loafmas, ghosts walk at mid-day.' I used to love hearing that, giggling with delicious terror at the thought of the bright summer landscape infested with phantoms. Now I felt a little of that same fear: primal, inexplicable, gut-deep. Loafmas, the first of the harvest festivals, is of course the Christian name for this time, being yet another holy day tacked on to earlier pagan celebrations. It was – and often still is – observed by farming communities, as thanks for a successful harvest, but for some it goes deeper than that. The land is alive to them, with its own intelligence: a personality to be appeased. Without its co-operation people would starve. And now I felt some vast, muscular yet invisible presence undulating through and over the land. I fancied I could even see it, an intense shimmer of heat, coming like the thresh of ocean waves upon me, up the hill, blaring with unheard trumpets and victorious cries. Then it passed through my flesh and for a brief instant I felt the most incredible joy – no, beyond joy, *ecstasy*. Then it was gone, as swiftly as it had come. The heat. My imagination. What strange tricks the mind can play, coupled with an ancient memory.

Mai was in the garden of the cottage, sitting next to a woman I took to be her mother, who was doing some mending, a sewing basket at her feet. When she saw me she remarked, without introduction or preamble, on how red I was and sent Mai to fetch me some lemonade. I sat in the shade of an apple tree, panting, and fanning my face with my hat. Bronwen was silent, concentrating on her work, apparently comfortable with the lack of conversation between us. She was a strong-looking woman with thick black hair, which was iced with the faintest threads of grey. The heat was becoming increasingly uncomfortable; even sitting down I still felt breathless, light-headed.

When the girl returned, and had sat down on the grass before me, I asked if we could continue our conversation from before.

'Of course,' Mai said. 'What else do you want to know?'

'Well,' I began, 'there isn't a saint called Galar known by the Church, and no saint like how you described her who has a festival today...'

Mai interrupted me in a shocked voice. 'I didn't make her up!'

I raised my hands to placate her, noticed a sharp glance in my direction from the mother. 'I'm not saying you did, but what do you know about her?'

Mai regarded me carefully for some moments. 'She's very old and has lived for ever and ever at the spring.'

Bronwen paused in her sewing. 'She was once joy but now she is sorrow, for some things are fading away.'

My head was pulsing with pain, and I held the

lemonade glass to my face before I took a swig of the contents. It was warm and the liquid itself was hardly quenching, being sickly sweet. I wished Mai had brought me water. 'What things?'

Bronwen looked around, at the copse behind the garden, the sky. 'The old ways. She doesn't like modern things, like cars, I suppose, and radios, and things like that. Neither do we.'

'And churches?' I asked crisply. The conversation was now between Bronwen and myself; Mai had fallen silent.

Bronwen's dark eyes were cold. 'What do you mean?'

I rubbed my neck, pulling my shirt collar away from my skin. I mean, is this Galar older than the church, say St Helen's in the village?' I looked at Mai, who was regarding me curiously and spoke to her directly. 'You do know that Helen was once Elen, a lady of ancient Wales, don't you?'

Mai nodded. 'We learned that at Sunday school.'

'Well, before that, she was a goddess in folklore. Are there people who perhaps still see Helen as that? Were you ever told that?'

Mai's mouth dropped open a little and she stared at me, as if horrified. 'You want to make her bad!' she cried abruptly. 'You don't want her to be part of God, because she's not in a book or written down, but everything *is* part of God, you stupid man!'

'Mai!' I cringed at her ferocity, which had seemed to come out of nowhere.

Bronwen did not chastise her daughter for insulting me, which was equally insulting.

'Go away!' Mai scrambled to her feet and pointed at me. The air shimmered with heat all around her. My vision was blurred, my head pounding. Mai pointed at me with a stiff arm, her hair over her eyes. I couldn't dispel the absurd idea that she was some ancient, vengeful priestess, somehow manifesting in the body of a girl. 'You're not wanted,' Mai hissed. 'None of us want you here. We don't need to be *investigated*.' With these words, she turned and ran into the house, slamming the back door behind her.

I felt as if the girl had slapped me.

Bronwen picked up her sewing again, her fingers moving deftly. 'People have always known Mai is different, sees things differently,' she said in a soft voice. 'Mr Coombe, our ways are not your ways, or anybody else's. If Mai sees the lady as a saint, and calls her Galar after the well, it doesn't matter. She's Helen, Elen, or merely the light of the land. I think you've learned all you can. You should go now.'

'I'm sorry if I've caused offence,' I said, 'but...'

Clearly, Bronwen didn't want to hear anything further I might have to say. 'You should go. You don't look well.'

A breeze fretted the foliage around us, then fell just as suddenly.

I stood up. The darkness of the copse nearby was watchful. I was being observed and what – or who – looked on was not benign. I fancied I could almost see it in the shapes created by the shadows between the branches and leaves, the shiver of the water; a vague figure, a face, eyes that were spots of sunshine. My flesh shrank against my bones and I turned my back on whatever loomed over me and poured the sticky lemonade onto the grass. A libation? A miserable attempt at appeasement? It felt the right thing to do. What had I stumbled on here? If there was an unseen wave approaching me now, it was one of repulsion; not sorrow, not joy. Mai's words echoed in my head: *Get out of here!* In fact, I had no choice.

I walked around the side of the house and back onto the path. I could barely see. Was this heat-stroke? The village seemed so far below, and all around me the pulsing landscape, the shimmer on the hillsides, pushing me away.

Somehow – and I can't remember all of that painful walk back down the hill – I reached Llanelyn and fetched my luggage from the inn. All I wanted was to get home, to lie down, recover. As I fumbled with my wallet to pay my bill, I remembered an old legend of a ferocious goddess: because she knew how to injure, her devotees believed she must also know how to heal. Could this not work also in reverse? This was superstition creeping up on me, the power of suggestion. How fragile is the human mind? Are we not all children at heart, frightened by the darkness, all that we do not know?

They were watching me as I stood waiting for the bus near the church. Mothers with children, elderly folk, people going about their business at the tail end of the sweltering day. Of course, news would have got around about me asking questions in the village the day before, but I knew it was more than simple resentment of my investigation that burned behind their eyes. I could feel it, as if the vast sentience of the hillside had followed me down the path and settled over the village and its inhabitants in a caul of ringing heat, looking out through every pair of eyes. Father Brynn was by the church door, but he did not come to me. He simply watched, as the others did. I knew they were all waiting for me to leave, urging it. And I was eager to do so. I did not want to make them feel threatened by my presence. Who knows how far they'd go? I would report what I'd seen and witnessed, what Father Brynn wanted me to believe. An imaginative young girl at the brink of womanhood. Credulous people who believed they'd been healed. Superstitions that still live in the heart of the countryside, perhaps made real in mind by an older faith.

Ill-health prevents me from further investigation at present. What I experienced and saw – and suspected – is certainly at odds with Christian teaching, of course, but to me the book is closed on this case, even if I suspect I read only half of it. The old ways have not died out completely, but it is my belief that when a community respects God and the Church, whatever else they might believe, they should be left to their own devices. Delusion it may be, but harmless, if we let them alone. This is what I experienced in the village of Llanelyn in the summer of 1959.

AT THE SIGN

OF THE LEERING ANGEL

This story was inspired by an amusing incident that took place at a party at our house a few years ago. Some of us had been dancing in the front room, and one of the women had taken off her shoes, which she'd left out in the hall. Later in the evening, a male friend, a rather well-built and macho man, marched into the living room, and, hands on hips, announced with aghast astonishment: 'These aren't my shoes!' He had rolled up the legs of his trousers and was wearing the woman's high-heeled pumps. Cue raucous laughter. But somehow this little incident stuck with me and wanted to be included in a weird story. This is what grew from it. It originally appeared in Dark Horizons *magazine in America.*

'*These* aren't my shoes!' A thick-set man, wobbling on women's spiky heels, filled the entrance to the building. Arietty could see – and sense – the crowds behind him. The tall old house was a smoky hive; humming, throbbing. Heat and dim light pulsed out of it, yet its top third story was in darkness. People seated on the front steps in the late summer night were laughing uncontrollably at the shoe man's antics. He struck a dramatic, supposedly feminine pose, laughing so much himself he must surely fall over soon.

'Idiot,' said Zinsa beneath her breath. She linked her

arm through Arietty's elbow, dragged her up the steps. Sprawling limbs moved sluggishly from their path.

'*These* aren't my shoes!' the man told them.

Zinsa bared her alarmingly white teeth at him.

The shoe man grinned, spat, 'Oooh, get her!', guffawed, and turned back to his friends.

Arietty really wanted to go home. She wasn't so much tired as people-drained, exhausted by all the faces, the yapping mouths, the heat and stinks of others, in bars whose names she could not remember, where baleful music thundered like the howl of demons, and there were too many glittering eyes.

Zinsa had turned up at Arietty's flat earlier that day – they'd been friends since school. 'Your trouble,' Zinsa had said, pointing a perfectly-groomed talon at Arietty, 'is that you're just rooted in your room, growing pale and yellow like a mushroom. You don't do anything, except sit in front of that computer.'

Arietty had never been as dark as Zinsa. She was naturally paler, owing to a white grand-mother. She didn't bother to argue about her genetic inheritances, however; merely braced herself against the onslaught.

'You should go out more,' Zinsa said, then smiled to soften the lecture. 'Anyway, that's not a suggestion. Get ready. We're going out *now*.'

Zinsa meant well but she didn't understand Arietty's world – that of the virtual realms of the internet. She didn't know about Arietty's artwork, all the online friends she had made, the virtual galleries in which her creations were displayed. To Zinsa, as the pictures weren't created in reality they undoubtedly wouldn't count as real. 'Do some proper painting,' she'd probably say – if she knew about them.

And so Arietty had been dragged into the circles of the city to suffer its torments in the name of fun.

After the bars had been exhausted, Zinsa had been told about a private club – *The Leering Angel* – which apparently was one of *the* places to go. *Whatever that means*, Arietty thought sourly.

'Great name,' Zinsa said.

The tall skinny man who had offered the information flicked his fingers and a card appeared, as if in a magician's trick. A pass. A key. The magic artefact that would provide entrance into a mysterious realm. Arietty had already decided to make the best of it all by imagining her excursion as some kind of fantasy quest. The man with the card was a trickster, probably not to be trusted.

So here she and Zinsa were, in a narrow road of towering old terraced houses, only one of which spewed light and noise and had a sign above its door: *The Leering Angel*. This was painted – quite expertly Arietty decided – upon a board, which had been fixed above the door. The picture was of a tall, skinny man, dressed in black leather, sprouting black wings from his shoulders, and winking at the viewer. Leering, Arietty supposed.

Passing the revellers on the steps and proceeding into the hall, Arietty guessed this must be a student house, because it didn't look like a club, rather somewhere people lived, albeit somewhat squalidly. A bicycle was shoved against the wall below the maw of the stairs. The old black and white tiles underfoot were grimy. One of the stained-glass panels beside the open door was broken and patched with cardboard and tape. This was a house that had once been grand but was now infested with vermin and rot. Sad. Arietty could see an illustration of it in her mind already; its walls leaning rather more than they did in reality, its dark windows like mournful eyes.

A long corridor led Arietty and Zinsa past three rooms, apparently full of people; in one of them dancing. They emerged into a large kitchen, brightly lit, where a table was covered in beer cans and vodka bottles, plus an array of lurid "alcopops". People were still yapping here, like in the bars. Their faces looked bloated. They were fizzed up with booze and recreational drugs.

I have nothing in common with any of them, Arietty thought, and glanced at Zinsa who was already chatting with some Asian girl covered in red tattoos. *Not even with Zinny anymore? Have I moved so far away? How is any of this fun?*

A voice spoke close to her ear. 'You want the next floor.'

'What?' She looked back, but whoever had spoken had already turned away, or perhaps they hadn't even been speaking to her in the first place. Her imagination wanted to believe it had been a disembodied voice and that this was the beginning of a strange adventure, but of course that was unlikely. The people here, although trying hard to be the opposite, were desperately unstrange. The crowd had moved in behind her, closing the path she and Zinsa had taken to this room. She was trapped. And where was Zinsa? The room was crammed with bodies. Arietty's friend had been swallowed by them. She decided to worm her way back outside, call a cab. She could make her excuses to Zinsa tomorrow.

A girl was vomiting at the threshold to the house, braced by one hand against the door frame. Again, Arietty could see an illustration forming in her mind: the shadowy forms, the dark, merging colours. All that was clearly visible of the girl was her stiff, supporting arm and the gleam of light on the viscous pool at her feet. Dimmer, losing focus, her bare legs were splashed with vomit. Her long pale hair, knotty with extensions, was blurry and wet, hanging over her face. She wore no shoes. Perhaps the man outside was wearing them. Arietty noticed others observing the girl, one or two reaching forward to assist, others drawing back with pinched expressions. They were frozen, as if in a photograph. The girl was a prophet, half feared, half revered. Her visions made her sick. This was a painting of the time she predicted the end of the world. Beyond her, far above the skyline of the city, the night sky was gartered with a band of deep red.

But not in reality. This was merely a pissed-up student, who if she had any shred of self-respect would wake up tomorrow cringing at herself. She would call a friend: 'Did I do anything embarrassing last night?' *Yes. Yes, you did.*

Arietty glanced behind her at the stairs, reluctant to edge past the retching girl. *Perhaps we have to make our adventures,* she decided. *There are pictures and strangenesses everywhere, but they're in the eyes, the heart, the mind. They're in dreams. We can follow them.* She put a hand upon the sticky stair rail. Again a picture came to her: a fragile girl, shadowy as the sepia dark above her, staring up into the unknown.

Arietty needed the bath room, and this was as good an excuse as any to find herself on an upper floor, looking for a queue of people, or an open door with light spilling out. She found neither. There were wall lamps with old-fashioned fabric shades, from which little pom-poms dangled, but most of the bulbs had expired. The carpeting underfoot was merely the memory of a floor covering and would have to be removed with a metal scraper, should anyone ever bother to renovate the house. Sad ghosts might walk this corridor, sickened by what humanity had become, wishing they didn't have to keep walking and witness it.

This upper floor was quiet, but not watchful, as Arietty hoped, simply empty, worn out. She walked along the corridor, trying doors. Two were locked, but one opened onto a room full of crates, with a window blind so torn that the street light glow came in as if through filigree. Arietty held up her hand towards the pane and it seemed that light came out of her fingers. She backed out of the room and closed the door.

Next she came to another flight of stairs, which was narrow and potentially frightening. There were more rooms to investigate on the floor she was on, but she opted to go higher instead. She could *decide* she was led. There would have to be something to find. The stairs led to another corridor, where attic rooms must have been converted into rented bedsits. Here, Arietty could hear faint music, not modern but classical. To her right, some yards ahead, red light fanned from a doorway. As Arietty drew nearer she saw legs sticking out of the room, a woman's legs. She paused a moment, staring.

This must be it, what she'd been led to.

The legs were still, lifeless, but perhaps their owner was simply unconscious. The feet wore no shoes. Arietty approached cautiously. She was intrigued, curious, but also aware there might be others around of whom she should be wary. If these were dead legs, why did she feel so detached? She didn't feel there was a picture in what she saw, which was odd. The scene was weirdly prosaic.

She wouldn't know why until she saw everything there was to see. She reached the door, peered in, and her stomach clenched.

The legs had no body. For a few horrified moments she imagined they were amputated, but then the coolest, most sensible part of her mind pointed out there was no blood – no flesh, in fact – and that the thighs of the legs ended in devices clearly designed to attach them to a human body: a legless human body. Arietty put one hand against her stomach. Where was the owner of these legs? Why would someone who used them leave them here like this, sticking out of a doorway?

The room was empty of living presences, although possessed the watchfulness Arietty hadn't felt on the lower floor. There was a bed, rumpled, with a duvet covered in scarlet imitation satin. Beside the bed was a small cupboard covered with a fringed shawl supporting a lamp with a red shade and bulb. There was no other evidence to suggest someone had been there recently, but there was another door to the left of the bed. Perhaps this led to a bathroom. The music Arietty had heard had grown faintly louder. She knew that when she opened the door she wouldn't find a bathroom. She would find what the clues had led her to, nothing more.

The glow within was also red but extremely dim. Arietty saw the lights first, small brass lamps that perhaps held night lights or candles. The room contained a mattress on the floor strewn with rugs and shawls. The walls were similarly adorned. On the bed...

Was this a picture?

The woman had shoulder-length black hair cut severely straight on the brow into a fringe. Her skin was leper white, her eyes panda'd with black and diamante.

Her lips were astonishingly red and wet, somehow bigger than should belong in her face. She wasn't pretty, because her chin was weak, nor even particularly striking, despite the metal spiked corset she wore – and the legs. These were black, chitinous, multiply-jointed, like those of an insect, ending in claws. This female creature regarded Arietty from where she fawned against a semi naked, emaciated male, this one rigged up in patent leather harness, and a mask over his face. His nipples were pierced by rings, from which screaming faces in silver depended. He wore a shiny, black false phallus that reared decoratively from his crotch, but one very human testicle peeped half squashed from the edge of this device.

Arietty's mind wasn't taking pictures. She simply stared, numb, at what she saw.

The woman leered. 'Cat got ya tongue, honey?' She held a glass with a lurid cocktail in it.

The man laughed, muffled.

How could a cat take my tongue? Arietty thought. *Those words are meaningless. Why do people still say them?* 'I'm looking for the bathroom,' she said.

'You can piss on me,' drawled the woman, encouraging another grunt from the male, who behind his mask might possibly be gagged in some way.

'Where is it?' Arietty asked. 'The bathroom?'

The woman straightened up a little, moved her insect legs. 'Two doors down, love.'

'Thank you.'

Arietty stared at the scene before her for a few more moments. She didn't want to forget. 'I'm sorry,' she said.

The woman reached for a cigarette from the packet lying on the bed, lit one. 'What for?'

Arietty shook her head. They wouldn't even understand.

'We too weird for you, love?'

'No.' Arietty paused but didn't speak her thoughts. *That's the trouble. You're not weird at all. You're... ordinary.* She went back to the corridor, down to the cramped bathroom, where two aged tooth brushes embraced in a broken glass on the shabby sink, alongside the body of a crushed toothpaste tube that lay contorted on its back. Arietty pee'd gratefully, glancing round herself. Old blue slippers behind the door, a towelling bath robe in faded pink leopard skin hanging from a hook. There were holes in the vinyl flooring. A tap dripped into the bath.

They were bikers, Arietty told herself. *She lost her legs in a crash.*

But maybe that wasn't true. Maybe she'd been born like that. So sad.

Downstairs, the sick girl was now sitting on the steps with other revellers, drinking from a bottle of spring water. The oracle soothed, her prophecies spent. Arietty paused before her. 'Say something to me,' she said.

The girl grimaced, bleary eyed and confused, then smiled a little. 'They weren't his shoes,' she said.

Arietty took out her purse and put a coin in the lap of the pale-haired girl. 'Thank you. You've inspired me.'

'Wow,' said the girl, uncertainly. Her fingers closed over the coin.

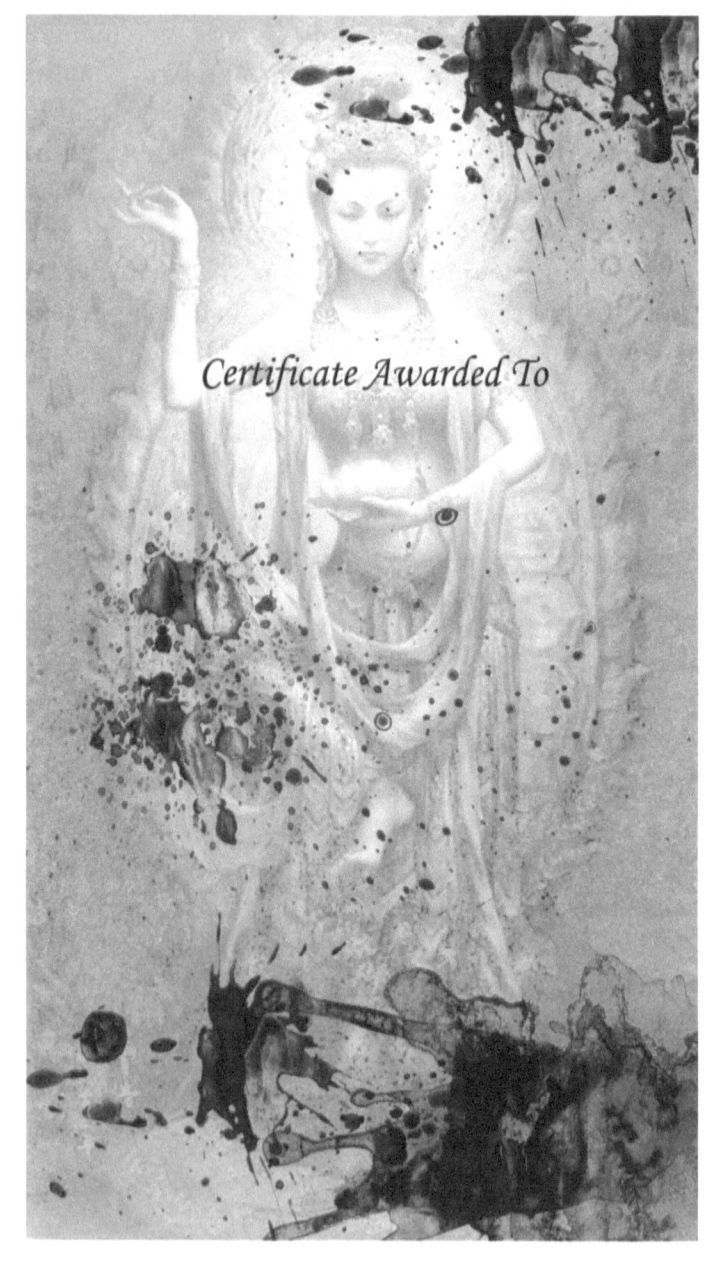

Certificate Awarded To

Master of None

This story was inspired by my distaste for the way the so-called 'healing community' developed that grew up around Reiki. When I was originally trained in this healing method, nearly 20 years ago, I was pleasantly astounded by it – and was eager to learn more. My curiosity led me to the internet, and what I found there was astounding but certainly not pleasant. Warring 'healers', each trying to outdo or undermine each other, and ever more bizarre variations of Reiki springing up with little or no associations to the original that had originated in Japan. There was a story begging to be written about this, and I had to write it, although it's specialised subject matter meant it couldn't be placed easily in a book or magazine. I doubt any New Age publication would have approved of my implied criticism!

The certificate lay beside Coral's plate on the breakfast table. She'd risen late that Saturday, which meant the mail had already arrived; one big, brown, fortified envelope in particular. Coral, mug of tea held in both hands, stared down at the pastel rainbow of the certificate. The teacher for *Five Seals Radiance* lived in Orkney. There was a seal rampant at either side of the title, each smiling and indicating with flippers the importance of the attainment. A slight shiver touched Coral's spine. *Five seals... Trite... Surely nonsense. No... Stop that.* She'd felt the energy wave as she'd lain on her sofa to receive the distant attunement; there could be no doubt. And yet.

Suppressing a sigh, Coral put down her mug and rose from her seat. Beneath the work surface by the cooker was a deep drawer containing unused picture frames, all of a size to accept most healing module certificates. Sometimes Coral had to trim the mount card; that was all. She opened up the back of a frame painted gold and inserted the *Five Seals* certificate. Job finished, she admired the effect. In a frame, the certificate looked better, less... no, there was no *less*. The healing system worked as well as any other and had been channelled by its founder Leearia from ancient knowledge that had lain hidden in the Orkneys for thousands of years. Coral took the certificate into her dining-room and saw that there was room for it near to the door; it would be hidden when the door was open. So much knowledge displayed on her walls, so much experience.

Coral's interest in healing systems had begun just over a year previously, owing to a woman she'd met at her Yoga class. Makayla Reed was a flamboyant new member of the class, a little younger than Coral, in her late 40s. She was something of a Pagan, but heavily into Reiki. Vocal on her favourite subject, she'd been happy to give demonstrations to other people in the class, which was held in the gym of a nearby school on Tuesday evenings. Coral had always been sceptical of things like this and had said so to Chloe Bowman with whom she had become casually friendly since joining the class.

'Yoga is one thing,' she'd confided, 'it's good for the body, the mind, the soul, but all this other stuff... I don't know. Seems like so much wishful thinking to me.'

Chloe had made a simpering sound that might have been agreement. She was altogether rather a *limp* person,

Coral thought, but kind-hearted and a good listener on the occasions they'd had time to talk. They always placed their mats next to one another at class now. Coral appreciated good listeners. But even so, sometimes the girl's lack of opinions tended to grate.

'Well, what do *you* think?' Coral said, rather too snappily.

'A lot of people swear by it,' Chloe offered. She hesitated. 'Why don't you try it, see for yourself?'

Coral wondered if she was correct in perceiving a slight note of criticism in Chloe's gentle remark: *don't judge what you haven't tried.* But perhaps that was merely her own conscience having a word with her. 'You're right. There's no harm in trying.' She laughed. 'Might even like it. Sometimes, there's pleasure in being proved wrong.'

'Yes,' said Chloe.

At the end of the session, Makayla was as usual holding court in the corner near the door, where water dispenser stood. The teacher, Jessica, had clearly become taken with Makayla's views over the past six weeks or so, and had begun Reiki training with her. Coral had to admit she didn't like the way Makayla had muscled into the group and subtly elbowed aside former favourites of the teacher, Coral among them. Makayla took care to give everyone attention, but even though no one had actually said it to one another, they knew she had become Queen Bee. She was a hearty, jovial person, with a generous but not dramatically overweight figure, given to wearing lots of beads and voluminous tie-dye skirts, which, at the start of the class, she always discarded like a skin to reveal exquisite soft linen Yoga garb beneath. She had a wide attractive face and expressive hands. Her hair was a riotous red mop, contained with artful messiness in a knot on her head, attractive tendrils always drooping down about her shoulders. Something about her meant she could not help being the centre of attention, perhaps even without trying. Beside her, Coral felt somehow stiff and conventional, unnoticeable, even though she was used to holding court occasionally herself. While she tried to dismiss Makayla as an embarrassing, attention-seeking extrovert, part of her was extremely envious and wished to be more like this other woman. For this reason, she generally ignored Makayla, hoping she'd eventually lose interest in the class and things could go back to how they'd been before.

But tonight, after Coral had put on her trainers and picked up her bag, instead of leaving the hall, she sauntered over to where Makayla was chatting with several of her class-mates. Chloe trailed behind her like the ghost of a drowned woman; she seemed always to have a cold and her long straight colourless hair somehow appeared perennially wet.

'Makayla,' Coral announced. She had enough of a commanding voice to get the other woman's attention immediately.

'Hi,' Makayla said, clearly having forgotten, or never known, Coral's name.

'Just wondering if your offer's still open – to have a sample of the Reiki.'

'Sure, sure!' Makayla enthused. 'Just a sec!' She began to rummage in the huge tapestried bag she always brought with her and eventually produced a business card. 'Give me a call, come over one evening, or weekend afternoon. We can book something.' She tilted her head at

Chloe. 'Both of you come!'

Coral was slightly appalled Makayla regarded her and Chloe as somehow a *pair*. Their friendship did not extend beyond the yoga class.

'Thanks,' said Chloe.

'Well... OK,' Coral said. 'Perhaps we can arrange something.' She took care to appear slightly flummoxed, so that Makayla would know she didn't generally socialise with Chloe. She decided not to offer her name so that Makayla would have to go to the trouble of asking someone else who she was. She turned to Chloe. 'I don't have your number...'

'Oh, yeah...' Chloe retrieved a mobile phone from her own bag and she and Coral enacted the ritual of exchanging contact details.

A couple of weeks later, it was arranged that Coral and Chloe would go to Makayla's house on a Saturday afternoon. Coral drove to Chloe's house to pick her up. Like several of the women in the yoga class, both Coral and Chloe were single – Coral divorced, and glad to be, Chloe unclaimed by any man, which was no surprise to Coral. Men, in her experience, were not greatly turned on by drowned ghosts. Chloe still lived with her parents at age 27. As they drove to Makayla's place in relative silence, Coral reflected on the fact that she loved her freedom. Most women she knew, from the office, the yoga class and her Latin dance club were chained by husbands and/or children to their homes. They could not do things spontaneously – ever. She realised that in this respect Chloe was not a bad companion. She would always be free to take advantage of an invitation. *Perhaps I've been too dismissive of her*, Coral thought, casting a covert glance at the pale girl staring out of the windscreen beside her. *Perhaps if she had a little guidance she'd come out of herself a bit.*

Makayla sailed down her garden path to greet them. She wore gardening gloves and carried a pair of secateurs. A kaftan wafted about her body in a bouquet of deep, jewelled colours. Her perfume smelled of incense and cut grass. 'Hi, hi!' she trilled. 'Right on time!' She opened the garden gate. 'Come on in.'

The house smelled deliciously of baking. *Could this woman get any more perfect?* Coral thought wistfully. Makayla led her visitors into a large, sun-filled front room. Flowers spilled voluptuously from antique bowls onto elderly tables. Thick Oriental rugs were strewn everywhere sumptuously. Plump sofas sagged seductively, claimed by sleeping cats. Pre-Raphaelite prints adorned the dark red walls. In the corner near the French windows, an immense flat screen TV lurked in what seemed a slightly embarrassed way.

'What a great place,' said Chloe.

'Thanks,' Makayla beamed. 'Now, I do have tea and freshly-cooked muffins.' She winked at Chloe. 'I have elderflower wine too, but perhaps it would be cruel of us to drink that in front of the designated driver.'

'Don't let me stop you,' Coral said, smiling. She was rather surprised a self-professed Master Healer drank alcohol, but then Makayla was rather *Bohemian*.

While Chloe and Mikayla drank a glass of wine, and Coral herself consumed a mug of satisfyingly rich, dark Assam tea, (thank God, not just herbal on offer), Mikayla talked about healing. 'The energy of the universe is all around us,' she enthused, gesturing wide with both arms.

'We're simply not aware of it. But we can connect with it, to effect healing or to touch reality in other ways.' She winked. 'That's why I get called an old witch!' She laughed heartily. Coral wondered if Makayla had had a few drinks before she and Chloe had arrived.

'But how does this healing thing work?' Chloe asked, frowning. 'Do we just have to believe in it or something?' She held out her hands in front of her, almost transparent in their paleness, gazed at them, perhaps wholly unconvinced the immense loving energy of the universe was prepared to course through her.

'You don't have to believe in it at all,' Makayla said. 'That the beauty of it. Once I attune you, you'll find it to be a completely physical thing. The most sceptical people are astounded. My husband, for example!'

Coral glanced around the room. There was no sign of a man in this house, no remnant, no psychic effluvium. Makayla perhaps caught the thought.

'We don't *live* together,' she said. 'I need my space.'

'Convenient,' Coral said, and laughed, to change the tone of what had sounded like a sharp remark.

'Certainly is,' Makayla grinned. 'Anyway, the bugger got me to attune him to prove me wrong. He *loves* trying to do that.' She rolled her eyes. 'But Reiki knocked his socks off. He could *feel* it. That was the last I heard of the sarcastic remarks, I can tell you!'

'I do find it hard to believe,' Coral said, 'that my body, my... er... *energy system*, can be somehow changed so I become a channel for Reiki.'

'Many feel that way,' Makayla said, in a kindly tone. 'It really doesn't matter. Once you've had a treatment, you can decide whether you'd like to proceed. Reiki *is* for everyone, in most respects, but I don't believe it should be forced on people. It will be entirely up to you.'

'Fine,' Coral said. 'I've an open mind about it.'

Makayla nodded. 'Well, let's get started. Coral, you can go first. Chloe, dig into my books and magazines or watch the telly, while we're away.' She smiled at Coral, gesturing at the door. 'I have a temple,' she said.

Makayla's temple was on the first floor, an erstwhile bedroom facing the garden. Looking out of the window, Coral saw a beautifully-cultivated space with curling pathways, a large white Buddha statue, ponds and a stream... wind chimes in the trees.

The temple itself had golden yellow walls that were caressed by the light. Various altars were positioned against the walls. Coral saw shrines coloured by different beliefs systems: Egyptian, Norse, even what seemed to be Voodoo.

Makayla unrolled a futon and gestured for Coral to lie on it. 'Take off your shoes,' she said. 'But that's all. I don't know how much you know about Reiki, but it's not massage or anything similar. I'll simply hold my hands in certain positions over your head and shoulders – we'll just stick with those for this session – and all you'll experience is a lovely heat, and great relaxation.'

Somewhat awkwardly, Coral lay down. It felt odd, like lying on the bare floor. She could smell a musty incense aroma rising from the carpet. Makayla inserted a CD of some tinkly New Age music into the discreet sound system and then went to wash her hands. Coral was finding it hard to breathe, as if each intake of air had to be drawn consciously, otherwise she wouldn't be breathing at all. Was it a frisson of fear she felt, or something else – something that felt as if was about to take a step into a different life?

When Makayla returned she moved silently, bare-footed,

across the room. 'Don't be nervous,' she murmured.

Coral smiled weakly. She felt as if she was at the dentist's, or somewhere equally nerves-inducing, but in a way this feeling excited her.

Makayla sat cross-legged behind Coral's head. 'Close your eyes,' she said softly. 'Drift...'

Coral obeyed the directive about the eyes, but was convinced drifting was a tall order. And yet, as the gentle heat from Makayla's hands seeped into her and the waves of unobtrusive music washed over her, she felt herself sinking... sinking...

Half an hour later, Makayla woke Coral up, by gently squeezing her shoulder. Coral opened her eyes. She felt almost... drunk... but pleasantly so.

'Lie here a while if you like,' Makayla murmured. 'I can see the treatment had a profound effect upon you.'

Coral couldn't even talk. She wanted to continue basking in the receding echoes of what she'd experienced. It had been like a dream, like being held. Really, this was ridiculous, her rational mind told her. Was she thinking so wishfully about being nurtured and cared for that her hungry feelings had blown everything up out of proportion? And yet... she just felt so good, so languorous.

Before she got downstairs again, Coral had decided she wanted to learn the system.

Chloe was not affected as strongly as Coral by the treatment Makayla gave her, but she too signed up for training. Makayla said they could learn at the same time if they wanted to, but separate was also good. Coral confided quietly, while Chloe was in the bathroom, that she'd prefer to learn alone. And Makayla didn't hesitate to comply, even though it would clearly have been far more convenient for her to earn her fee only for two training sessions rather than spread over four.

Back home, with a date for her training written neatly in her diary for the following weekend, Coral went to the internet to find out more about Reiki healing. She knew the facts from Makayla – a system inaugurated in the early 20th century by a Japanese Buddhist, how it spread to the West via a Japanese American and was once available only to the very rich. Clearly, thousands believed in the system, but what astonished Coral more than that were all the permutations of it. She found Reikis of every sort, as well as systems with completely different names, but which were incredibly similar. It was as if each new teacher over the last thirty years or so had added to and expanded it, even in some cases renamed it. The amount on offer was mind-boggling. While Makayla claimed to be "old fashioned" and liked to train her students in face-to-face sessions, there were teachers online offering what they called "distant attunements". For as little as ten dollars someone could buy one of these. How could they possibly work?

Because Makayla had told Coral to call her if she had any questions at all, Coral did so that evening. 'How did so many systems spring up?' Coral asked. 'And what are these distant attunements?'

Makayla sighed down the phone. 'You simply pay ten dollars for a certificate to say you've done the training,' she said, then made a tutting sound. 'Oh, that's harsh of me. I know some of those teachers are sincere about their work. They "send" attunements to their students, through meditation, but with most of them, that's it. No follow up support, simply a case of "we takes ya money, then we're gone". I don't agree with it, but then I believe this kind of training should be more than just a "wham bam, thank you, ma'am", attunement. It's an education, an unfolding even, and teachers have a responsibility.' She drew breath. 'Oh, listen to me, I'm ranting.' She laughed. 'Let's just say people get what they pay for. People react differently to the treatment and to the training. You yourself, Coral, had quite a strong reaction. Some people shouldn't be left to deal with that alone, if they even experience attunement properly through that method. I don't know. But I'm not a fan. You asked. You got. Anything else you want to know?'

Coral laughed. 'No, you made everything clear. But how bewildering it all is.'

'There's money in it,' Makayla said darkly.

Coral resolved not to look at any more web sites about healing. She had been lucky enough to meet someone who would teach her in the way it had originally been taught, and the rest was mostly the territory of charlatans or wishful thinking.

So began a new phase in Coral's life. Reiki became another of her hobbies. She enjoyed the training, which Makayla went to considerable lengths to make "special", a rite of passage. Incense burned, curtains were drawn, candles were lit. Makayla padded barefoot around the temple, while Coral sat with closed eyes and hands in prayer to receive the attunements. She felt this process, with its poetic words and ritual, had a religious feel to it, but of course, no, it was *spiritual*, and that was different.

Afterwards, like all those astonished students of Makayla's in the past, Coral could feel a sinuous energy travelling through her, out of her hands. The effect was physical. She could experience the heat and so could others.

For some weeks after her first-degree training, Coral offered treatments to people for free. Everyone complimented her on the results, saying how good the treatments made them feel. Coral was clear to point out this wasn't down to her personally, but the energy she channelled. Privately, she was amazed. This *wasn't* just down to wishful thinking; there was a tangible effect. She couldn't explain it. And yet, even though her experiences were exciting and satisfying – even ego-boosting – Coral couldn't dispel the feeling that there was yet something more to discover. Perhaps this was simply later stages of the system.

Chloe also appeared impressed by the training, and she and Coral now met once a fortnight or so at Coral's home to exchange treatments and talk about them. Coral perceived, however, that Chloe's interest wasn't as keen as her own. Coral had her eye on Reiki Master already and could imagine herself padding softly around her own temple barefoot, uttering soft words, making flowing gestures, in a robe of incense and candlelight. She'd begun clearing out the small box room in the house, which had been the dumping ground of everything Coral didn't want to throw out yet didn't actually need or use. This act in itself was therapeutic; a clearing.

The room, when it was bare, looked bigger. Coral painted the walls a soft gold, furnished it with large cushions in ethnic designs, hung prints on the wall – a stylised Buddha in red and gold, dolphins leaping from a dark ocean against a sunset, an angel depicted so faintly against a glowing background you could only see it when you concentrated on the picture. Good for meditation,

Coral thought. She purchased a low table of Nepalese design, on which she arranged a new incense burner, vanilla-scented candles as thick as her wrists, and a small white statue of Kwan Yin, whom the woman in the New Age shop she'd visited had told her was a Japanese goddess associated with healing. Coral began to spend time in the room every evening after her yoga exercises, practicing Reiki on herself and meditating. This felt as if she was doing something that was good for her, like exercise or eating properly.

Coral detected the faintest whiff of...what? disapproval?... from Chloe when she showed the girl the finished room. 'You're really getting into this, aren't you?' Chloe said.

'Yes,' Coral said, firmly.

'Well, the room looks nice,' Chloe said.

Their attunements to the first degree of Reiki were three months past. Coral felt she now wanted to take the training to its next step. She mentioned this to Chloe, expecting her to feel the same.

Chloe wrinkled her nose. 'Oh, I don't think I'll do any more,' she said. 'Reiki 1 is fine for me.'

'But... don't you want to learn how to use the second-degree symbols, take it all a notch higher?' Coral asked her.

'No, not really.' Chloe smiled wanly. 'But, yeah, you should. You'd be good as a teacher.' She went to examine the picture of the angel.

'Well, it's too early to talk about that,' Coral said. She was faintly horrified when Chloe turned and gave her a knowing glance and felt herself colour.

'You really get into things,' Chloe said. 'I just dabble.'

Coral wondered how Chloe could come to this conclusion when the girl didn't really know her very well.

'I want to do it because it helps people,' Coral said, a little stiffly. 'If you can make a difference in the world, however small, surely you should do so.'

Chloe shrugged.

Coral realised she'd anticipated embarking on all the training with Chloe, having someone with whom to share and discuss it. She now felt disappointed, not just in the lack of a companion for the journey, but in Chloe herself. She'd wanted Chloe to be more than she was. *My assumption*, she told herself firmly – and somewhat proudly at her self-honesty. *A wrong one.* Still, if Chloe was happy to continue their meetings, she could be someone for Coral to practice on and get feedback from. That would have to be enough.

When Coral phoned Makayla later that day she was nervous that Makayla would tell her it was too soon to continue the training, but the woman agreed that Coral should now take the second degree. 'You've really taken to it,' she said. 'With some people, I'd advise waiting a little longer, but not with you. I can tell you're more than ready.'

'Yes, I'm eager to learn.' Coral laughed. 'I've even made myself a little temple. A room that needed clearing out.'

'Cool. Would you like me to come and do the attunements at your place, then? Wake the room to its purpose?

'Oh... yes. Yes, that would be great.'

'I'm free this Saturday evening.'

'Me too.'

Coral considered inviting Chloe along, then decided against it. The doors to the inner sanctum must remain closed to the unbeliever, she thought jokingly, smiling to herself.

Although the Reiki symbols had traditionally been secret, passed on from teacher to student, the secrecy had broken down after the advent and rise of the internet. Now, they could be seen on hundreds of web sites and in books. In a way, Coral was disappointed this was so. She imagined how important the symbols must have seemed in the days when a teacher revealed them reverently as part of the attunement ceremony. In those days, Makayla told her, students hadn't even been allowed to draw the symbols to take home with them. They'd had to be memorised. This, she said, had given rise to the vast variation in detail of the more complicated symbols.

'People didn't remember them correctly and passed them on to their own students in the incorrect form,' Makayla said. 'I don't think it matters, really. The intention behind the symbols is what counts. Some say they were even added to the system later and that the founder, Usui, originally taught it without symbols.'

'Symbols fascinate me,' Coral said. 'I'm looking forward to working with them.'

'You get three of them at Reiki Two and the final one when – or if – you take the third degree.'

Coral already knew this from her internet research but didn't say so. She didn't want to appear a know-it-all to her teacher.

'I usually charge a hundred and fifty quid for Reiki Two,' Makayla said, 'but to you – a hundred and twenty. Is that ok?'

'Yes, *thanks*.'

'Only one session for this,' Makayla said.

Makayla arrived at seven o'clock on the Saturday. All she brought with her was a photocopied training manual for

Coral to keep, which contained the symbols and gave tips on how to use them. 'You'll find your own uses,' Makayla said, carelessly handing the stapled papers to Coral. 'This is just a guide.'

Makayla enthused over Coral's temple room, which was lit softly by candlelight and smelled warmly of jasmine joss sticks. Coral had added to the room a very expensive ochre-coloured Oriental rug made of silk.

'Great energy,' Makayla remarked. 'I can tell you've created this temple with love.'

'Well... yes, yes I did.' Coral smiled at Makayla.

'Let's get started, then!'

If anything, the second degree attunements felt more powerful to Coral than those she'd experienced before. As she received a treatment from Makayla at the end of the session, she drifted in a half-conscious state, and found herself thinking about the thousands of people all over the world who had taken this training. She thought about the different systems that had sprung up. So many of "the attuned" were eager to work creatively with what they'd learned, symbols and ideas cascading through their minds as they channelled the energy. *I get it*, Coral thought. *I get how it happened.* The healing energy was fluid, formless, yet could flow into shapes to take on form: the empty vessels of people's creative imaginings. For each person it touched, the energy could change, mutate, become something new, yet simultaneously retaining its pure self. And the deeper you delved into its heart, so the more permutations would be revealed. The secrets of centuries, perhaps even millennia. The revelation made Coral breathless, excited. What was that little New Age saying Makayla had once shared? *Where intention goes - energy flows*. And human intention was a fathomless ocean, waiting to be energised.

The following morning, Coral went to her computer in her dressing-gown, holding a mug of tea and finishing off her breakfast toast. She still felt high from the previous evening's adventures. After the attunements were over, she and Makayla had drunk some wine, which had gone to their heads, and had later required a giggling phone call to Makayla's husband to come and pick her up, since she was in no state to drive. Makayla scorned people who she called "miserable ascetics" and claimed – as she sloshed the wine into glasses – that hedonism was as much a spiritual discipline as monkish abstinence. 'Look at the celebrations of Dionysus,' she'd said.

Coral, being unfamiliar with the excesses of Dionysians could only nod, as if she knew.

'Don't be afraid to celebrate,' Makayla had said. 'Free your mind.'

During the evening, Makayla had led Coral on meditational path-workings, and either from the influence of the alcohol, or the Reiki, or both, Coral had visualised magnificent vistas, cyclopean temples in endless landscapes below a nebula-splattered firmament, both temples and sky scored with complicated symbols and patterns, seething with energy. Makayla had told her to draw these symbols, write down all that she remembered. She had to do it right then, *that* moment – 'mustn't wait, remember what happened to the original Reiki students and their symbols' – so Coral had somewhat woozily done her drawings, written her notes. Today, catching sight of the wine-ringed papers on the kitchen table next to the empty glasses, Coral felt the scrawls upon them were the revelations of an oracle.

Something was waiting for her. Something huge.

She sat down at her computer, turned it on, waited as it whirred into life.

First she typed "Reiki symbols" into the search engine, then went directly to "images". A waterfall of pictures splashed before her eyes; symbols, cupped hands, praying hands, ying/yang, more symbols, the universe, swirling light... She blinked, had to scoot backwards on her chair, click once more to "all" to stem the tide of visual information. Was she that hung over? She finished off her tea in one gulp. Her hands hovered, poised, over the keyboard.

Even in a few months, there was more information than ever before. She changed the search to "healing systems". Now, with the knowledge she had, the revelations she'd experienced, Coral was curious about all that other people before her had invented. While many systems were clearly and heavily influenced by Reiki, with simple embellishments, some seemed to soar far away from the original inspirations. Shamanic Reiki, animal Reiki, angelic Reiki. Belief systems were even mixed, some part Christian/part Pagan, a stylised crucifix symbol nestling unembarrassed beside a pentagram, with the principle Reiki symbols looking on from a different row in the table of pictures, perhaps wondering what they were doing there. Other systems were greatly influenced by Egyptian mythology and magic. Coral spent hours reading all the web sites, making notes, until her stomach demanded to be fed.

She went to the kitchen to prepare herself pasta and salad, realising how hungry for knowledge she was, as hungry as an empty stomach. One thing she'd noticed, though, was that all the colourful new systems she'd read about required potential students to have already taken the Reiki Master Degree. The books Coral had bought, albeit most of them written at least twenty years previously, stated that between six months to a year was a suitable gap between second and third degree. While Coral knew Makayla wasn't a woman to stick to tradition, and would no doubt be happy to attune her to that level after another couple of months, Coral was impatient she'd have to wait that long. Now she'd started, she wanted to draw upon the patterns of the universe, interpret the messages offered by other teachers, taste the different flavours of the energy. She remembered the cyclopean temples of her visualisations and craved to revisit them, explore that alien landscape within. She felt these images were intrinsically part of her training.

After her meal, she went back to her computer. One site had particularly drawn her attention, that of Lunarshadow Stardaughter, an American who styled herself a "Grand Master" of Reiki and a whole list of other systems. She specialised in distant attunement and offered literally hundreds of different modalities to students, some of them as cheap as ten dollars, the most expensive being around fifty, with the majority somewhere in between. It seemed sad to Coral that unadulterated Reiki 1 was in the ten-dollar bracket, as if it were an inconvenience to get out of the way before more exotic wonders could be revealed. Lunarshadow's site was beautifully designed and easy to navigate. Unlike some of the others Coral had seen, it wasn't plastered with flashing Buddha GIFs or screaming pink starry backgrounds. The colours were muted, the design unornamented. An arty photo of a single white lotus, voluptuous with dew, adorned the home page. On the

"About Me" section, Coral saw a picture of a hippyish, middle-aged woman, dressed in white gypsy skirts and blouse, showing a deep cleavage, where a silver pendant of a goddess snuggled. She had tousled, dusty-looking, ash blonde hair, half-pinned up, half trailing, a style Coral had tried hard to emulate in the past but had since given up in favour of a tidier style, given that her hair had refused to tousle wantonly and had just looked a mess. The smile on Lunarshadow's face looked welcoming and genuine. She didn't hide her wrinkles and appeared supremely confident; an attractive older woman who didn't care about ageing. This, Coral realised, in a moment of self-awareness, was an ideal she admired. It was why, despite her initial envy, she had been so drawn to Makayla. This was what she wanted to be.

Coral read that Lunarshadow's drive to be a teacher, and to make healing accessible to all, had led her to offer distance attunements, although she ran workshops continually at her ranch in California and was prominent on the New Age festival circuit. Despite Makayla having uttered withering remarks about the quality of distance training, Lunarshadow claimed to offer a full backup service to students. Skype meetings cost fifteen dollars, but, well... the woman must have to make a charge or she'd spend all her time talking to people about their problems and not teaching. Coral read all the articles on the site, and the gushing testimonials. She looked at the photo gallery where Lunarshadow held court at various festivals in glorious sunshine, surrounded by beaming women. But always Coral was drawn back to the page featuring that cornucopia of modalities, including the forlorn Reiki Master with its pauper price of twenty-five dollars.

Coral did have a moment of doubt and remembered

Makayla's words. *You just pay ten dollars for a certificate to say you've done the training.* Some people, she knew – because Makayla had told her – simply collected certificates. Coral had no idea what these people must do with the healing. Did they even use it? Or was it simply wheeled out at workshops, where a circle of practitioners would sit chanting, holding hands, believing they glimpsed infinity?

So. The path forked. The moment of doubt came. And went.

Coral filled in the online form to receive the Reiki Master attunement. She told herself she was merely enquiring. She knew she should discuss this with Makayla, give her friend the chance to say yes or no, but for some reason she found herself shrinking from that. She knew, instinctively, that this time Makayla would advise her to wait a couple of months. 'What's the rush?' she'd ask, and then Coral would feel bad. She'd feel thwarted. Like in all online shops, what she wanted was simply there on Lunarshadow's site, immediately at her fingertips and the entry of her payment details. It was so easy.

When she got home from work on the Monday evening, Coral was delighted to see she'd received an email from Lunarshadow. The mail thanked Coral for her enquiry and explained how distance attunements worked. She'd have to choose a time to receive it and Lunarshadow would send it to her at this time. She elaborated that the energy worked beyond normal space/time, so the attunement could be sent into the past or future, if needs be. Should Coral be happy to proceed, a time could be arranged for her to receive her attunement. If she wanted to receive a signed certificate, in the form of a document to print out herself, there would be no charge, but should she want a printed certificate, on parchment card, there would be a small fee of twenty dollars, including international shipping.

That simple. No questions asked, such as if Coral had taken her first and second degree. There was no instruction on how to pass on attunements, or anything about teaching. No mention of a training manual or even a JPG of the Master symbol. *Wham, bam, thank you, ma'am*, as Makayla had said. Well perhaps such things could be discussed on Skype.

Coral remembered the solemn ceremonies of her earlier training, the sense of occasion. She remembered Makayla proudly showing her their lineage and that Coral was only five teachers away from the Reiki founder. What was Lunarshadow's lineage? How could she even know that Coral would bother to compose herself to receive the attunement? She could just pay her money and then pass herself off as a Master. How could the energy be passed on in this way?

Determinedly, Coral hit "reply" and wrote back to Lunarshadow. She spoke of her certainty about taking her healing studies further and that... She paused, thought, then continued by saying that her teacher for the previous degrees had moved away and didn't do distance training.

Coral went out that evening to her Latin dance class, and when she came home hurried to look at her email. She wasn't really expecting a reply this soon, because of the time differences, but no, there it was: another mail from Lunarshadow. Coral was pleased to read that a manual would in fact be forwarded as a document file once she'd made her payment. The mail ended with Lunarshadow asking if Coral still wished to proceed, and if so to let her know the time for her attunement in the relevant time zone and submit payment on her web site.

Coral wrote back, specifying Wednesday at 7.30 pm, her time. She faltered over whether to order a physical certificate, then decided to pay the extra, because it would feel more "real".

On Wednesday, Makayla sent Coral a text message, asking how she was getting on following her Reiki 2 attunement. Coral felt distinctly uncomfortable seeing the message. She texted back that all was fine, thank you. Normally, she'd have felt moved to suggest a meeting for coffee after this week's yoga or arrange a night for Reiki practice. She realised she'd been too abrupt in her reply. Makayla would think this was strange... wouldn't she? Coral sent another message saying how hellishly busy she was for the next fortnight, but perhaps they could meet up one evening early next month. Smiley face. A row of xxx's.

She'd not go to yoga for a couple of weeks.

Coral was aware she risked jeopardising her new friendship with a woman she liked and admired, and who lived close to her, simply to pursue a bizarrely urgent need to further her training.

It'll be fine, she told herself. *Once the training's done, it's done. I can forget about it and look at the other modalities I want to learn, which Makayla doesn't teach.*

But Coral, said that annoying inner voice. *Why did you even bother with the Reiki Master? That woman would have taken your money for any of what she offers without question. Does any of it mean anything? Is it not just writing on a page?*

But... Coral knew she could not argue with herself over this. She would undergo the distance training with as much genuine commitment as she could muster, and her conscience would simply have to live with that.

Later, in her temple, Coral did some yoga exercises, then composed herself ready to receive the attunement. She had to say a little phrase Lunarshadow had mailed her, and now recited it aloud: 'I open myself with full awareness to accept and receive this Reiki Master attunement, from Lunarshadow Stardaughter and the love of the universe.'

And there was something, wasn't there? A rush of heat, a hastening of the breath?

Coral had memorised the Master symbol and visualised it now, hanging before her, radiating light. She willed it into herself. She could feel it sinking into her body, filling her with a healing glow. It was done.

The next day she mailed Lunarshadow. 'Thank you for the attunement, which was wonderful. I'll be in touch concerning further training in the near future.'

A greater part of spiritual studies, Coral thought, was belief. She must believe in her training. This wasn't too difficult, because she was adept at drowning out or ignoring her nagging inner voice, although she would have liked someone upon whom to practice attunements. All the likely candidates were people known either to Chloe or Makayla, and she didn't want to risk them finding out what she'd done. Oh well, she didn't have to become a teacher to continue her training. And presumably, at some point, she could actually undergo the Master training again with Makayla. Wouldn't hurt anyone. Her spiritual studies were personal, private, and she would pursue them alone.

When her Master certificate arrived, it was quite beautiful, and Coral wished she could hang it on her temple wall, along with the two that Makayla had given her. Should she just stop inviting Makayla and Chloe over to her house? No, it would seem odd. She paused in her thoughts. Just how valuable were these friendships to her? *Have I ever really had close friends in the way other women have?* She wondered. She'd never been one to confide in others or pour out her heart to them. She'd never even had a pet, and her marriage had been a bloodless affair that neither she nor her husband had felt any qualm about discarding. She realised that she had always dealt with life's difficulties alone.

To appease nagging feelings of guilt, and an odd kind of remorse, Coral practiced her Reiki almost furiously. Every day she spent an hour in her temple doing yoga and then giving herself some healing. She meditated on the symbols. She performed an attunement on a spider plant and was sure it became perkier thereafter. Yet even though she was a "master" now, and could call herself that, there was still within her an itch of yearning. But for what? More training? Was she heading to become one of those people who merely collected certificates to hang on a wall? She was sure this wasn't the case. There was something waiting for her that would not only change her in the gentle way that Reiki had but open her up to something so immense she could not yet imagine it. This unknown thing was alluring in its distance and yet – she felt – tantalisingly close.

After her two week "retreat" from classes and other social activities, Coral re-emerged. She called Makayla and Chloe and suggested they go for a Chinese meal together in town at the weekend. Her treat.

Coral didn't want to lead a double life forever. She found that keeping her Master training secret from her friends wasn't difficult, although she'd experienced a frisson of disquiet when she'd given Makayla a treatment one evening. This had been nearly a month after the Master attunement, and Makayla had remarked the energy had felt different.

'In what way?' Coral asked, aware of an increase in her heart beat.

Makayla sat up on the mat in Coral's temple. 'Just... different,' she said. 'Must be because we haven't swapped treatments for a while.'

'I've kept up my practice,' Coral said, 'so the Reiki doesn't feel weaker or anything, does it?'

'Oh, nothing like that,' Makayla said. 'It's probably just me! I tend to think the way people channel Reiki is similar to a fingerprint; each person has their own...' She wrinkled her nose. 'Well... feeling.' She shrugged.

'I hope it isn't anything to worry about,' Coral said.

Makayla waved an arm at her. 'No, no, don't be daft. The feel of the energy can change as you become more confident. It'll be no more than that.'

But perhaps it *was* more than that. Coral had already bought from Lunarshadow a "Star Guide Reiki" attunement and also "Reiki of the Birds", the manual for which had included meditations on various totem birds. She'd enjoyed receiving the attunements, if only for the small ceremony she performed herself: a ritual bath, a soft robe about her body, a new incensy perfume daubed on her skin that she'd bought from an online store. She did her exercises beforehand, trying to make them like a dance, and then lay on her yoga mat on the temple floor, an open vessel to receive the energy pulsing through the ethers to reach her.

Coral loved receiving attunements and then working with the ideas behind whatever system she'd chosen to learn. And yet? And yet...

The brief manuals she'd received were adequate for her needs and any questions she wanted to ask could be provided by the infinite knowledge base of the internet. Lunarshadow didn't enquire how she was getting on, and Coral didn't offer any information about this herself. She ordered her attunements and paid for them. She received them. These were simple business transactions, which gave her the ability to take her training further in her own way. The certificates were stored in a drawer, waiting for the day they could be brought out into the light.

Impatient to reach this day, three months after taking her second degree with Makayla, Coral made what she hoped sounded like a casual but keen enquiry about Reiki Master. She did this on an evening when she was visiting Makayla, and her friend had already consumed several glasses of wine.

Makayla pursed her lips. 'Well, with anyone else, I'd suggest leaving it a bit longer, but you're so keen Coral, and you've taken to the energy so well, I can't see any point in keeping the last degree from you.' She clasped one of Coral's hands. 'I'd be very happy to share this with you.'

'How much?'

Makayla frowned a little. 'Oh, Coral, we're friends now. I don't like charging friends.'

'It's also part of your business, your living.' Coral

smiled. 'Please. I want to pay you.'

'All right. Fifty quid?'

'Be quiet. You'll get a hundred and not complain, OK?'

Makayla grinned. 'Well, if you're sure.' She sighed. '*This* is why I'm not rich – or so my husband tells me!' She laughed heartily and drained the glass of wine in her hand.

The attunement would take place at Makayla's house; Coral felt sure this was the right thing to do. Makayla suggested they invite Chloe over for a meal after the attunements, of which there would be two this time. 'Master Degree can be quite a blast,' Makayla said, 'so we'd better not spend much time worshipping Dionysus that night.' She laughed.

'Not drink? You?' Coral laughed also.

'I *can* be responsible when it's needed,' Makayla declared, then shook her head, grinning.

Quite a blast... Could that honestly describe Coral's distant attunement? Well, that wouldn't matter now, would it?

As before, Makayla went to great effort to make Coral's attunements memorable. The house was filled with incense and candle light. Soft music played. There was a sense of reverence in every room. They'd arranged for the training to take place in the afternoon, giving them time to relax before Chloe turned up for dinner at 7.30. Coral did indeed feel very spacey, but perhaps that was mostly down to the atmosphere. The attunements, when she received them, were like waves of sound and light. She was rocked by them. She felt like weeping but breathed her way out of that. She didn't want to cry in front of Makayla, because what was there to cry about?

Questions would be unwanted.

But after the ceremony, Makayla seemed uncomfortable, so much so that Coral had to ask if something was wrong.

'No, no... I'm sorry,' Makayla said, shaking her head. 'It's just that during the attunement, I felt there was...' She stared at Coral. 'You might think I'm losing it, if I say.'

'Say what?'

'Did you feel anything... different?' Makayla asked, then added tentatively, '*see* anything?'

'The energy felt very strong,' Coral answered, 'but I didn't *see* anything, as such. Just soft colours in my mind, perhaps a suggestion of...' Now that she thought about it, maybe she *had* visualised something. 'Perhaps flowing water, or seaweed. Nothing unpleasant, though. Why?'

'I saw a dark temple,' Makayla said, 'and perhaps it *was* underwater. It was immense... pulsating with energy... almost watchful. I felt there were *beings* inside it.' Again, she shook her head. 'I must've been thinking of those images you came up with after Reiki 2.'

'You seem to find them sinister, yet you didn't then,' Coral said, a trifle sharply.

'No, not sinister.' Makayla smiled. 'I think you're a natural, that's all. Reiki has opened you up. Don't you feel that?'

Coral nodded. 'Yes. I do.'

'Keep a note of your meditations,' Makayla said. 'There may be messages for you there.'

Coral left it another couple of months before mentioning to Makayla she'd found some "amusing" healing systems on the internet and was going to give them a try. 'Your ten-dollar fixes,' she said airily. 'Still, I'm curious.'

Makayla gave her a strange, guarded look, then laughed. 'Well, it's your money.'

'Oh, come on, aren't you curious about what on earth the "Healing Rays of the Blessed Virgin" must entail?'

'Morbidly, I suppose,' Makayla said.

There was no stopping Coral after that.

She knew that Makayla was somewhat bemused by her enthusiasm for the motley array of healing hybrids into which Coral threw herself. They didn't talk about them very much, and Chloe simply wasn't interested. Coral mounted her certificates upon the walls of her least used room – the dining-room, since she always used her large kitchen in which to eat and socialise – so that Makayla wasn't likely to see them. Sometimes Makayla would ask cheerfully, 'so what malformed bastard child of Reiki are you learning this week?'

Once Coral replied, '"Frankenstein's Rays of Joy", which made both her and Makayla laugh.

But privately, Coral enjoyed receiving the attunements, telling herself they all had different flavours and feelings. Some, she had to admit, did nothing for her, but others she was sure had a kick to them. She amassed certificates over the months. They crept across her walls like slow-moving rays of sunlight. By this time, she was buying attunements from other teachers. She'd almost exhausted Lunarshadow's catalogue, and the few modalities that remained were rather too religious in flavour for her taste.

The certificates and the training seemed to Coral like the bricks of a temple she was building – her personal temple – and the more she added bricks, the faster it was raised towards the sky. In her mind, it was a ziggurat of pale granite against a beautiful sunset. Sometimes, in her meditations, she'd wander this structure, add details to it as she traversed its chambers and corridors. Symbols of many different healing systems adorned the walls, and were inlaid as mosaics into the floors. The building hummed with power, like the throb of a thousand distant bees. Something lived there.

One night, Coral dreamed of the various healing rays tumbling around her bed, a swirling plait of rainbow colours and soft sounds. They sang to her, called to her, almost as if by learning them she was weaving something greater than their parts, was indeed creating a living hybrid, but not – she told herself on waking – a monster. This dream came the night before she received her "Five Seals Radiance" certificate. As she put the certificate upon her wall, fitting it into the space behind the door, she thought perhaps the mirror over the mantelpiece would have to come down, and also the remaining pictures between the light fittings.

Rather than sating Coral's desire for knowledge, "Five Seals Radiance" seemed to enflame it. She craved more, even though she generally left a few days at least between attunements. She felt light-headed, *hungry*. Was her yearning for training becoming an addiction, the subtle jab of the attunements the drug? *No, it is near... Just over the hill, beneath the wave, above the silvery clouds...* Coral drank coffee as if recovering from a hangover.

That evening, Coral went to her computer and browsed for more teachers. Nothing caught her eye. Most of the modalities she viewed seemed somehow drab. But then a site bloomed across her monitor that claimed to offer "deep and hidden knowledge, the wisdom of the elder gods". What was this? She'd not come across it before. *The Ancient Legacy*. Pictures adorning the site depicted deep, underwater caverns, filled with waving weeds, illumined by globes of wan light. Coral shivered, but pleasurably. *My visions...* In the darkness beyond the weeds, she could make out dim outlines of creatures rather like mermaids, their eyes reflecting the faintest pinpoints of light. The artwork was beautiful, if somewhat eerie, but not overwrought.

'Become attuned to the most ancient system of self-development in creation,' claimed the site. 'Meet with entities of many kinds, each with a symbol to bestow that embodies the great wisdom personified by each being. Visit the secret temples of prehistory. Receive knowledge from the secret order that dwells within these sacred walls.'

There was no "About Me" section on this site, no pictures of smiling teachers surrounded by grateful students. There was a *silence* to it; Coral could not explain it better than that. She'd clicked the enquiry button before she'd even finished reading the pages. Her breathing had become shallow and fast. Excitement made her fingers tremble as she typed the words.

When her message had been sent a message flashed up on her screen: *Not Everyone Finds This Temple*. This disappeared before she was able to react, never mind take a screen shot. She stared at the web page. Had she just imagined those words?

Two days passed before Coral received a reply to her enquiry. This was from an email address called "knowledgelibrary", not even a person's name. The attunement cost $100. The cost included a bound manual, but a full colour art book was also available, which could be purchased separately as an aid to meditation. This extra volume cost an additional $40, plus shipping. Impulsively, Coral ordered the course and the book. Next day, a follow-up email advised her the attunement would be sent the following day, held in an etheric repository for her to pick up at any time convenient for her. (Did it have an expiry date? She wondered. This wasn't mentioned.) She had to visualise and chant the word *teramatfall*, which was a personalised astral password for her. Once she used this to establish contact with the repository, she should compose herself and recite the chant: 'I am ready and open to receive this update from the universe, channelled from Ancient Legacy and its partners.' Odd words. Perhaps they were meant to be "cyber" and "cool". Still, the mysteriousness did much to help create an atmosphere, similar to how Makayla did. Coral felt sure these attunement would be different to any other she'd received.

Next morning, Makayla texted Coral at work, asking if they could talk on the phone. Coral stared at the message for nearly a minute, but then put the phone back in her bag. An hour later another message came. *It's vital we speak.* At lunch time, Coral relented and called her friend. By this time, she'd received five messages.

'What is it?' Coral asked when Makayla answered the phone. 'Your messages sounded desperate, but I couldn't reply. I was working with my boss.'

Makayla's sharp intake of breath came through the phone. 'I had the most... I *dreamed* of you last night,' she said.

Coral laughed uncertainly. 'It doesn't sound good.'

'It *wasn't.*' There was a pause. 'Coral, are you planning

any more attunements, in particular for tonight?'

'Why?

'It's just...' A pause. 'If you are, please don't.'

'I don't understand. What's wrong?'

'Have you seen Chloe recently?'

'Well, of course, at work, but not socially for a couple of weeks. What *is* this?'

'I feel very strongly you mustn't take any more attunements for a while. In the dream... it was dangerous, Coral. I saw you drawn into a void, reaching out for me. You were screaming but I couldn't hear your voice. Then I saw those weird temple buildings again and these... well *creatures* who looked like Chloe.'

Coral laughed. 'Chloe creatures?'

'It's not funny. Please believe me when I say I'm afraid for you. I don't need to warn you of the dangers of what you might find on the internet. You can't be sure of its integrity. It's potentially harmful to open yourself to unknown energy. I feel you've stumbled on something bad. You must trust me on this, Coral. I'm an old witch, remember?'

For a scant moment Coral found herself transported to Makayla's dream. She *was* being drawn away from her friend, but not screaming. She wasn't reaching out, but waving farewell. The void was a tunnel of transition and amazing vistas waited at the other end of it.

'OK,' she said soothingly to Makayla. 'Please don't worry. It was just a dream. Really.'

'Will you come and see me tonight?' Makayla's voice was restrained yet still frantic. 'Please, Coral. I need to see you're all right. I need to protect you in some way. It's crazy, I know, but...'

'OK, but not tonight. Tomorrow evening. I'm sorry.

That's the earliest I can make.'

Makayla sighed. 'Fine, but please don't do anything with any more healing systems before I see you. Will you promise me?'

'Yes, of course.' Coral didn't feel what she was about to embark upon could be termed a healing system.

Poor Makayla. Left behind. The weeds closing over her like a veil.

When Coral returned to the office after her lunch, she saw Chloe hunched over her desk, her hair hanging over her face. Why on earth would Makayla mention the girl in that way? Perhaps she felt threatened by Coral's training. Perhaps she was just a little crazy.

That evening, Coral intended to receive her attunement in her temple, but for some reason felt compelled to sit among her certificates in the dining-room, as if the one she was about to receive would be the crown above an imagined set of mystical robes, sandals and jewellery. As she made her way to the room, dressed in a soft saffron caftan, and trailing tendrils of musky perfume, Coral heard her computer making a noise, as if its hard drive was grinding. She should go to see, and yet... She couldn't spoil the mood. She'd look later.

She sat at the head of the table and laid her palms down upon the polished wood. Before she began to visualise the password, it seemed to her that in the candle-light all her certificates were faintly glowing, power radiating from them. The sum of all she had learned. She took a deep breath and closed her eyes.

Chanting aloud, it was as if she were falling into a trance. She was swimming down through the ocean between vast cliffs, so vast they were almost beyond imagination So ancient and so deep. The light below was dim and yellowish green. Coral saw shadowy shapes swimming through it. They were waiting for her.

'Are you home, Coral?' said a damp voice, close to her ear. This sounded real, right beside her. If she turned, would it be Chloe standing there?

'Yes,' Coral said. 'I am.'

A cold, wet hand closed over her right shoulder. 'Come to those of the water through the fire of initiation,' lisped the voice. And the hand was cold no longer.

A day later, when they found Coral, dead in her dining-room, a couple of the more imaginative police investigators wondered whether spontaneous combustion was to blame, because of the state in which the victim was found. Burned through, black as charcoal, and just as crumbly. There was no evidence of a fire in the house, and the chair and table at which Coral sat were unmarked, although the mass of picture frames on the walls had rings of soot around them, some including faint traces of red, gold, green and blue pigment. Bizarrely, all of the picture frames were empty.

IN THE EARTH

This story was written for Creeping Crawlers, *an anthology edited by Allen Ashley. My inspirations were drawn from my own childhood – including a combination of friends I'd once had and adventures we'd got up to. Jeryl isn't a real person, but rather a composite of personality fragments that has been embellished and changed to fit the story. However, one aspect is based on truth. Some years ago, I spoke with someone who knew an old childhood friend of mine. When I asked if I could have their contact details, I was met with the reaction you'll find at the end of this story, but that's the nearest Jeryl gets to reality.*

The centipede was cut in two. 'Why did you kill it?' Mawde asked.

Jeryl pursed her lips. She was squatting in the dirt of the lower cellar, the frilly skirt of her white Sunday dress pulled up over her knees. 'Don't you know what they *do*?' she said.

Mawde shook her head. 'Run about?'

'They *burrow* – into *any* hole of your body, and then they start eating.'

Mawde grimaced. She couldn't believe that. Why would a humble creature like a centipede do that?

'They *do*,' said Jeryl. 'I've seen pictures. They ate a woman's eyes from the inside.'

Mawde was sentimental about all creatures, whereas her cousin Jeryl seemed fixed with the idea that if anything was small enough to slaughter with a quick stamp of the foot or a blow from a trowel, then it was her treat – or perhaps her duty – to kill it. Mawde's mother said that all animals, however scary and unpleasant they might look, were all part of the Nature's creations and must be respected. Loved.

Jeryl's mother didn't believe in anything. Now Jeryl poked the centipede parts with a stick she'd found.

Outside, the summer was gloomy and thundery, pressing down on the tall wooden house, making its labyrinth of cellars a cauldron of shadows and lifeless air. A smell of old earth surrounded the girls; pungent and musty. Jeryl was staying with Mawde's family for a whole month during the school holidays. She liked to play in the cellars. She said there were tunnels down there, hidden behind the sagging wooden racks and shelves, which snaked right into Pike Mountain, dating back to the start of time. Even when dressed in feminine flounces, within this confection lurked the heart and mind of a grubby little boy. No amount of dressing up would change that.

Jeryl had been looking for tunnels, (hence the digging that had unearthed the doomed centipede), but to Mawde's relief so far none had been found. She liked her cousin's company but wished sometimes her favoured pastimes didn't have to involve danger or fear. It wasn't enough simply to sit in the sunshine on the porch roof; Jeryl insisted they had to jump down from this height onto the lawn, which hurt Mawde's ankles and feet. They couldn't just play make believe in the cellars but had to look for tunnels – undoubtedly haunted, or so Jeryl said. Neither was it enough to climb the tall old yew trees that clustered like hags at the garden's edge; they had to hang upside-down by their knees from the highest branch they could reach... then right themselves and drop to the ground. Jeryl was always on the lookout for higher places from which they could jump and was unconcerned that yew wood was relatively soft and therefore not the best support for weight, even of a child. She was obsessed with heights, but also liked to push herself physically. 'This *could* be too high,' she might say solemnly, before holding out her arms and throwing herself into the air. Mawde was afraid of these antics – demands, even – but couldn't bring herself to refuse them. Jeryl's scorn was worse than her challenges. But that aside, she was the most fascinating playmate, unlike any other girl Mawde knew.

Neither set of parents were aware what the girls got up to during their holidays. In all the households Mawde knew, it was common for the children to be shooed out of adult company after breakfast, tolerated briefly at lunch, then sent out again until tea. Unless it was bad weather, when they were allowed to play indoors, but out of adult hearing, such as in the attics or cellars. Bizarrely, neither Jeryl nor Mawde had ever hurt themselves, which perhaps – Mawde thought – meant that her mother's stories about guardian angels must be true.

That night another storm came up from the south, crotchety and fevered. When lightning pierced the hot sky it had the look of bruised flesh being punctured by needles. The heat, the anxiety of the sky, infected the old house. It groaned in what sounded to Mawde like dread. Her cousin Jeryl slept in a bed on the other side of the room, but had fallen asleep soon after the curtains had been drawn, and did not wake, even when flickering storm light illumined the room. The unseen inhabitants of the house – vermin and insects – were skittish, pattering behind the walls and in the cavities above the ceilings, below the floors. Mawde lay awake, thinking of the centipede her cousin had killed, how the halves had curled in on themselves. The creature had felt pain, and it had been so big. What if...?

No, Mawde told herself, *no. It was an insect. Didn't have feelings.*

The rain, when it came, was of the kind that Mawde's grandmother often referred to as the tears of the world – that is, a deluge beyond measure. Even through the curtains, the stormlight now seemed watery, running down the walls of the room, threading between the somehow sickeningly large roses of the wallpaper. Despite the rain, the air was hot and Mawde's body felt sticky and uncomfortable beneath her light summer blanket. She drifted in and out of sleep, images flickering across her mind's eye, her head aching. She dreamed of earthy tunnels and myriad feet in the dark. On her hands and knees, she crawled through the dirt, then it was as if she slithered along it on her belly, and the scent of loam and rot was like the sweet hearth of home. She was comfortable in this dream, neither scared nor excited, simply... doing her business.

Then, as dreams do, the world shifted, and she was standing barefoot in the middle of her bedroom with the watery light over the walls and the blanket-cocooned hump of her cousin's shape in the bed before her.

Was this a dream?

'Jeryl?' Mawde breathed.

The hump in the bed twitched and a strange little sleeping-noise came out of the blankets, such as a slumbering dog might utter, as it ran across its dream-fields.

Mawde went to the bed and placed hand on her cousin's shoulder, shook it. 'Jeryl?'

Another noise came out, like dead branches rubbing together, or a bowl of dried peas being thrown down the stairs. Dream-Mawde pulled back the blankets, saw what lay there. A centipede, cut in half, the size of an eleven-year-old girl, the parts curled in on themselves. But the face between the feelers at the head was Jeryl's and now she looked up at her cousin with all the pain of the world, its deluge of tears in her eyes.

Mawde woke with a cry. She felt sick, wanted to vomit, but then the feeling passed. She sat up, glanced fearfully at the bed to her right. 'Jeryl?' she murmured. And then louder: 'Jeryl!'

'Wassamatter?' came a grumpy reply.

'I had a dream,' Mawde said.

Jeryl sat up in her bed too, scraped hair from her eyes. 'You're awake now. Open the curtains'

Mawde shuddered. 'No!'

Jeryl expressed a disappointed sigh and clambered from her bed, went to the window.

'Why?' Mawde asked.

'There might be angels in the windows,' Jeryl said. 'I see them a lot at home, especially when I wake up from a dream.'

Mawde had not heard Jeryl mention this before. 'You *see* them?' she asked timorously.

'Yes, they fill the window, very tall. They tell me things, but I never want them to step out and get into the shadows. It's important to keep them where they are, because then you can see them. They can't hide and whisper things.'

An angel is a kind, beautiful creature, Mawde thought, but in that moment the idea of seeing one seemed the most terrifying thing possible.

But all that was in the window was the fluid mosaic of running water and Jeryl's face, half asleep, dripping with the light.

The storm passed away moodily to the north, and summer returned in its wake. The morning was magnificent, inviting, and any echoes of the disturbing dream and its unsettling aftermath faded from Mawde's mind. Now the weather was better, the cousins could ride their bicycles out into the country lanes around Mawde's home, which were empty of traffic during the week, except for the occasional farm vehicle or someone riding a horse. No longer required to wear what Jeryl referred to as "stupid doll dresses", they were attired in shorts, T-shirts and pumps, riding their bikes from village to village. In nearby Elmslane was a tiny shop that sold ice cream, which they always aimed for before returning home for the day. In every village, Jeryl was drawn to the moss-robed old churches, looking for ghosts or evidence of people being buried alive. She would examine headstones for mysteries. 'Look, this woman died two days before her baby, and she wasn't much older than *us*. The father killed the baby because it had killed her. That's obvious.'

Ever since Jeryl had started visiting her cousin in the holidays, one of her favourite pastimes was to hide and frighten people, especially those who came to tend graves. As graveyards were often thick with yew trees – Jeryl's favourite kind – she would order Mawde to climb into the branches and stay very still. A woman might come, or an elderly man, and then Jeryl would coo something sinister, such as, 'Nooo, nooo, tooo soon.' Or simply hoot like an owl or utter a sound like an exclamation from a startled dog or cat. They were rarely caught, and if the victim did spy them, the girls would throw themselves from the tree and run off like deer. Mostly, the people would pay no attention, but it was satisfying when a frightened face looked up, glanced around themselves, hurried away. Then the cousins would giggle uncontrollably. 'Let's go to the next place,' Jeryl would say.

But that day, the graveyards were empty of sport and Jeryl became restless. She suggested a visit to another of their haunts.

At the western end of Dappleheath, Mawde's home village, was a row of old houses with long gardens. At the bottom of these summer-time jungles was a "no-man's-land" that didn't appear to belong to anybody. This was a narrow ribbon of woodland – holly, birch, thick stands of elderberry, some domesticated fruit trees that had perhaps escaped the gardens – through which a stream ran. On the other side of the trees was a school playing-field that seemed inordinately huge and was rarely used. Not that Mawde ever saw it that often in term-time; her school was somewhere else. After heavy rain, one section of the stream would swell to fill a shallow sandy pool. Naturally, as the pool's width varied, and offered on some occasions a greater challenge, Jeryl liked to take a run and jump it. Mawde was afraid of getting wet, even though the water was hardly treacherous and less than three inches at its deepest point. There was simply something disturbing about the way it was so important to Jeryl that they succeeded in their jumps, as if, should they fail, some calamity would happen.

Today, of course, after the storm, the waters would be engorged and swift – as much as they ever could be – and Jeryl was eager to see how wide the pool would be.

Mawde liked the wood, even if she didn't enjoy the jumping that much. There was such a variety of life within it, as if it were a miniature, and therefore magical, ancient woodland. Rabbits braved the boundary between this small wilderness and the shorn playing-field. A woodpecker lived there; always heard, sometimes seen. The petals of flowers – periwinkle, forget-me-not, campion – seemed more vivid there amid the emerald forest grass that was springy underfoot. Mawde liked to think it was a sanctuary for benign magical creatures, but to Jeryl it was the fortress of capricious fairies, who would steal babies, swap them for a blackened tree stump. They could suck out a beautiful girl's youth, or curse a man to fall in love, then go blind, mad. Jeryl searched for the spoor of these beings relentlessly.

On that day, as Jeryl rooted in the soft, dark earth, like a terrier rummaging for a buried bone, Mawde wondered why – for her – angels were golden and good, and fairies were simply aloof and mysterious, yet for Jeryl these creatures were always cruel and vengeful, full of hate for humanity.

'Look at this,' Jeryl said, wonder in her voice. She had uncovered something beneath a stone, perhaps evidence of a fairy atrocity.

But before Mawde could come to look, a harsh male voice rang out. 'Hoi! Get out of there! This is private property! Gerrout!'

The cousins stared at each other in alarm, before

jumping to their feet. Mawde had a glimpse of an unfriendly male face – elderly – staring over the fence at the bottom of the nearest garden.

'Don't you come back here, you little pests!' he roared as Jeryl and Mawde scampered away. 'Private property, you hear?'

Usually, when caught out, and a swift retreat was called for, Jeryl laughed and poked fun at whoever had yelled at them, but this time, when they emerged through a hole in the fence by the lane, where their bicycles lay hidden in the long grass and cow parsley, Jeryl's face was pinched.

'Stupid old git,' Mawde offered, hoping Jeryl would then smile and say something even more insulting.

'I'll get 'im,' Jeryl said simply, not even with darkness in her tone, just stating a simple fact. She lifted her bicycle from the grass. 'No one uses that land. It's wild. No one should stop us.'

'*How* will you get him?' Mawde asked.

Jeryl said nothing. She mounted her bike and jerked her head to indicate Mawde should follow.

They went to another woodland place they liked – a copse of oaks and beeches in a hollow in the middle of a hay field. But sometimes other children were there, which neither Mawde nor Jeryl liked particularly. Today, mercifully, they had it to themselves. Jeryl was still not speaking, despite Mawde's efforts to lighten the atmosphere. Jeryl simply rooted, clawing at sodden dead wood and beneath the bracken. She turned over a large log that had to be pulled forcibly from the earth, making a sucking sound. Beneath, the ground teemed with insect life – wood lice, beetles, centipedes. 'Oh, look,' Mawde murmured. 'So many of them.'

Jeryl stood up, then, methodically, she began stamping on the tiny creatures, grinding her foot against the soil, all the time making a soft, grunting sound.

'Stop it,' Mawde said. 'Stop, Jeryl.'

Jeryl wouldn't stop, and for the first time, Mawde ran away from her cousin, out of the shade of the wise oaks, across the sun-soaked hay field, and went home alone.

Jeryl did not reappear until tea-time. To protect her cousin from any parental chastisement, or indeed herself for leaving Jeryl alone in the copse, Mawde hid in the garden until she heard the whirr of Jeryl's bicycle wheels on the gravel of the drive. Then, Mawde ran from her hiding place, across the lawn. At that moment, Mawde's mother came out the house, no doubt to advise them their tea was ready. She caught sight of Jeryl, muddied and unkempt, then glanced briefly at her tidier daughter. 'What have you been doing?' she snapped. 'Where have you been?'

Jeryl stared defiantly, shrugged.

Horrified at what this insolent response might evoke in her normally fair-minded mother, Mawde said, 'We went fishing and Jeryl fell over in a muddy place.'

'Mud?' said Mawde's mother in a voice that might easily have been saying "entrails?" so disgusted was her tone. Mawde realised then – one of the chiming epiphanies of childhood – that although her mother considered nature beautiful and to be respected from a distance, in her view no girl had any place getting *into* it and letting it dirty her.

'Get changed,' she said severely to Jeryl. 'And wash yourself as best you can. Bath later.' She turned to Mawde, 'As for you, young lady...'

'I'll wash and change too,' Mawde said, even though she wasn't very dirty. She ran after Jeryl, who was stomping into the house.

In the bathroom, Jeryl was still quiet, although she hummed to herself softly. 'Are you all right?' Mawde asked.

'Of course,' Jeryl answered.

'Jeryl...' Mawde began. She knew she had to speak, say *something*, but the words were reluctant. 'You shouldn't kill things like that.'

Jeryl flicked a sharp glance at her. 'They don't mind dying for me. They expect it.'

'*Dying* for you...?'

'How else can I tell them what I want? Beetles don't have brains, but they have eyes. You have to show them.' Jeryl threw water over her face, rubbed mud from her arms.

Mawde remembered her dream then, the insect Jeryl in the bed, cut in half. 'You're wrong,' she said.

Jeryl expressed a contemptuous snort. '*You* don't know anything. Keep your trap shut.'

The look in Jeryl's eyes was frightening, so cold and dark, like winter earth; small scuttling things moving behind it. A distinct thought formed in Mawde's mind: *don't make her angry with you.*

'Sorry,' she said, and went to the bath where she washed her hands. She didn't want to share the sink Jeryl was using.

That night, Mawde slept deeply and did not wake. To her, it was an ordinary night and the morning that followed it equally ordinary. Jeryl seemed brighter now, for which

Mawde was grateful. The sullen, quiet Jeryl frightened her; she'd never been like this on previous visits.

While they were washing-up for Mawde's mother after breakfast, a knock came at the back door. Friends and family never used the forbidding front door, which was rarely opened. This visitor came right inside without waiting to be invited – a friend of Mawde's mother called Mrs Cherry. She had a sickly son, who went to the same school as Mawde and was excused sports and swimming.

After the ritual offering of tea, and with Mrs Cherry established at the kitchen table, the woman lit a cigarette, inhaled purposefully and on her exhale, announced with relish, 'The Hensons had dreadful trouble last night.'

'Who?' asked Mawde's mother.

'Live in End Lane, the one with the green door.'

'Oh... yes... I don't know them personally. What trouble?'

Mrs Cherry chewed her words with satisfaction before sharing them. 'Vandals got in their garden. Made a terrible mess. Ruined it, you know. Ruined it! Even the greenhouse gone. It's just a mud patch now, I heard. And you know what?'

'What?'

'They didn't hear a *thing*. Got police round now, of course.'

'How dreadful...'

Mawde's head had begun to buzz. She felt strangely dizzy and disorientated. End Lane... the wood at the back of the houses where she and Jeryl had been yesterday. She knew her face had gone bright red and that it was important her mother didn't notice this. Jeryl was still washing dishes in a serene manner, as if her mind was far away, as if she hadn't heard.

'Susan Ross just told me that May Henson's kitchen was absolutely crawling with beetles this morning. Unearthed, I expect. They were in *everything*.'

Mawde put away carefully the last dish she was drying. 'Can we go now, Mum?'

Mawde's mother nodded distractedly. 'Yes, sweetheart. Don't be late for lunch.'

Outside, as the cousins walked to the shed where the bicycles were stored, Jeryl was again quiet, although she was smiling – a private expression she clearly had no intention of sharing. Mawde wanted to say something, *ask* something, desperately, but was afraid to do so. She sensed endings and change, the summer fading, without understanding why. At the shed, as she wrestled with the padlock – unlocked but as recalcitrant as if it were stuck fast – she said, 'Wonder if it was the man who shouted at us... whose garden was wrecked.' She glanced up at her cousin.

Jeryl stared back for a moment, the put out her tongue. Mawde jumped backwards. There was a centipede on Jeryl's tongue, still and wet, just lying there. Jeryl uttered a squawk of laughter, then spat. Mawde winced away.

'Told you,' Jeryl said.

After that summer, the cousins grew apart. Further details of the holiday became blurred in Mawde's mind, but then perhaps Jeryl had returned home only a couple of days after the garden-wrecking incident – a crime for which no one was ever caught. Later that year, Mawde overheard a couple of whispered, coded conversations that her mother held on the phone with friends. Listening carefully from concealment, Mawde deciphered Jeryl had been in severe trouble at school. Phrases such as, "difficult child" and "a bit touched" were breathed down the line. Mawde gleaned that for Jeryl a new and different kind of school had been in order; her mother and father had moved a couple of hundred miles away to be near her. There had been no further holiday visits, and the relationship between Mawde's mother and her sister inexplicably cooled. Mawde couldn't divine the reason, and her mother kept her secrets until she died, quite young. Mawde had no idea where her aunt lived, and any questions made to her father resulted only in: 'let it lie, Mawde. They don't want us contacting them.'

Jeryl became a childhood memory; a strange yet intriguing girl. Mawde never spoke about her, and eventually forgot her, except for moments during summer storms, when she lay awake in the dark at night and heard insects in the walls.

Then, by chance, many years later, when Mawde was in her late thirties, her work brought her into contact with Meredith Jones, a woman who'd known Jeryl as a child. Mawde had even met her a couple of times at gatherings of Jeryl's family, not that she recognised Meredith's grown up face, and – unlike Mawde – she had married, so her name was different. After an office meeting, as both women were putting away their laptops, Meredith said, 'You're not the Mawde Emsley who's a cousin of Jeryl Ashman, are you?'

'Yes, I am,' Mawde said, surprised. In an instant, the past came hurtling back, and she felt faintly disorientated. She smelled earth.

'You probably don't remember me,' Meredith said. 'I was a friend of Jeryl's.' She laughed. 'Well, went to the same school, and was invited to birthdays and so on, but Jeryl didn't really have friends, did she.'

'I... well... it was a long time ago,' Mawde said, in a colder tone than she intended.

Meredith blinked in a non-plussed manner, clearly unsure what to say.

Mawde made a vague gesture with one hand, looked away, fiddled with her computer bag. 'Family thing. There was a rift...'

'Ah.' Meredith sighed, then ploughed on bluntly. 'Can't say I'm surprised. They had a terrible time with her, terrible. So sad for the parents, having to move away and virtually take on new identities.' She offered a pitying expression. 'But of course you must know that.'

Mawde grimaced, which she trusted would indicate she didn't wish to speak further on the matter, although part of her was itching to interrogate this stranger. The problem was, she didn't know *anything*. This childhood acquaintance of Jeryl's knew more.

'Are you still in touch with the family?' Mawde asked, as lightly as she could muster.

'My mother is,' was the reply.

'I wonder...' Mawde now spoke impulsively. 'Jeryl and I had no say in... becoming estranged when we were children. I wonder whether I should contact her.'

The woman gave Mawde a glance that was full of meaning, bursting with it: a keen arrow of a glance. 'That's up to you,' she said carefully, 'but... she's a very *troubled* person, Mawde.'

Polite euphemism, Mawde thought. She nodded. 'Yes,' she said, 'I expect she is. Cut in two.' She hadn't meant to say those last few words, but Meredith Jones nodded.

'Yes, you could put it like that,' she said. 'Tragic.'

Mawde muttered a hasty goodbye and fled the room.

Outside, it was thundery, the lawn beyond the office building oozing and mulchy. Mawde saw a brief image before her mind's eye of Jeryl crouching in the dirt, glancing up, her smile as secretive and cruel as that of the fairies in which she believed. There were insects on her skin, like a living tattoo. Then she sank into the wet earth until only her eyes remained, peering out.

FROM THE COLD DARK SEA

This story appeared in Dreams from the Witch House, *edited by Lynne Jamneck, which is an anthology of Lovecraftian stories by female authors. I thought that if any hint of Lovecraft's mythos was to exist in the British Isles, Cornwall would be one of the places where it could be found – memories of an older race haunting the ancient landscape, and strange progeny bred from denizens of the sea. In the Lovecraft stories – and others since written for the Mythos by other writers – the hybrids of land and sea are typically grotesque, monstrous. I wanted to write about people who weren't* that *different, but were unnervingly not quite normal, either.*

The house stood on a cold finger of land that poked out grudgingly into a sullen sea. Cara could see it from far off, because the peninsula appeared scoured of life, covered only by heather and wiry grass, with the occasional salt-stunted tree – leaning sorrowfully away from the winds – and lichen-covered rocks. The house was square, bereft of gardens, ornate or otherwise. There wasn't even a fence, just a narrow, neglected road, full of holes, and an enormous backdrop of miserable sky, where sinister spirals of rain cloud pushed blackly down over the far ocean.

Cara's car whined as it negotiated the bumps and pot holes. She passed a solitary wooden post, from which colourless tattered ribbons hung. Surely not the site of an accident? Any driver would have to aim very carefully at that post to hit it. She grimaced, fumbled on the dashboard for a cigarette, the last she would smoke before leaving the car.

A commission had come from the house, *Maples*, asking for a book restorer – Cara's specialty. Since leaving university ten years ago, her job had taken her to many hidden corners of the country, to dim museums and crumbling houses with wormy libraries. Mrs. De La Mere, the inhabitant of *Maples*, had contacted Cara via a letter handwritten on creamy headed notepaper. Usually her clients got in touch with her by email and, if not, letters were typed. Mrs. De La Mere was concerned about the condition of a valuable family heirloom and included two photos with the letter: grainy pictures of a huge old book. But – the older the better, as far as Cara was concerned. There was more chance of restoring an ancient book that had been created before the acids of relatively modern paper-making had doomed books to a finite life.

Cara finished her cigarette on the front drive of *Maples*, while her car ticked and cooled. She could hear the wind beyond the car windows, its voice rising and falling in bitter song. Mean rain, menaced by the spiteful squalls, rendered the scene blurry and vague, like a water-colour painting. Drenched and sombre, Maples was a gaunt-looking residence; two turrets and constructed entirely of dark stone. Cara imagined it would feel arthritic inside, with unstable banisters and groaning stairs, a haunting of creaks and sighs. Also, houses simply didn't look right if they had no garden. Not far from it, the sea pounced against the cliffs and savaged them, perhaps goring away the finger of land so that one day *Maples* would fall into the bullying waves. *Maples*. What a stupid name for a house where no trees grew.

Cara got out of her car, locked it, and went to the front door that stood above three worn steps of black slate. She lifted the bulky brass knocker, which had apparently been polished fairly recently, and let it fall three slow times. She wondered with some amusement what apparition would eventually shamble forth to answer her.

The door opened. A tall, teenaged girl stood there, dressed as if she'd expected the day to be warmer than it was – red shorts and a lime green T-shirt with a cartoon duck printed on it. Her greeny-blond hair was tied in a pony-tail. Her feet were bare. How disappointingly ordinary.

'Hi,' Cara said. 'I'm the book restorer. Cara Milltop.'

The girl nodded vaguely. 'Come in.'

Cara entered the hallway, which was naturally dark, it seemed, but lit by a sufficient array of wall lamps. Stairs rose majestically, branching at the foot of an immense stained-glass window. Overhead a chandelier hung, with coldly glittering pendants. The wood panelling on every wall was intricately carved. The hall was beautiful – in a Gothic, fairy-tale kind of way. 'Amazing,' Cara said feebly, her head thrown back to squint at the vaulted ceiling high above. She peered at the colourful window at the point where the stairs divided, seeing now that it depicted a seascape hectic with storms, a great ship rolling, mermaids clawing its sides, taking drowned sailors into their embrace. 'That's dramatic,' Cara said, pointing.

The girl smiled as if she didn't care. 'Yeah, guess so. It's my grandmother you want.'

She began to walk away, then paused, turned to see if Cara was following her. Cara blinked quizzically.

'This way,' said the girl.

Cara found that the house wasn't completely without garden, as when she entered the room where the reigning matriarch awaited her, she could see a walled yard through the long windows. She glimpsed a washing-line bearing a few wooden pegs, turned earth with garden implements, straggling growth.

'Ms. Milltop,' announced the elderly woman seated by the hearth. A fire burned there, licking wood as an elderly dog might lick its own paws. The woman sat straight-backed, blessed with remarkable bones that anchored beauty still to her narrow face.

Cara strode forward, hand extended. 'Mrs. De La Mere,' she responded, smiling.

The woman indicated the seat opposite her with a pale graceful hand. 'Do take off your coat and sit down.' She gestured at the girl who was loitering at the door. 'Judy, put the kettle on, dear. Make us tea.'

The door closed.

Cara removed her jacket and put it carefully over the back of the chair. She sat, in a way she hoped conveyed businesslike purpose.

'It's the damp that's always a problem,' said Mrs. De La Mere. She sighed, stroked her coifed silvery hair. 'Well, you must know that.'

'The book...'

'Yes, *Marvels of the Deeps*. It's been in our family for perhaps hundreds of years. I understand it's quite valuable. The children have always loved it. The illustrations, you see.'

'Like the window in the hall? That's quite stunning.'

Mrs. De La Mere nodded vaguely. 'Yes, that sort of

thing. It's a shame when something so beautiful and so *meaningful* to children can no longer be handled. Is there anything you can do?'

'Well, naturally I'll need to see the book first, make an assessment.'

'Oh yes, of course.'

'But the good news is that the older a book is, the healthier it can be. It's because of how paper was made. Wood pulp is flimsy in comparison to the old linen-based paper. That can withstand quite a lot and is more amenable to being restored.'

'I see. Well, I hope that's the case.' Mrs. De La Mere paused. 'Do you love your work, Ms. Milltop?'

Cara nodded. 'I know I'm privileged to have this job, and yes I love it very much.'

'I imagine it's similar to working in a beauty parlour – restoring old things.'

Cara wasn't sure whether that was a joke.

Mrs. De Le Mere grinned. 'It's quite all right. I'm not asking you to restore me!'

Cara laughed uncertainly. 'I suppose it is, in a way.'

The girl Judy was swift with the tea. It didn't come in delicate ancient tea cups but sturdy modern mugs, each with a different print. Mrs. De La Mere talked a little about the house and the village – Mordarras – nearby. Cara listened but didn't feel as if she was actually hearing anything. Perhaps she was more tired than she felt.

The library of *Maples* seemed tall as a cathedral. The De La Meres were certainly a family of bibliophiles. Cara itched to explore every shelf. Book cases rose to a mezzanine where more books huddled in shadow. Sliding ladders reared on three sides of the room.

'I used to adore swinging on these when I was a girl,' said Mrs. De La Mere, gently fingering the satiny wood of one of the ladders. 'We all did.'

She indicated the way to a table where the muted colours of another stained-glass extravaganza – an abstract pattern rather than a picture – splashed over the wood. Here, the family treasure, *Marvels of the Deeps*, lay waiting for Cara's attention. It was as big as a Bible. Cara opened her work satchel and drew out a pair of latex gloves, and also her old-fashioned dictaphone and other instruments she might need during her preliminary inspection. She put on the gloves and turned on her machine. 'Book title *Marvels of the Deeps*,' she began. 'Dimensions approximately 30 centimetres width, 40 centimetres height. Thickness 8 centimetres.'

'How very *forensic*,' murmured Mrs. De La Mere.

Cara smiled reassuringly at the woman. 'I just like to keep thorough notes and record progress. It's not an autopsy.'

'Well, I would hope not.' Mrs. De La Mere laughed charmingly.

Cara laid her fingers lightly against the front cover board. This appeared to be made of leather, originally dyed dark green and embossed with gold, but now faded. Almost all of the embossing had gone. There was also staining to the cover, perhaps water damage. Reverently, Cara opened the book. The first folio was severely spotted and clearly suffering disintegration. The book hadn't been stored correctly. And yes, as Mrs. De La Mere had suggested, damp had had its way with the ancient fibres. Fortunately the binding appeared still strong; as far as Cara could tell, the book would not need rehinging. She used felt-tipped tongs to turn the page. The book certainly predated the mid-nineteenth century, when new paper-making methods had brought in the dreaded death sentence of fibre-destroying acids; but at first glance, she wasn't entirely sure the base material had been linen.

'Is it rescuable?' Mrs. De La Mere asked tremulously, as if enquiring about the health of a frail relative.

Cara flashed a smile at her. 'I'm sure I can do something.' She paused. 'Really, Mrs. De La Mere, this book should be stored under careful conditions. If you want children to play with it, I'd advise getting a copy made for them.'

'Oh, but that wouldn't be the same...'

'I know, but this book is really too old to be handled by little fingers. No one should touch this without wearing gloves, like I'm doing.' She turned the blank page that had followed the title page. 'Oh!'

'Yes,' breathed Mrs. De La Mere.

Even though the folio itself was ancient and delicate, the woodcut upon it was still dark and clear, printed with thick, shining black ink. Staring at the picture was like looking down a tunnel deep beneath the ocean, rocks to either side thickly gemmed with anemone growths and crystals. Weeds hung like drapes, drawn back to reveal the path. Paler shapes suggestive of eyes winked between the weeds. Was that a tiny hand reaching out? And at the distant end of the path, soft rays of light, an intimation of space and height. Anyone looking at that page would want to go further, to see the end of the path, to walk it. The pages beyond were the portals to this secret place.

Cara carefully closed the book. 'It's late now,' she said, 'I'd like to examine the book properly and start work tomorrow. Hopefully the light will be better. I like to work in natural light. Is there a hotel you can recommend in Mordarras?'

'Don't be silly, dear,' said Mrs. De La Mere, making a sweeping gesture with both arms. 'You can see the size of this place. You will of course stay here for however long it takes.'

'Well... thank you,' Cara said.

Judy showed Cara to a room upstairs that had windows in two walls, one overlooking the walled garden, the other providing a dramatic view of the sea. It was a pleasant, airy room – in spite of the dull weather – although somewhat featureless, almost as if Cara had walked into a generic hotel.

'We keep this for guests,' Judy said, as if sensing Cara's disappointment not to find herself in a gloomy, shadowed chamber.

'Do you get a lot of guests?' Cara couldn't help asking, depositing her luggage bag on the bed.

Judy shrugged. 'At certain times of year. We have a big family.'

'This must be when the children come,' Cara said, 'the ones who like the book.'

'Yeah.' Judy paused, then said, 'There's a bathroom a little way down the passage to your right. Hot water whenever you need it, but if you want a bath, better wait. We'll be eating soon. Shall I call you?'

'Yes. Please.'

Left alone, Cara stood at the window, staring out across the ocean. The sounds that came muted to her ears were soporific, the plunge of the waves, the wail of the winds.

At dinner, Cara ate what she could only describe as a *polite* meal of roasted chicken breast, with what tasted like home grown vegetables, full of flavour. Not exactly exciting or exotic, but well-cooked and satisfying. For dessert there was honeycomb ice cream, which Mrs. De La Mere explained was made on a farm near Mordarras. 'The girls from Morbenyn Farm help us out here,' she said. 'It's a big house for the two of us.'

'Has it been in your family a long time?' This was a question Cara often asked, a staple of her conversation with clients.

'Oh yes, a very long time. Our ancestors were seafarers, you know.'

After dinner, Mrs. De La Mere wanted to show Cara DVDs of the local area, mainly because *Maples* was mentioned a couple of times as being something of a curio. Cara was conducted to a large comfortable sitting room, somewhat over-furnished in a Victorian manner, but dominated by an immense, flat screen TV. Mrs. De La Mere used a series of remote controls expertly and swiftly in order to begin the presentation. In one film, she was interviewed, standing regally before her domain on a bright sunny day, wearing a wide-brimmed hat. All she had to say was that in the summer *Maples* offered cream teas and that several of the rooms in the house were then open to the public. The hall, apparently, was faintly famous for its carvings and window. The camera panned round to show tables set out on the flat ground in front of the house. No one was sitting there. Mordarras was also featured; a typically picturesque Cornish village huddling in a deep hole beneath the cliffs as if it had fallen there. The single road that led through it was punishingly steep to either side. But there wasn't anything that interesting in the documentaries, which were clearly aimed at tourists, who wanted only an animated guidebook to take them to pretty spots and tell them where to eat, where to stand to view the sea.

Mrs. De La Mere was lavish with her sherry while they watched, so that Cara felt quite inebriated by ten o'clock. 'Do you mind if I turn in?' she asked. 'It was a long journey today.'

'Not at all. You go ahead.' Mrs. De La Mere poured herself another sherry. 'Judy can wake you. Not too early. We're not early risers.'

Cara dreamed of the illustration she had seen in the book. This wasn't of some fantastical journey, swimming down through the ocean deeps, but merely of standing in the library, staring at the picture and saying aloud to someone unseen behind her, 'but there must be a way to it, there must.'

She woke up in darkness, pulled abruptly from sleep by what she could only describe as a racket. This was a rhythmic clacking, thumping sound, which as she listened became faster in tempo until it was a wall-shaking rattle. 'What the hell?' she said aloud and leaned over to turn on the bedside light. She glanced around the room, unnerved, but not exactly frightened. She saw that despite the relative modernity of the fittings, the radiator in the room was of the ancient, cast iron type. The noise came from that. Cara got out of bed and went to touch the radiator, which was mildly warm. Her fingers registered a faint vibration that surely should have been greater. The noise was so loud. And then it wasn't. The room fell silent. Cara looked out through the open curtains. The night was overcast, drizzle still falling. And yet it seemed the sea was glowing. She watched this for some minutes, even took some photos on her phone. Then she returned to bed and slept till morning.

'It's the pipes,' Judy supplied, rather unhelpfully, when Cara mentioned the noises in the night. Judy had come at 9.30 to rouse Cara, who had already been awake.

'Well, I gathered that, but it sounded like your boiler was about to explode.'

Judy stood in the middle of the room, hands stuffed into the pockets of cut-off jeans. 'It comes through the pipes,' she said, 'from the sea.'

'The sea?'

'Gets amplified, I guess. Knocking and that. It won't blow up.'

'*What* comes through the pipes?'

'Just sounds from the sea. Waves, water moving things.' Judy shrugged. 'Our drains go into it, so the sounds come back up. Always been like that.'

The explanation seemed plausible, and of course old buildings were renowned for temperamental plumbing arrangements. But Cara plunged on, refusing to be deterred by Judy's dismissive tone. 'The sea, too... it was strange, but when I looked out of my window it appeared to be glowing, as if lit from beneath.'

'Algae,' Judy said abruptly. 'They let off light. Sometimes.'

'Oh.' Cara paused, then added brightly, 'that must be where lots of old legends spring from – lights beneath the sea.'

'Yeah,' said Judy. She smiled insincerely – apparently bored – and turned to leave the room, Cara following.

Mrs. De La Mere wasn't at breakfast. Judy, draped awkwardly yet strangely graceful in her seat at the table, rather like an unstrung puppet, explained her grandmother liked to have her morning meal in bed. There were boiled eggs, cooked to perfection, thick-sliced brown bread, laid in a basket upon a paper towel, and a glass dish of dark yellow butter. All this produce, Judy said, came from Morbenyn Farm.

After breakfast, Cara went directly to the library. She'd left her tools laid out neatly there. The day wasn't much brighter than the one before, but when Cara turned on a desk lamp it threw a powerful, interrogatory light over the table. She drew on her gloves and examined the book's cover more carefully. She had cellulose products that could help restore its condition and lustre, even if the embossing was lost for good. The interior pages could be subtly laminated with professional tissue, which would protect them while being almost invisible. She had been called upon in time. The invalid could be nursed to health.

Before starting her gentle therapy, however, Cara wanted to look through the book. She stared once again at the opening illustration, the invitation to explore. A tunnel of weed and rock, hiding shy inhabitants, who watched the viewer as their eyes strayed down the path. At the end? A suggestion of ruins or a huge building of some kind, but so faint within the light it was impossible to discern details.

Cara turned the page. On the left folio was text, heavily printed in dense black ink, but in a language with which she wasn't familiar. She didn't recognise many of the characters. They weren't Russian or Greek, but around half were similar to Latin letters. She must ask Mrs. De La Mere about that. Her eyes wandered to the illustration on the right-hand page. She'd deliberately kept her gaze from it until that moment. There was the city beneath the sea, to which the path had led her. She was gazing at it from the mouth of the tunnel, from which curtains of weed hung down, half obscuring her view. But now she could glimpse towers and staircases, colonnades and balconies. She could not see people, of any kind, but fishes in abundance – some seeming to fly in blurred flocks like birds, others swimming stately and alone; huge, and adorned in gowns of fins.

She turned the page. Now she had stepped beyond the mouth of the tunnel onto a paved pathway. The stones were inlaid with shells and crystals, depicting stylised sea creatures and curling waves. She could see now that the entire city was walled. Sentinel statues, as tall as three storied buildings, stood guard at the immense gates, which were slightly ajar. The statues had the torsos of men, but their heads hung down, so you could not see their faces, and were further obscured by swathes of weedlike hair that fell to their waists. Below that, they were *of* the sea; not with fish tails, like mermen, but a mass of squidlike tentacles. These creatures were not fearsome but to be respected. She did not want to wake them.

Cara turned the page. She was right by the statues now, close to the alluringly barely-open gates. The portal was made of stone, and carved with octopi rampant – that was the only way she could describe them. On each looming panel a creature faced inwards, four of its tentacles raised towards its partner on the other gate.

Cara put her hand upon the stone, then jumped, as if woken abruptly from sleep. 'What?' she said aloud. She'd *been* there, just for an instant. Not merely looking at a picture, but ready to push open the gates. How evocative these old illustrations were. They'd drawn her in that much. She took a step back from the table.

For several long seconds she stood motionless. Her head was aching slightly. Then she became aware of a presence, another living thing, and her gaze snapped to the doorway. She couldn't suppress a small cry and jumped in alarm.

A young woman stood at the threshold; tall, thin, with a small, round head. Her pale hair streamed to her waist and she wore a long ocean-green dress. Her large, rather protuberant eyes were fixed on Cara. For some agonising moments, Cara thought this person wasn't real, couldn't be, but then the woman said. 'Sorry, didn't mean to scare you. Would you like some tea? Just making some for the missus.'

'Oh...' Cara shook her head. 'Sorry, I was miles away. Yes, that's kind of you.'

The woman smiled. She had a wide mouth. 'I'll bring a tray.'

Was she beautiful or hideous? Cara truly couldn't say. Arresting, perhaps. Strange.

Cara closed the book; she would begin work upon the cover. As she mixed her cellulose paste, the woman returned, gliding into the room like one of those peculiar cat-walk models, who were striking to behold yet not anyone's idea of conventionally pretty. She did not seem to be the sort of person who would serve tea, or indeed engage in any menial task.

She appeared curious about what Cara was doing, peering somewhat indirectly, perhaps to be polite, so Cara felt she should say something. She held up her pot of cellulose mixture. 'This is to mend the cover. The paste will soak gently into the leather without damaging it, simply binding its fibres, protecting them.' She smiled, not comfortable enough to look directly into the woman's round-eyed stare. 'It won't look new, but it will be strong again.' She risked a quick glance. 'You work here, then?'

'I help,' said the woman.

'You're from the farm, Morbenyn?'

'That's right. We help out.' She smiled in her oddly face-stretching way. 'I'm Minny.'

'Cara,' Cara said, managing not to laugh at the other woman's name, which was so inappropriate it didn't sound feasible. 'This is a very beautiful book.'

'It is. We're very glad there are people like you to save it.' Minny laughed in an entirely normal way, which coming from her seemed completely odd. 'Oh, what does that sound like? It's not *our* book, of course, but the legends mean a lot to us around here. The old sea stories. And they're not saved anywhere, are they, some of the old legends?'

'I know what you mean. It's horrible to think how many wonderful stories are just lost.' Cara pointed at the book. 'Disintegrating away in old libraries.'

Minny nodded. 'Well, happily this will not be one of them.'

'So...' Cara began carefully. 'This book is about a local legend?'

'The deep city, yes.'

'I thought at first it would just be about marine life and so on.'

'Well, it is that too. Perhaps half the species are dead now.'

'A very old legend, then.'

'Oh yes, very old.' Minny straightened up. 'Sugar?'

'Yes, just a little bit.' Cara inspected the woman as she poured out the tea. She could be a mermaid herself, with that pale colouring, the streaming hair, and – it had to be said – somewhat fishlike features. Did this indicate inbreeding?

'Do you know what the language is, in this book?' Cara asked as Minny handed her a mug. 'It doesn't look like old Cornish.'

'It's a dead language now,' Minny replied.

'From what part of the world?'

'Oh, far away. I don't know, really. No one does.'

'Where did the book come from?'

'It's been in the De La Mere family for a long time, that's all I know. They were seafaring people.'

'But you said it was a local legend...'

'It is.' Minny grinned widely again. 'Well, perhaps legends repeat themselves, in different places. I'm not sure where the book came from exactly. You'll have to ask the missus if you want to know more.'

'Well, I'm just being curious. I don't need to know the book's history to restore it. I just think it's so fascinating.'

Minny nodded. 'The pictures are magical. I loved them when I was little. The missus always lets the children look at them.'

The book didn't look like a children's book to Cara, mainly because the era in which it appeared to have been made didn't tend to produce books specifically for children. Still, it had illustrations, and to many people a book with pictures was for the young.

By lunchtime, Cara had finished work on the cover and left it to settle for the rest of the day. She was still curious about what else the book contained, but would have to leave further exploration until tomorrow.

Judy called Cara to a modest lunch of sausage rolls and tea. The weather had cleared somewhat; at least the rain had stopped. 'I'm thinking of going into the village this afternoon,' Cara said.

Judy nodded disinterestedly, nibbling at her food. Cara wondered about the girl. Where were her parents? Why wasn't she at school or college or at work? Did she live off her grandmother?

'Are there any local sites of interest?' Cara asked.

Judy shrugged. 'Not really.'

Determinedly, Cara said, 'Perhaps you could tell me something about the book I'm working on? It seems to have a history!' She laughed a little.

'It's just a relic,' Judy said.

Cara gave up any pretence of conversation and finished her lunch.

A winding lane led down to Mordarras, past the Morbenyn Farm. A sharp wind hurried clouds across the sky, making the watery sunlight dappled. Early spring flowers groped for light beside the path. Above, sea birds surfed the air, uttering those bleating cries that always reminded Cara of childhood holidays. Did people still have holidays like that? A hotel at a seaside resort, buckets and spades, ice cream melting over cardboardy cones? Cara's walking boots crunched upon the loose gravel of the lane. Gorse bushes spiked the sides of the roads stiffly. And to her left, far below, surged the sea. Mordarras was held in a circle of rock providing a natural harbour. It looked bleak though, small white buildings cowering beneath the black cliffs. Perhaps in summer it was different. Cara hoped there would be a café she could sit in; she'd brought a novel with her.

Halfway to the village, she heard the hard tap of horses' hooves behind her, paused and turned. A pony and trap was approaching; how quaint. Cara saw it was driven by Minny from the farm. The woman pulled the pony to a halt. 'Want a lift, m'love?'

'Oh... oh yes, thank you.' Cara climbed up beside the driver. 'I've never had a ride in one of these.'

'People take the car, don't they,' the woman said, 'even when it's two steps down the road. What's the rush?'

'It's far nicer to go to the village like this,' Cara said. 'Thanks, Minny.'

The woman laughed. 'Oh, I'm not Minny, I'm Tally.'

Cara stared at her.

'Her sister,' the woman said. 'Twin.'

Cara shook her head. 'Sorry, the resemblance is... well of course I've only met your sister today.'

'Our own people still make the mistake,' Tally said amiably.

'I'm Cara...'

'Yes,' Tally interrupted, 'she told me.'

The café was still closed for the season, but Tally said that the local post mistress served tea to visitors. 'Not that we get many at this time of year, but I take a cup with Sissy when I'm in town.'

Cara suppressed a smile. *Sissy. Town.* She didn't need a novel to read; she was in one.

Tally dropped her by the door to the post office. 'If you want a lift back up, I'll be an hour or so.'

'No, that's fine, thank you. I could do with the walk.' Cara patted her stomach.

Tally stretched a wide-lipped smile, clucked to her pony, and moved on.

Sissy the post mistress was clearly a relative of the Morbenyn mermaids, since she shared the same appearance, except she was older and wore her hair in a neat bun. Also, her eyes bulged so much, she seemed not to blink. Cara half expected a nictitating membrane to slip across Sissy's eyes. Like the others, she was friendly and perhaps bored, all alone in her shop in the empty season. The makeshift tea room amenities comprised two small tables at the back of the store, with chairs crammed round them. It quickly became clear that Cara would not be allowed time to read in silence.

'How's your work going?' Sissy asked, looming gauntly over the table.

Really, these specimens should be secretive and aloof, Cara thought. Their sociability seemed incongruous but then, she reflected, most fishes swim in schools. At least now she could look them square in the face and not feel faintly freaked.

'Oh, the treatment is going well,' Cara said. 'Does Mrs. De La Mere make the book available to tourists in the summer? It seems quite a local celebrity, in its way.'

'Oh no,' Sissy said, 'it's not for them. The children like it. Do you have any children?'

'No.' Cara hoped the hardness of the word would stem any further enquiries down that path. She decided to make some of her own. 'Does Judy De La Mere have no parents?'

Sissy's wide mouth opened and closed a few times. 'The missus is all she has now,' she said dramatically.

Perhaps they drowned out in the bay, Cara thought, rather maliciously, and wished she could ask, but realised the question might be offensive.

Leaving the post office earlier than she planned, because Sissy refused to leave her alone and wanted to witter on about the problems of running the place, Cara decided to explore the village. Rain clouds had begun to threaten the horizon again. She hoped they'd hold off, or perhaps she should seek out Tally for a lift home shortly. There were hardly any people about. The shops, mostly for tourists, were closed. Small houses clung to the cliff walls like barnacles, and there were lights in the windows of some of them. Cara saw figures down on the beach, perhaps shellfish gathering, as they were stooped over rock pools, panniers hanging from their shoulders. All of them were women – from a distance appearing tall and strong, their long legs clad in heavy thigh-length boots. Cara hadn't seen a single male since arriving at *Maples* the day before, but then she'd hardly been out. Perhaps the men worked away in a larger town.

Later over dinner, Mrs. De La Mere – again fortified by sherry – offered more information about her family. 'In days gone by, there were fortunes to be made,' she said. 'De La Meres brought many strange and wonderful things home from their travels and used to sell them. Not here, of course – not much call – but in the towns, and even up in London.'

'And your book came to you in this way?' Cara asked, then added, 'Minny said it depicted a local legend, though.'

Mrs. De La Mere laughed. 'Well, not exactly that. There is a local story of a city beneath the sea, but then there are stories all over the world like that. The families here like to think the book is about this area, *their* sea, but that's romance, isn't it?'

'The language in the book,' Cara said, 'I didn't recognise it.'

'No one does,' said Mrs. De La Mere.

'Have you ever thought of having the book examined by experts?'

'I understood *you* were an expert.' Mrs. De La Mere's tone was somewhat tart.

'I meant someone who knows languages, antiquity... Aren't you curious?'

'It's a much-loved old book that means a lot to my family and, as you have seen, to others. I don't want *experts* tramping about, thinking they know it all, and I wouldn't let *Marvels* leave this house.'

Cara sensed the slight hostility entering the conversation, inspired, she thought, by the drink. 'Of course, that's understandable,' she said in a soothing tone. 'I'll start work on the pages tomorrow. It'll soon be mended again.'

Cara went to bed early to read her novel, but she couldn't concentrate on the words. She had always made up stories in her mind, and a new one was forming now, of a town comprised of peculiar land-walking mermaids, where there were no men, and a sacred book resided in a wind-scoured old house on the cliffside. The lady who lived there was the guardian of this book and her grand-daughter? What role did she play in this story?

Laying her open book face down on the bed, Cara blinked at the ceiling. The grand-daughter must be the oracle, the sea priestess, and at night the sea moaned, lit up, and something came from it.

Cara smiled to herself. Yes, that idea worked. She turned off her bedside light and turned onto her side. After some minutes, the tapping began.

Roused from a half sleep, Cara lay for some time

listening to the hollow knockings from the radiator. They sounded too regular to be random noises from the plumbing and were softer than what she'd heard the previous night. She turned on her light again and padded across the room to the radiator. Tap. Tap-tap. Tap-tap. Pause. Tap. She ran her fingers over the rugged, painted metal, which was again comfortably warm. Almost without thinking, she rapped back: Tap. Tap-tap. Tap-tap. Tap. This was repeated to her. She shook her head, remembering then how when she was young, staying with her cousins, they had communicated with each other like this at night, pretending to be secret agents. Code through the radiators. Now she rapped out a different code: Tap-tap-tap. Tap-tap-tap. And it was sent back to her.

Could this be Judy? She doubted Mrs. De La Mere would be responsible.

Cara rapped again, a more complicated rhythm, but all was silent. She looked out of the window at the sea, but it wasn't shining.

At breakfast, Cara told Judy bluntly. 'I heard the noises in the radiator again last night. And the strangest thing was, when I made the same tappings, they were copied, sent back to me.'

Judy glanced up from her meal inscrutably. 'You think so?'

'That's what it sounded like.'

Judy shrugged. 'Well, I doubt it was.'

No further interrogation seemed possible.

In the library, Cara was pleased to see that her work the previous day had been successful. The cover boards looked good – not new, of course, but *restored*, which was the idea. Now she could start work on the pages. Reverently, she opened the book. She would resist looking through it now, but would discover each illustration as she worked. She laid out her materials and plugged her small Teflon iron into the nearest wall socket to heat up. Then, from a package of protective sheets, she peeled a single tissue, which she trimmed to the relevant size. This she laid carefully over the first page. When her iron was ready, she applied it to the tissue gently but firmly, so that resins within it were released and adhered subtly to the fibres beneath. What odd fibres they were too. When the page had cooled, she turned it and bent down to peer at the other side. It wasn't fashioned from wood pulp, that was obvious, but neither did it seem to have the exact consistency of linen, or any plant derived fibre. Some kind of treated animal skin? Yet the laminate had behaved as if it had been applied to a linen paper page. Must be that, just somehow altered by storage conditions and age.

Pausing to allow some time to gaze upon the illustrations she'd seen previously, Cara worked to the point where she reached a new picture.

Beyond the city gates, a wide avenue of tall, branching corals, like a processional way, unrolled before her. Ahead, an immense building reared. It was roughly pyramidal, but built of tiers. Statues similar to those at the gate guarded its walls. They were almost angelic, Cara thought, but for their obviously aquatic features.

She turned the page.

This building was a temple, she could see that now, and she had reached the steps that led to its yawning entrance. Beyond was only darkness. But from within, faint sounds emerged, chanting perhaps, or singing.

As on the day before, Cara jerked from the dreamlike state she was in, finding herself in reality. And didn't a faint song still tantalise her ears? She went quickly to the stained-glass window, put her hands against it. No, too indistinct to hear now. The sounds must have been the wind, the distant waves. Her grandmother used to say to her: *Too imaginative, young lady. That's your trouble.* Cara had always preferred make believe to reality. As an adult, she hid this more effectively than she had as a child.

At this point, Minny manifested at the doorway, today already carrying a tray of tea things. She came silently, but Cara was aware of her arrival, nonetheless. 'Hi,' she said, turning from the window, 'I thought I heard something. Like singing.'

Minny glided to the table and put down the tray. 'They say that seals can sing,' she said, and smiled. 'You've been looking at the pictures. Don't get lost in our old book, now, will you?'

'I think I already am,' Cara said with a laugh that sounded too bright, too loud.

Minny smiled back as she poured the tea. 'They weave a spell, that's for sure. When we were girls, we were always playing in that world, down on the shore.'

'You look like a mermaid,' Cara said, unable to stop the words. She was pushing the story, she knew. Perhaps this was unwise.

Minny's smile widened to a grin. She lifted her long skirt a little, struck a pose with dainty feet. 'You see, no fish tail. Don't be disappointed.'

'Maybe you can change, shed your skin,' Cara said.

'Maybe I can,' Minny said mischievously. 'May I see what you've done?'

Cara returned to the table and showed Minny the first few pages she'd laminated.

'Oh, that does look better,' the woman said. 'How clever.'

'Minny,' Cara said tentatively, and the woman glanced up at her, a little sharply, perhaps because of Cara's tone and what might follow.

'What, m'love?'

'Oh... nothing. I'm just fanciful!'

'It's this place,' Minny said warmly. 'Mordarras is like a little dream in the cold of the world. And there's nothing wrong in being like a child again, full of wonder.'

'You're lucky to live here.'

'Well, perhaps, but surely others choose to live where they do?'

Cara was silenced by these words, thinking about them.

Minny said, 'Well, must get on. Judy won't be here for lunch, but I'll lay something out for you. Eat when you're ready.'

'Yes. Thanks.'

Cara didn't feel like eating lunch. She worked on, part of her wanting to proceed swiftly, while another part – perhaps the child Minny had spoken of – wanted to delay, to prolong the work. Yet *Marvels of the Deeps* was a remarkably cooperative patient. The protective sheets slid onto the pages, hardly needed moving or shaping, never wrinkled, but adhered perfectly.

Does it want me gone? Cara thought.

The pictures had continued to guide Cara around the city, down into phosphorescent grottoes, up into forests of weeds. She met astounding sea creatures – immense squids who were ancient and wise, barely moving; fluttering veils of fishes who danced before her in fractal patterns; grouchy old crustaceans weighed down with dependent limpets. She stepped through a crowd of haloed anemones, which opened and closed as she passed. She came to a fan of coral in a shrine that glowed with its own eerie light. All of this within the half-ruined arches and colonnades of the wondrous city. No people, though. The sea creatures didn't count. Cara was sure there were people, but they were hiding. The pictures were leading her away from the central temple, but she wanted to return. Surely the book couldn't just finish without revealing its greatest secret? She wanted to skip to the end, but she couldn't. She was held back, forced to reveal each new picture only as she worked on its page.

By late afternoon, Cara was exhausted and very hungry. Judy came to find her. 'You didn't eat your lunch,' she said accusingly.

'Sorry, engrossed,' Cara said, 'but I'm starving now.'

'Is it nearly done?'

'A lot of it's done, yes.'

'Well, dinner's nearly ready.'

Judy walked away, and Cara followed. She paused in the hallway to stare at the stained-glass window. That too could be a picture from *Marvels*. The mermaids were absent from their city because they were up in the storms of the world, assaulting sailing ships, seeking husbands to drown. She climbed the stairs to stand directly beneath the window. How strange. She hadn't noticed before but the creatures reaching up to the terrified sailors weren't mermaids at all – they were male. These creatures were lithe and strong, with wet shawls of hair clinging to their pale flesh. Their faces were like Minny's, somewhat fishlike but still beautiful. The ship had rolled on its side and soon the sailors would drown. Irresistible arms would drag them down into the merciless waves, but not in desire. Cara could see now that in the distance, beyond the struggling ship, were the lights of home – the coast, the village, so near. And the women were watching there, in a row at the seashore, drenched by rain, their hair hanging down like weed.

No. There were no such details, just murky colours and suggestion.

Cara shivered and ran back down the stairs to the warmth of the dining room and another appetising dinner.

She was working again. She could lift the tissues with one hand and let them float down on the page waiting to be preserved. No other action was required. Simply the heat of her hand against the fibres caused them to meld. The tissues sank into the pages, became invisible.

Her steps led her back to the heart of the city. As the pages turned so did the pathways. Now the temple was ahead of her again, its summit haloed in a pulsing glow. She saw presently that an immense jellyfish enclosed it, tentacles hanging down, dotted with pinpricks of radiance like fairy lights.

She became aware of movement in the doorway to the temple, which must be the rear entrance, since she'd not yet returned to the front. At ground level, something seethed. As she drew nearer, she saw these were small creatures, which were half swimming, half crawling – very swiftly. Soon they were swarming round her feet, almost tripping her up. What *were* they? Some eight inches long, slim like fishes, yet with rudimentary limbs. They had gills, small round heads. They were fry – more developed than tadpoles – making for land. Although still drawn to the temple, she had to follow these little creatures. She had to find out where they were going and why. There were so many of them. All along the ocean floor they scrabbled and flapped, and then the safe walls of the city were behind them and the terrible dark and cold of the open sea surrounded them. The fry were bigger now, yet still defenceless. Lithe forms undulated in to take bites of the vulnerable swarm, fishes with cruel teeth. Still the survivors struggled on. When finally they reached the surface, crawling onto the land, dawn had come. And then the vicious seabirds came down to take their fill. Now, thin shrieks filled Cara's ears, as the fry were snatched and taken. Grimly, those who escaped beaks and talons hurtled on. The women of Mordarras were waiting for them beyond the tide, calling, leaning down to pat their bent knees, encouraging, *begging*.

By the time the little creatures had reached the dry sand, they were running on two legs, upright, their plump white arms held out to the women. Little girls. A dozen little girls. Thousands more dead behind them.

Running with them, Cara could see that the women were sobbing, yet still encouraging and calling. For their daughters. Birds still tried to take the children, but Cara beat at them with wild arms, screamed in anger. The moment came when the girls were within reach of the women, who grabbed at them desperately. There were trills of joy and relief. Far more than a dozen women, though. But who could tell which child belonged to who? All the women looked the same, as did the girls.

The greedy sea birds circled and screamed, but they'd

taken all they were allowed. The rite of passage was done. The daughters had come home to their mothers.

Cara woke and sat upright in bed, panting. Her hair was wet with sweat, as was her skin and the bedclothes around her. She clawed herself into her dressing-gown and on bare feet ran downstairs. The stained-glass window in the hall glowed softly, lit by the moon, perhaps. Cara went to the library, turned on the desk light. She turned the last few pages of the book hurriedly – they were *all* laminated. But she'd been in bed, hadn't she? Had she finished this work in her sleep, then somnambulantly returned to her room? There were the pictures of the daughters of Mordarras making their arduous journey from the city beneath the sea to land. One crucial aspect of the story didn't appear in the book. How did the process actually work? Did the mermen come to land to mate with the women, then took the spawn back with them? Or did the women take on fish tails and dive beneath the waves to join their husbands for the marriage rites? But when the spawn hatched, no fathers appeared to protect them during that horrifying journey through the predators. Of course, if every child survived there would be far too many of them. How cruel, though, how barbaric. Yet, little different from the way baby turtles started life, Cara thought. Just the cruel barbarism of Nature herself. The strongest survived – or the luckiest.

From what Cara could discern from the last few pictures, the girls grew quickly. Four seasons were shown to pass, so that within only a year or so, the girls were women – or looked like women. Some returned to the sea, and their sisters waved to them from the shoreline. Some,

Cara thought, must always stay on the land to maintain the ancient ways. And then a season would come when the lady of the house on the cliff would open the book and speak the words that would make things happen all over again.

Cara glanced up at the stained-glass window, and it seemed to her that the abstract pattern within it was moving, the colours swirling to create something tangible. She could see an immense creature, somehow not understandable to her mind even though she could discern its details: a suggestion of the arms of an octopus, myriad arms, a great goatlike eye, a maw of anemone tendrils. Silhouettes clustered about it, men who were not entirely men and not entirely fish. Their arms were held up as if in supplication or worship. And then the colours ran down, as if they were a child's paints doused with water, and the picture swirled into abstract patterns once more.

Cara felt – *knew* now – that the De La Meres had brought back rather more than material treasures from their travels.

Dazed, holding her breath, and in fact finding it hard to breathe, Cara turned to the very last page of *Marvels of the Deeps*. All that was on it were seven sentences, composed like a poem, but of words she could neither understand nor pronounce.

At breakfast the next day, Cara said to Judy. 'The book is finished. Will you tell your grandmother?'

Judy raised her eyes from the magazine she was perusing. 'OK.'

'I'm going into the village this morning. I'll leave tomorrow, if that's all right.'

'Sure, don't start your drive today. The weather's bad again.'

A rare moment of warmth from Judy, Cara thought, most likely because soon she would be gone.

Cara drove down to Mordarras and parked on the sea front. Through the rain, she could see children splashing around the rock pools as their mothers collected shell fish. She wasn't surprised. In the post office, she asked for tea and sat at one of the tables. The excited shouts of the children came to her ears as she sat waiting for her order.

When Sissy arrived with a tray, Cara said, 'It happened last night, didn't it?'

Sissy stared at her. 'What, m'love?'

'The children came.'

Before she could say anything further, Sissy said, 'It's half term, m'love,' and moved away quickly to the back room of her shop.

Cara sipped her tea. Outsider. They'd never confide in her, include her.

Sissy did not reappear, so Cara left some money on the table and went outside. The rain had thinned to a hardly more than a mist. She considered going down to the beach but then decided against it. They might not all be girls. They might be different ages and not all look the same.

Cara trudged back to her car and returned to *Maples*.

Once there, she searched for Minny, but the woman wasn't to be found. Neither was Judy. She presumed Mrs. De La Mere was in her private rooms and knew she couldn't intrude there. The house felt empty and cold. Cara went to the library and examined her work. *No, this can't be real. It's a story book, a fairy tale. A story you might want to be real.*

For the rest of the day Cara looked through the books in the library. Many were extremely old and valuable, but there were no more mysterious tomes to further her knowledge of what lay within the pages of *Marvels of the Deeps*. Occasionally, she went back to look at the pictures. There was an ache in her belly, for tomorrow she would leave *Maples*, and no one would stop her or ask her to stay. She'd done what she'd been hired to do.

At dinner, Mrs. De La Mere complained of tiredness, and did indeed appear frail and exhausted. Perhaps she'd had a busy night. 'I can't stay up long, my dear,' she said. 'But thank you so much for all you've done. And so quickly too! You've earned a bonus for that.'

'Really, there's no need...'Cara began feebly.

'Nonsense,' interrupted Mrs. De La Mere. She paused. 'And it's quite safe now for the children to look at the book?'

'Well, perhaps you could turn the pages for them, but use gloves, Mrs. De La Mere, *please*. I wouldn't let many people handle the book again.'

'Well, that's better than nothing, I suppose.'

Cara fixed Mrs. De La Mere with a stare and the woman returned it blandly. 'It's quite a story,' Cara said.

'It's a wonderful story,' said Mrs. De La Mere.

When she went to her bedroom, Cara was in no mood for sleep. She sat by the window, gazing out at the restless sea. There was nothing untoward to witness. Idly, she ran her hands over the radiator beneath the window. Then she began to tap. Various patterns and rhythms. *Please answer me... I will come to you. I will...*

Nothing.

She had to look at the book one last time, so went back

downstairs. The house was silent and still. All she could hear was a clock ticking.

In the library, she found the book had gone. Mrs. De La Mere must have put it away somewhere, denying her that last glimpse of a hidden world. Cara stared up at the stained-glass window, tried to interpret its random pattern, force an image to form. No picture within the swirls would show itself to her, but even so, she wanted to believe it was there, for those who had eyes to see.

IN EXILE

This story was written for the Tanith Lee tribute anthology,
Night's Nieces. *Many writers count Tanith as their greatest
inspiration, and a lot of them became her friends, myself among
them.* Night's Nieces *contained stories by some of the writers
who were closest to her.*

*In Exile was inspired by aspects of the world — real and
imaginary — that Tanith enjoyed writing about: the sea, an
outsider in an exotic land, and a touch of the weird. I thought
Tanith would have loved a story I'd come across of a bell that
had been punished for sounding an alarm — an anecdote from
Russian history (Uglich, in the 1500s). So that had to go in the
pot too.*

Mabelise watched the slave ships come to port. She
recognised the flags of *The Curse of the Sea Witch* and
Hasten Home. Behind them, *Blue Mercy* — slower and
smaller. Mabelise heard the crews singing odes to the
harbour spirits, their words so ancient no one knew what
they meant anymore, which was probably just as well.
The ships were empty, of course; their cargo had been
sold across the shining sea. Slaves were bred in the
temples now, rather than simply taken from them.

The peninsula, as always, shivered with heat, its white
rocks blasted and dead, its small trees stringy and
parched. The sun, indifferently murderous, desiccated
everything. A villa with a turquoise-tiled terrace hung
from the side of Seven Eyes Hill. The white, tiered
building shimmered, ghostly yet solid, sparkling with

quartz. Its terrace was shaded with huge awnings that resembled horizontal sails. The young woman who sat there, curled upon a stone bench in partial shadow, would never be mistaken for a native. Her skin was baked to a reddish brown, her auburn hair bleached in streaks by the relentless sun. Inside the villa, in a pale room, Mabelise's sister Eileenia panted on her bed; the air in this hot land far from home was supposed to help cure her strange malady, which was quite clearly killing her. Their parents had arranged the trip, and a foreign travel agent had accompanied them to this isolated spot, dealing with all official requirements along the way and across borders. Now, they were alone among strangers.

Mabelise was unsure whether the local air was of benefit or not, since she'd noticed no change in her sister's health during the couple of weeks they'd already spent in this cruel country. Perhaps it would take more time. Eileenia's stomach was still intolerant of most foods, her lungs were at best a set of faulty bellows, and her general state that of deteriorating weakness. Mentally, she was disinterested, listless, beyond sadness.

Mabelise was a companion who had no company. Only in the evenings, did Eileenia perk up a little and want to talk, or listen to her sister reading aloud. The rest of the time Mabelise was mostly alone, wandering the house and garden, reading, sometimes attempting to make sketches of the landscape. She had to admit it was liberating not to have to wear stockings and shoes, and to adorn her body with long, loose dresses such as the local women wore, but while the slow pace of life, and the fact there were few demands upon her, gave an illusion of freedom, Mabelise felt trapped. How long must they stay here? Until Eileenia recovered or died? What if neither of these things happened and they were stuck here forever, baking and fading away? Generally, the weather made walking and exploring unbearable, this being one of the hottest months of the year, so Mabelise could only be a witness to the land, not a participant. She watched the ships through her spyglass, a gift from her father, and knew their names.

A festival was approaching – old and forbidden, garbed in another name, with different trappings to its past – so the hillsiders were engaged in preparing the land. Pointless to decorate it with flowers, since even if the blooms could be procured they would be swiftly crisped. So the winding lanes, the necklaces of the hills, were dressed with cairns of painted stones. No symbols, but splodges of colour, the most innocent reminder of ages past.

Gazing upon this landscape, the small carefully-placed piles of stones, made Mabelise sad – not an immense feeling, but an acute yet wistful ache, like a star reflected by daylight in the deep water of a well. Grief, she supposed, for a time she'd never known.

Shala, the woman who owned the house where the sisters were staying, stepped out onto the terrace. She was dressed in a cream-coloured robe and head-covering veil, the fabric of which had an ornate border in black and gold thread. A golden ring blistered with pearls pierced her left nostril. Her lips were painted with ochre. Mabelise thought that the skin of the hillsiders was like olives dusted with gold. Never voluble, but always kind, these people had so far kept their secrets. Mabelise knew there were secrets. They were hidden in the stones of the cairns, in the faintly-reflecting sorrow in her heart.

'The girls have made ice peach,' Shala said. 'Come to the kitchen. Take a cup. You're becoming one with the air out here.'

Mabelise realised she could barely move. She felt like a sun-drunk snake, perhaps about to shed her skin. 'The ships have come in,' she said, in a voice that even to her sounded intoxicated.

Shala padded to the edge of the terrace, shaded her eyes to look down upon the harbour. 'The local sailors must be home before the festival,' she said. 'Old beliefs die slow, or not at all.' She turned to Mabelise and smiled. 'Come now, come inside.'

This was the first time the invitation had been made; before this Shala had always brought food and drink to Mabelise as if by instinct whenever she felt hungry or thirsty.

The kitchen, at the back of the house and reached by a flight of wide steps, overlooked a sloping garden that was part of the hill. Here, Shala's four girls planted onions and garlic, and tended the bent and wizened trees that nevertheless – Shala insisted – every year became heavy with fruit – peaches, lemons, olives, persea. The girls were not Shala's daughters – she had no man and no children. They did not appear to be staff exactly but were not quite relatives. They looked so similar they could be sisters, with their pale flowing clothes and thick dark hair that tumbled around their veils. Mabelise had no idea where they'd come from or what their true function was. They weren't very interested in her, even though she was foreign and unknown, but maintained a polite distance. She didn't even know their names, since Shala always addressed them as *fya*, which meant "loved one".

Sometimes Mabelise heard the girls laughing softly together in some other part of the house. She knew that if she needed them they would be at her side instantly, but other than that she might not exist.

Now, in the dimness of the kitchen, the air cooler than outside and fragrant with peach juice and rose oil, Mabelise was aware of a sense of imminence. Perhaps it oozed from the skins of the girls, from the brightness of their eyes: something about to happen. The girls spoke in whispers, still cutting up fruit at the table, conspiratorial with flashing knives.

'What is the festival about?' Mabelise asked the room in general.

Shala, of course, was the one to answer. 'In the olden times, there was a festival for every day of the year, because a god or a goddess owned each one of them. Ruka Gusa falls over two days and is the feast of Ruuko and Zalgusa.'

'A god and a goddess?'

'No, two goddesses. Ruuko fashions the flesh of children but cannot give them souls. Zalgusa distils new souls from the matter of the heavens and these are dripped into the mouths of those who will be born. But these are just old stories. No one believes them anymore. Nowadays, people simply see the festivals as a reason to get together and celebrate.'

What Shala did not say, but which Mabelise nonetheless knew, was that the hillsiders were actually proscribed by law from believing in such stories, ever since the Oords had come in their cruel narrow ships, nearly a hundred years before. All of this land, from the peninsula to the sky-piercing mountains of the cold north belonged now to the Oords and their implacable god. His symbol was a lidless eye that could see everything, everywhere and at all times. He had blinded the spirits of Seven Eyes Hill – a story which Mabelise had heard – so perhaps it should now be called Sightless Hill.

'Do you ever wonder what happens to the gods and goddesses people are forced to abandon?' Mabelise asked, her chest fluttery with daring. From the edge of her vision, she noticed the four girls pause at their work for a moment.

Shala raised an eyebrow at her, somewhat stern, then smiled. 'If something isn't real, then it can't have anything happen to it.'

The girls went back to their fruit-cutting, murmuring together, a soothing sound like the insects of evening.

Mabelise wanted to think that Shala and her girls still believed in the old goddesses, even if their devotion was no more than placing a coloured stone beside the road.

That evening, Eileenia felt well enough to sit on the terrace. Shala wheeled her out there in an invalid chair, after having carried her from her bed to the ground floor. Shala was tall and strong, but Eileenia weighed hardly more than feathers anyway. When they'd first arrived, Mabelise had pointed out politely that perhaps Eileenia should have a bedroom on the ground floor, since she could not walk, but Shala had said gently, 'Then she would have no reason to *want* to walk again.'

Shala did not know Eileenia, but perhaps soon she'd realise – as Mabelise had done reluctantly – that Eileenia feigned interest in things to please her sister, that was all.

The evening was warm, and breezes gambolling down the hill brought with them spicy scents of pine and myrrh. A table for dinner was laid beneath the awnings, gentle food of noodles and soft fruits. For Mabelise there was a leg of chicken in a fiery peach sauce. Eileenia couldn't eat meat; it made her stomach hurt too much. One of the girls came out silently into the evening and took a seat at the far side of the terrace. Here she played the *aluud*, a kind of lute, and hummed a wistful tune.

'This could not be more beautiful,' Mabelise said, taking a deep breath of the scented air. She leaned across the table towards her sister. 'How are you feeling, dearest? Is it any better?'

Eileenia shrugged her sharp shoulders and curled a noodle around her fork. This she stared at for a moment before putting it into her mouth, chewed slowly. She did not find joy in food, no matter how fragrant and appetising Shala made it. Mabelise, on the other hand, felt she must have put on far too much weight over the past couple of weeks. She was incapable of refusing any of the delights Shala placed before her.

'I hate being here so much sometimes,' Mabelise said, cutting into her chicken, 'but other times, like now, I wouldn't want to be anywhere else. This land comes alive at night, once the sun stops bullying it.' She frowned. 'I think I'm just lonely. I wish you were better, dearest, and we could go walking.'

'I'm sorry you have to be here,' Eileenia said, and there was no bitterness in her voice. 'I don't think it's doing me any good, anyway.' She raised her head and stared out at the sea.

Mabelise shivered in the balmy air. *She wants to be dead.* The thought came unbidden but sure. 'Don't talk like that,' she said. 'You're certainly not any worse, and that *has* to be good. You have to get better because I refuse to live without you.'

Eileenia smiled a little, shook her head. 'I think it's something you might have to get used to.'

'Stop it, Lina!' Mabelise snapped. 'Remember all the lovely times we've had together. I want them back, and so must you. You have to want it so badly it can't help but happen.'

'I've been ill for less than a year,' Eileenia said in a dull voice, 'but all I can remember is being this way. It was another woman all those good things happened to. They can't come back.'

'Don't give up,' Mabelise insisted, although she knew her words weren't reaching her sister, not really.

At that moment, Shala drifted out onto the terrace, bringing with her a jug of cold milk and a plate of sugared pine nuts.

'There's a moth in your hair,' she said brightly to Eileenia. 'That's good luck.'

And so there was: a small, pale fluttery thing. It folded its wings and remained still on the side of Eileenia's head like a hair ornament.

'How is it lucky?' Mabelise asked.

'Mother Moth brings healing pollen,' Shala said, 'or so our older people say.'

She's used to this, Mabelise thought. Of course, others like Eileenia must have stayed here, because a friend of their mother had recommended it for invalids. Mabelise wondered how many died and whether any had got well.

Shala placed the milk and nuts on the table. 'Tomorrow evening we'll go down to the port,' she said. 'All of us.'

'For the festival?' Mabelise said. 'I'd love that.' Shala had not offered to take her out before, and she'd been nervous of walking around alone after dark, when it was cool enough to do so.

'I can't do that,' Eileenia said.

'Nonsense,' Mabelise retorted. 'I'll push you in your chair.'

'Your sister is right,' Shala said. 'You are well enough to do this.'

There was something in Shala's tone that made Mabelise think that some words were missing from the end of her speech: *you just don't want to be*. But perhaps that was simply what she thought herself, and she wanted to believe Shala was a knowing ally. So far, the woman had given no indication what she thought of Eileenia's illness or state of mind.

2

Lights filled the village, along with the scent of spiced meat and rose-flavoured sweets. Over the western ocean, the sun descended in a festival display of crimson and orange rays. The masts of the ships were black against the light, the ships as still as phantoms, since all their crews were on land. On the plaza before the harbour, there was a bonfire, and here children danced to the music of the *aluud* and the rhythm of hand drums and finger cymbals. Adults watched indulgently but did not dance themselves. Within the crowd were the tall blue-white figures of Oord beholders, making sure none of their conquered people ever contravened their rigorous laws.

Mabelise had glimpsed Oords on their journey to the villa, but the travel agent who protected them had been the one to speak to any officials, show them the precious green wafers of permission to travel. Now, as she pushed her sister's invalid chair towards the fire, she saw them;

tall creatures almost inhuman, with skin like that of the dead, mottled with blue tattoos that could equally be lines of rot. They either shaved their heads or wound their hair into complicated knots. If there was a Hall of Judgment in the realm of the dead, Mabelise imagined its overseers would look like Oords. She'd yet to see one smile or speak, but that was perhaps because the only ones she'd met had been militia or bureaucrats. Mabelise's country was not part of the Oordish empire, but even she knew that her leaders treated the Oords very carefully. There was trade between them, and it seemed Oordish ambitions of conquest did not extend to the alliance of lands of which Mabelise and her sister were natives. Possibly, the Oords considered a trade agreement was more convenient than the expense of invasion, in terms of resources and personnel. While they were no direct threat, the Oords were tolerated, appeased even. Mabelise's people could tour freely in Oordish lands, as long as they kept their green wafer travelling permits close to hand; it was considered dangerous not to.

There were stalls set up around the plaza selling sizzled lamb or glazed chicken legs, salads, sweets, fruits and nuts of every type. While strong liquor was frowned upon by the Oords, since lack of personal control was considered the worst of behaviours, a light beverage called *kuana* made of pomegranate, jasmin and other herbal ingredients was permitted – a person would have to drink an awful lot of it to get extremely drunk. This beverage was created solely for festival times; it was light and floral and had the unique gift of, even after a few sips, making you feel as if everything in the world was just fine; it tinted life with gold. Perhaps that was why the Oords allowed it. Shala's girls went to purchase a jug of *kuana* and returned with a tray also holding seven clay cups. Shala poured out a measure and handed it to Eileenia.

'I can't have liquor,' Eileenia said.

'Drink this,' Shala said serenely, 'it's mild, and a good medicine for the soul.'

Eileenia took a sip and grimaced, then held the cup in her lap.

Mabelise drained her cup in about four gulps. She'd never tasted anything so *bright* and airy, if a drink could be such a thing. Surely, the ancient goddesses would have drunk it and no doubt gave the recipe to humanity, if not the ingredients themselves.

'You go explore with Jaleya,' Shala said to Mabelise.

One of the girls glanced up, rather startled, from gossiping with her companions, but said nothing.

'I'd rather stay with you,' Mabelise said, 'and Eileenia.'

'It's perfectly safe,' Shala said. 'I'll stay with Eileenia. You should explore. You haven't seen the port yet. You're interested in history, I can tell. There's much of it here.'

Jaleya peeled away from her companions and took Mabelise by the arm. 'Come,' she said.

They walked away from the plaza, up a winding lane. Here there were shops, all shuttered and dark, although lamps burned on the thresholds of the buildings, accompanied by a few painted pebbles. Jaleya didn't converse, but hummed softly, a tune both melancholy and uplifting. Mabelise felt relaxed in the girl's company, as if – through her song – Jaleya was whispering to her like a friend. The doors and windows to the buildings were tall and narrow, the former ornately carved and painted in dusty colours – blue, green, russet. Pots of herbs grew on the window sills, filling the night with bittersweet scent. The port was incredibly ancient and perhaps had not changed for two thousand years. There might have been blood on the streets in the past, but that could be washed away; the buildings, untouched, were eternal.

They came to the top of a hill and here there was a cross-roads. 'I will show you the exile,' Jaleya announced, rather tonelessly.

'Who is that?' Mabelise expected a statue.

'You'll see.' A hint of mischief in Jaleya's voice now.

Ahead of them was a flight of wide, shallow steps, at the top of which was a tall building, much like all the others they had passed, only far bigger. There was a set of double doors in front, high and narrow, and shuttered windows in odd positions, as if they'd been thrown at random at the wall. Jaleya went up to the doors and opened one of them. Mabelise followed her through it. Beyond was a square courtyard with high walls, again studded with dark windows. Steps led to doors on two of the walls. Ornate lamps hung from high sconces, emitting a buttery light. Leafy creepers tumbled down from small iron balconies, and there were flowers – Mabelise could smell them. In the soft lamp-light, blushed with red from the setting sun, she saw them – a host of tiny white stars among the lush leaves.

In the centre of the courtyard was a miniature tower around six feet tall and within it a bell – seemingly too large for its campanile. It was more like a model than anything with real function, the whole structure being so small. There was no room for the bell to swing.

'Here is the exile,' Jaleya said, coming to stand before the shallow steps that surrounded the tower.

'A bell?'

Before Jaleya could speak, an Oord appeared as if from nowhere. Mabelise couldn't help uttering a squeak of shock and grabbed Jaleya's arm again.

'This is Zecksis, beholder of the exile,' Jaleya said, patting Mabelise's clutching hand. 'My friend here is a visitor,' she continued in a louder voice, addressing the Oord, 'I've brought her to see some history. Perhaps you could tell her the story.'

There was a certain tone to Jaleya's voice, which did not indicate fear, submission or hate, as Mabelise might have expected, but humour. Jaleya found the Oord ridiculous, perhaps, yet there was something else. The Oord, Mabelise realised, was young, so perhaps that explained it. He was dressed in a long looping robe that exposed part of his chest. Tendrils of colour crept across his skin, like plants. His head was fairly small and round, covered with knots of hair stiffened with blue-white pigment. His features were also small in comparison to Jaleya's or her own, yet not unattractive. He towered over them.

'Where are you from?' he asked Mabelise in a thick, halting accent.

'Floriland,' she answered and then felt compelled to utter an explanation. 'My sister is very ill. We have come to stay here in the hope the warmth will make her better.'

The Oord nodded. 'Do you know the history of this place?'

Mabelise shrugged awkwardly. 'A little, no great detail.'

Zecksis threw back his shoulders – rather dramatically Mabelise thought – and began to speak. 'In the beginning, when Zamander, our great Darm Lug, sought to bring the word of the Eye to all in this region, he first went to the great city of Askilia, further north along this coast.'

He spoke, Mabelise thought, as if reciting from a script. Clearly, he had learned these words by heart.

'Here, the priests and priestesses of Aska resisted the Word of the Eye and would not change their ways. They were fighting people and took up arms against Zamander, who sought to bring only alliance, enlightenment and peace. They were led by the oracle Moora-Tet, who they considered to be an avatar of their high-god. After much needless slaughter, suffering and bloodshed, Moora-Tet was captured and executed. The Askans laid down their arms and peace came to their land. But, as the oracle was flung from the cliffs above the sea, onto the rocks below, one priestess fled to the bell tower of the temple. Alone she pulled the rope of Nilufah, the bell rung only on the shortest day of the year to signify the death of the light. It rang out clear and loud, mourning the passing of Moora-Tet, who had brought only death to his people. Zamander was incensed. He had his soldiers smash down the campanile. He tore out the bell's tongue with his own hands, so it might never speak again. He did not destroy it, but sent it into exile, here, in a courtyard of flowers. He was not a cruel man.'

'What happened to the priestess?' Mabelise couldn't help asking.

'She was no longer part of the story,' Zecksis said, meaning he didn't know, but Mabelise could guess.

Only a mad man would regard the clapper of a bell as a tongue, rip it out, and then send the bell into exile, Mabelise thought. It was not the bell's fault, after all, that it had been rung. And yet the bell had remained in legend, while the priestess was mostly forgotten, just a nameless agent, and here Nilufah was now, silent and dark and motionless. Mabelise shivered. She could almost hear that distant tolling, see the bloodied, weeping woman hanging from the thick rope, pulling with all her strength to let her people know their light had gone out.

'Moora-Tet was said to be very beautiful,' Jaleya said in a coquettish tone. 'The priestess was in love with him, and that was why she rang Nilufah. It was the only way she could express her terrible grief.'

'That is a children's tale,' said Zecksis sternly. 'She rang it out of defiance, and paid for it.'

'And now Nilufah hangs here in her prison, unable to move an inch, forever pondering her dreadful crime,' said Jaleya lightly. 'I hope she is full of regret.'

'She is. You can be sure of it,' Zecksis said, clearly unable to interpret Jaleya's tone.

'There are no bells anymore,' Jaleya said, 'tell my friend why, Zecksis.'

He inclined his head. 'To the Great Eye, the clamour of a bell is dissonance, the voice of debauched gods. The instruments he finds pleasing are the harp and the small flute.'

'Thank you for the story,' Jaleya said. 'It was entertaining, wasn't it, May?'

No one but Eileenia had ever before addressed Mabelise by that nickname. 'Yes,' she answered, 'I feel educated.'

The tall Oord shifted uncomfortably and bowed his head to her. 'Come again,' he said. 'Visitors are always welcome. I can show you the museum inside.'

'Thank you,' Mabelise said. She didn't want to come to this place ever again.

'I will offer prayers for your sister,' Zecksis said.

'You are kind,' Mabelise murmured. She took hold once more of Jaleya's arm.

The two young women returned to the cross-roads and here they stood for a moment, staring down at the motionless sea.

'Mother Ocean is so calm among the ships tonight,' Jaleya murmured, 'yet further along the coast, in either direction, she crashes and sprays and mauls the rocks. She would eat all the land.'

'They take slaves from the Temples of Aska, don't they?' Mabelise said abruptly, although she knew the answer.

Jaleya did not flinch, answering firmly, 'Yes. Boys and girls are bred for it there. They are taken across the sea to serve the Eye. It is a reminder that our tongues too could be cut out and silenced at any time.'

'It's dreadful,' Mabelise said inadequately, unable to express the disgust she felt.

Jaleya took her arm. 'Don't grieve for us,' she said, smiling. 'We are the sea.' She sighed. 'Poor Zecksis, you have to feel sorry for him.'

'Do you?' Mabelise said sharply.

'Yes, of course you do. Nilufah's voice might have been silenced, but she can dream and think. I don't think Zecksis can. That's more dreadful, don't you agree?'

'I suppose so.'

There was peaceful quiet for a moment, then Jaleya said, 'Your sister doesn't realise she is free. She traps herself.'

A shiver ran through Mabelise's body. 'Are you talking of death?' she asked, expressing a fear.

'No, no.' Jaleya squeezed the hand that was hooked

through her left elbow. 'Come, you've seen the history and it's gone. Let's go back to the others.'

They descended the hill in silence for a while, but before they reached the harbour, the music and the laughter, Mabelise stopped walking and said, 'Is this a dream I'm in? After tonight, will you go back to being one of those mysterious creatures I can't approach, who barely seems to see me?'

Jaleya laughed. 'You had to settle,' she said. 'And we had to be sure you wanted to speak. We heard you and now things are different.'

'Oh...'

'Think on it,' Jaleya said, 'The buildings stand around us, but so much was destroyed. Not a single statue remains, not one inscription. We are all that is left.'

'I understand.' Mabelise looked Jaleya in the eye. 'Like the sea.'

3

In the harbour, they found Shala sitting on the sea wall, legs idly crossed, a clay cup held in one hand in her lap. She was smiling dreamily at the horizon but came out of her meditation when she sensed Mabelise and Jaleya approach. 'Ah, here you are,' she said. 'I hope you found the tour interesting.'

'Yes, very,' Mabelise said. She looked around for her sister, and then spied with horror the empty invalid chair some feet away. It looked grotesque. 'Where's Eileenia?' she asked. 'Where is she?'

'Hush, no need to worry,' Shala answered. 'My girls took her to shore.'

'She'd never go willingly... She...'

Mabelise ran along the wall, past the quays, until she was above the beach. Here, she peered frantically, but it was too dark to see properly, despite the small fires that had been built on the sand. She climbed over the wall and ran down over the soft, spilling dunes. Had she been separated from her sister on purpose? Had she unwittingly become part of some terrible rite? Ancient gods, passionless sacrifices. A sick woman no one would be surprised to find dead. And few would care; she was a burden, a half-life.

Mabelise ran between groups of people gathered round the fires. She ran towards the water, where the sand was damp and shining, the tide far out. She saw four figures, silhouettes against the sky, right at the water's edge. Dizzy, she hurtled on, barely able to breathe.

Then she saw Eileenia, supported on either side by two of the girls, ankle deep in the water, holding up her skirt so it wouldn't get wet.

'Eileenia!' Mabelise cried and her sister turned.

She smiled. 'It tickles,' she said, 'when the water runs over my feet. It tickles.'

THE SECRET GALLERY

I wrote this story for Dark in the Day, *an anthology of weird stories I co-edited for Immanion Press. I have a great love for weird fiction, stories that tantalise, reveal hints to the light, then pull back into shadow. I like to be tantalised in this way, to think about such stories after I've read them. Some can be interpreted in several different ways, others can't be interpreted at all, only experienced.*

The protagonist in this tale is ambiguous, and akin to the Wraeththu. But I don't want to say more. It's a weird tale, after all.

Had I heard of the *Galleria Buiocuore*? Of course. Who hasn't? A hidden salon that houses a private collection of the most provocative of the *buiocuore*, or darkened heart, artists who worked in the last century. People have always talked about it in my circle, but until I met Levayze, I'd never known anyone who'd claimed to have been there. I didn't believe it truly existed or, if it did, had to be fake, created by someone who ached to make it exist, because it *should* be real.

The Fellowship of the Darkened Heart had included both hedonists and ascetics among its members, who claimed they'd "opened to door" into the *giardino crepusculo*, the "dusk garden", and painted what they'd found there. They wandered, they said, the shadow of the world, the truth of nature, its darkness. They had a fondness for opiates, I was sure. The big pictures they had displayed at popular exhibitions had only been "glamours" apparently – the true work of the Darkened Heart had never been shown in public. Some said these more mysterious works were dangerous to view; the secrets they revealed would haunt you.

I was living in Italy when I was introduced to Levayze. This was at a presentation of modern artists – a dull show, I thought, brassy and shallow. Critics called my own work "antiquated", but in an indulgent, quasi-affectionate manner. I was harmless, I suppose, and invited to events like this because I was slightly famous, with a small but loyal clique of patrons. I was also a curiosity, a bauble to decorate their gatherings. Everyone had drifted out into the garden of the museum, into the breathing heat of that gilded summer evening. The chatter, the chink of talons against glass, melted into the sizzle of insects around me. All day, I'd been aware of this country's history, the prickle of the unseen against my skin. Something to do with the heat maybe, the weight of the past in the simmering air, ghosts of dryads among the trees in my garden. I suspected this heralded the germination of a new painting within me, its struggle for growth, but as yet it hid its face.

I'd dressed for the evening event to reflect my mood, in a pale gown like the robe of a Roman goddess. I still felt odd – full of excitement, a strange kind of yearning and expectation, yet simultaneously I was bored, wondering when it would be polite to leave. But then, Signora Sanguerosa, beckoned me to her with an enamelled claw. 'Come here, Alex, you dove. There's someone you must meet.'

She bought my work regularly. Of course I obeyed, my sandals sinking into the sweating lawn as I approached.

The small crowd around her parted, and there *he* was: glorious and golden, the most devastating of poisons.

'This is Levayze,' the lady said, 'he *buys*.'

Good reason enough, I supposed, to meet him. He smelled of opulence. Levayze was his family name, but he was addressed by no other. I knew his sort and was aware he saw that judgement in me. We bantered, crossed our swords lightly. He intrigued me, yes, because I like beautiful things, but I could always see through a predator's dazzling camouflage. The temptation he offered to win my approval was a visit to the *Galleria Buiocuore*.

I laughed. 'Really, Levayze?'

But he didn't laugh in return. He leaned towards me and said softly, 'You may only find the gate at certain times of year. And even then, you might not get in. But...' A killing smile. 'I'm confident you'd be welcomed.'

Only a fool would refuse. I doubted the experience he offered me would be genuine but, even so, entertaining. We arranged to meet at noon the next day.

I dressed scruffily in shorts and a loose shirt that was carelessly repaired in places, because I thought he'd expect the gliding twilight goddess of the previous evening. It amuses me to perplex people, so they're never sure what they've got. By daylight he was still glorious – a vain stallion of a man, his pale hair falling over his face. He treated me no differently than he had the night before. He had impeccable manners and a self-effacing manner. Quite the actor. He led me from the open piazza into the narrow ways of the city, into shadows – naturally. We didn't speak much, but the silence wasn't uncomfortable.

The entrance to the *galleria*, when we came to it, was

unimposing, a cramped gate half hidden beneath draping ivy, in the high wall of a common, nameless lane. No plaque to announce what lay beyond. No bell to pull to advertise our arrival. The air there was close; the sounds of the baked city muted but for the frenzied rub of cicadas. Was there a warning in that chirring? It would be easy to think so.

'You see?' Levayze murmured. 'We have found it. I knew we would.'

Did he think me so gullible? 'Let the adventure begin,' I said lightly, smiling to show I shared the joke.

Beyond the gate was a courtyard, where tamed trees grew in pots decorated with gargoyles and mermaids. Tables of green wrought iron were set out, and chairs, but no one sat there. The paving was of pale marble; a barely visible emerald thread ran through the stone. The walls of the yard were blanketed in green, vines so clean it was as if every leaf had been polished, every stem dusted. No dead growth, no insects lurking there. Against the right-hand wall was a rose garden; the blooms achingly white, the deep foliage behind them accentuating their purity.

Across the yard, the doorway to the *galleria* yawned open; beyond it darkness. I felt dizzy, and for a moment couldn't remember how we had got there; all memory of the walk had gone. Had I even agreed to come that day? When had I decided?

Focusing my mind, for I hate to feel vulnerable, I found the previous evening in my head, recalled the agreement, and then the walk earlier through the shimmering city, but even so I had become nervous, my breath shallow, one hand at my throat. I felt now my companion's claim was authentic, and I had perhaps been foolish not to believe him.

I didn't want Levayze to see how I was affected, but frankly it was impossible to hide. 'The heat,' I said, weakly, hoping that would be credible.

He took my right elbow, murmured sounds I couldn't interpret, leading me into the shadows at the threshold.

The building was so dark within that at first I could see nothing, but I could smell wood polish, and an intensification of roses. I thought I heard a strain of music, but it vanished swiftly. There was no other sound, but for the squeak of our sandals on the glossy oak floor. There appeared to be no other visitors, no staff to be seen or sensed.

Gradually, my eyes adjusted to the dimness and I could make out the dark oblongs and ovals of the paintings hung around us – only four of them. The room had a high, shadowed, domed ceiling and was roughly circular, yet even the largest of the paintings seemed to lie flat upon its curving wall.

I hung back, reluctant to draw closer to the pictures, thinking there might be no going back. But Levayze was braver – after all, he had been here before, or claimed to have. He still held my elbow and now I put my other hand over his arm, like an invalid. His vague form seemed to swim towards the wall through the dimness, me drifting in his wake.

'This is the first salon,' he whispered close to my ear. 'The works are quieter perhaps, but a taste of what's to come… Look, Alex.'

He led me to a picture, the first to our left, and now I could see that a narrow plank of sunlight fell down upon it from a slit in the domed ceiling, bringing certain details into high relief. A plaque to the left of the picture held the words '*Midsummer*', *Angelina Cuoroscuro*. The scene was painted from a viewpoint at the edge of a wood, where the foliage was thick and dark. The foreground was almost completely black, the vista beyond it startlingly bright. Standing before the picture, you peered through tangled branches and gazed out across a sunlit meadow, which sloped down towards a farm comprised of several low, pastel-coloured buildings and a high barn with a blue roof. White cows grazed in the meadow – you could almost smell them. Beyond the buildings was a further meadow, leading to more forest, which loomed over the farm, its trees being incredibly tall. The pale stone farmhouse, glowing in the light, looked strangely *exposed* – menaced – but I was sure it didn't realise this. It was dreaming in sunlight, didn't feel the eyes upon it.

I couldn't help but murmur, 'What happened?'

And Levayze squeezed my clutching hand and replied softly, 'That is for you to decide.'

He led me on, not to the picture further to our left, but back across the doorway, to the first on the right.

This painting had no light upon it but seemed to glow softly with its own faint radiance. The plaque beside it said: *'Rainy Day' Antoine Crevecoeur*. It depicted a window of four panes, puttied into an old frame of peeling paint and fibrous wood. The detail was incredible, almost photographic. Rain ran down the mottled glass. Thin blades of grass – brilliantly, acid green – grew at the corners of the sill, feeling its way through the mulchy wood; it must be spring time in the picture. You couldn't see into the room beyond the window; all was dark. But you could feel someone in there, looking back at you – desperately. I fancied I could hear the soft pat of rain, the hiss and shiver of it, and nearby the plink of drops falling from a blocked gutter into water, perhaps a barrel.

'What will happen?' I breathed.

Levayze laughed quietly in reply.

We moved on, further round the right-hand wall. I felt that by the time we reached the fourth picture something hideous would be revealed. Tension was building all around me in that dark chamber. My steps dragged but my blood pounded hungrily in my head. My apprehension had faded. I wanted to see.

The next picture was entitled *Path Across the Hills* and was another Cuoroscuro, perhaps even painted in the same countryside as *Midsummer*. The viewer stood upon a hill path that filled nearly all the foreground, tapering quickly as it snaked away into a late afternoon. There was one bush, a hawthorn, I think, to the right, a few feet up the path, but no other vegetation except for the sage green of the softly-bundling hills, here and there lightly smudged with pastel lilac heather. The horizon seemed farther away than it should be.

The scene was empty, plain even, but the more you peered at it, so a creeping fear spread across the pale of the sky. The landscape thrummed and hummed, not simply with heat, but the oppressive spirit of high summer, that which sends travellers mad, running like hares across the fields, through forests. It was as if an immense godlike being had been painted invisibly within the faint clouds, gazing down with a satyr smile.

'What is happening?' I asked, then added quickly before Levayze could answer, 'No, don't say. I know. They have already escaped.'

'Have they?' said Levayze.

I made to walk to the last painting in the room, but Levayze shook his head. 'Not yet. The next salon.'

The last painting of the first chamber hung in darkness, keeping its secrets.

The second salon was slightly brighter, but not much. It was again circular with no windows, but here the shafts of sun allowed through the domed ceiling were less constrained. There was a smell of greenery, as if someone had recently removed plants from the room, and the leaves had been slightly crushed in the process. Again, only four paintings hung upon the wall.

The first picture, by an artist known only as Zuko, was *The Garden*. It featured a mirror in an ornate mahogany frame: carved wooden birds strained their heads backwards within a profusion of foliage. They looked as if they were being devoured by the vines. One stem, I noticed, entered the mouth of a bird, pierced its throat and emerged from its back, between the startled wings. In the mirror, you could see the reflection of French doors leading to an old-fashioned garden, where lavender grew in untrammelled abundance, and white daisies reached for the sun. There was a gravel pathway leading through a high dark hedge in the distance. Not much could be seen of the room where the mirror stood, but I knew that someone was standing where I stood. They looked into the glass, yet saw no reflection of themselves, only that sliver of summer beyond the shadowed room. Staring at the picture, I felt trapped.

'Are they a ghost?' I said aloud.

Levayze said nothing.

'These pictures are nearly all of summer time,' I said.

Levayze murmured wordless assent, then said, 'Have you never felt that fear?'

I had, but didn't say so.

'Some think that autumn is desperately sad, because it

heralds the conclusion of life, and winter terrifying for the death it holds, the silence, but summer…' Levayze narrowed his eyes. '…that is when the secret is revealed for those hardy enough to withstand it. The secret of life, my friend, is horrifying.'

I stared at him. 'This is the theme of the gallery?'

'There is no theme,' he said. 'My words are whimsical.'

We moved in the same pattern as before, to the painting to the right of the door. The gallery sought to surprise me. Here was a winter scene by Zinaida Safronov. It depicted a sprawling manor house in a snowscape, where the sky was the same colour as the land. Heavy snow bent the immense branches of stately trees that framed the building. Bulky tarpaulins of snow oppressed the ancient roof. You knew at once the house was empty, abandoned, desolate, yet a curl of smoke sneaked from one of the tall narrow chimneys. The banks of windows were the staring eyes of a lunatic. You wanted so badly to see a misshapen form in one of them, or a white face, or a hand pressed against the dull glass. None of that. Just the house with its deceitful smoking chimney. The painting was entitled *Tomorrow.*

The next picture featured a lawn, neatly-clipped and tamed. In the distance, a border of dark blue delphiniums could be glimpsed. But the subject of the painting, which I didn't or couldn't perceive until I was close, was a peacock. He emerged from the green to fill nearly the entire canvas. His tail was folded, but so huge it looked as if it would be almost impossible to drag around. A train of brilliant feathers. The peacock stood with his back to you, but had turned his head to look behind him. There was something bizarrely human in the gesture, and you knew then he wasn't really a bird, but something else, incredibly beautiful and yet in some way ungainly because he was earthed. Do you ever see a peacock fly, his tail like a kite on the wind? This picture was named *The Looking Glass* and the artist was Toby Smatterpond.

We walked then to *At Home*, a painting by Anna Winfrey. Evening was coming down over a white square house. Bare trees clawed at the coral sky around it. Lawns spread away like an ocean. The house was in darkness, but for one window, high up, right under the roof. Here, yellow light spilled out of tiny panes. You felt lonely at once, aching with it. But in this picture, there was a figure, the first I'd seen in the collection. Just a shadow, long and thin, upon the driveway to the house. You felt they weren't moving, and perhaps had no intention of going closer; they were watching.

I turned away. 'These are sad, Levayze. I'm depressed now. Do we skip the last in this room and go to the next salon?'

'Not at all. We need to see if you may go in further.'

'What?'

He smiled, guided me. The painting was huge, a forest scene, although there was little to see other than tangled roots and branches. You must lean in close to see the eyes. And then, you couldn't see them, realised what you'd taken for eyes were only green berries. There was something obscenely fecund about this picture, which unsettled me. You could almost hear things growing, crackling, sucking, rustling, slithering. And within all that fecundity something hid. And yet there were glimpses of it, the suggestion of bare brown skin that became a tree, a swatch of hair that became ivy. A softly echoing laugh that grew louder and became the call of a yaffle in the foliage. The artist, again Zuko, had named the painting *Threshold*.

'There is a story here,' I said. 'The paintings are chapters.'

Levayze nodded. 'In a way, although you may read the chapters in any order. I'm merely showing you the one I learned.'

'How did you find it? Were you invited?'

'Of course. It's the only way to gain entrance. The gallery was built by the Fellowship's patron, Cosima Giocinta, an eccentric lady of wealth. I know her grandson.'

This explanation seemed sadly prosaic. 'Why the secrecy?'

Levayze smiled. 'Oh, come now... isn't that what makes it interesting? Desirable?'

'I don't believe it's only here at certain times,' I said. 'You have a membership, of course.'

Again he laughed and said, 'no', taking my arm again. 'Come, you can go further.'

'But how can you tell?'

He didn't say.

'Oh, stop it, Levayze, you're just being mysterious on purpose. Tell me.'

'Leave your doubts at the gate, my friend.'

He led me to the next doorway, which was curtained by thick drapery of deep crimson velvet. Swags of fabric, bound with golden rope, decorated its crown. I'd not noticed it before, yet now it seemed the most obvious feature of the salon. Before the entrance was a spindly table of gilded wood, upon which rested an old-fashioned oil lamp with a tall shade. It was lit, but the flame was low. Levayze lifted the lamp in one hand, drew aside the curtain a little with the other. 'After you.'

I gave him a hard glance but eeled through the gap into a darkened room. I felt space around me, the salon was no doubt circular like the rest, with a high, domed ceiling. Levayze's lamp cast a wan glow that didn't extend beyond us, creating a small vehicle of light for us to travel in. We walked to the left of the room as before, and eventually the light picked out the edge of a frame. As we drew closer, I saw that it was enormous, the painting within it yet hidden.

Levayze raised the lamp, illuminated a portion of the picture. I saw glimpses of jewels, spilling from gem-encrusted coffers, the fingers of a long, elegant hand, whose skin was almost golden, laid lightly upon the treasures. I drew closer, but could barely see beyond the small circle of light. Levayze took a few steps to the left and now more details bloomed. I saw a shapely leg – yet apparently male – its calf sandalled in coiling ivy. Levayze raised the lamp to reveal the figure's thigh. He was lying upon a couch of flowers, on his stomach, one leg beneath him, the other extended. A wisp of shimmering cloth, hardly more than air, covered his hips. Lush, fleshy blooms surrounded him, trailing over his body. I couldn't yet see his face but, in the shadows, the hand I had previously seen was still glowing.

'Who is it?' I murmured.

'Their model,' Levayze whispered back. It was as if we were in a shrine, standing before the image of a god. 'All of the pictures are of this... how would *you* say it? *Espíritu?*'

'Were they all in love with him?'

'Enthralled,' said Levayze.

I thought of the scenes of abandonment and bitter

loneliness, the depictions of fear and menace in the most ordinary surroundings, the knowing peacock stumbling over his tail.

'Who painted this?'

'All of them.'

'Show me the face.'

Levayze lowered the lamp. 'If I do that, you'll crave return, and you won't find the gate. Do you understand?'

'No, I don't. Don't be ridiculous.'

Levayze took my elbow, began to propel me back towards the entrance.

'The other paintings…' I said feebly.

'This is all we should see. You *will* understand why.'

At these words, I felt suddenly and overwhelmingly exhausted, as if I might faint. I let Levayze guide me, craving now to be outside again, in the sunlight. We passed through the curtain, and Levayze replaced the lamp upon its table. As I faltered dazedly at his side through the previous chamber, I felt as if I'd looked for hours upon scenes of unutterable brutality and vileness. Were there pictures beneath the pictures, hidden by paint, but which I'd somehow penetrated? I couldn't speak because of nausea, couldn't ask.

In the first salon, he took me towards the painting we'd not yet seen. I struggled a little. I didn't want to see. Not now.

'Hush,' he murmured at my protests, touching the fingers of one hand to my face. 'You must, because this will end it – for now.'

'How much more is there?' I asked.

He didn't answer the question, saying only, 'I knew you should come.'

The picture was of a filigree metal gate in a wall.

Beyond it was darkness, but lamps upon the wall, to either side of the gate, spilled light upon the foreground. A figure was standing there, a woman... perhaps. The figure was veiled, dressed in black, but facing outwards, about to walk away. You could see that person was me.

When we went outside into the courtyard, evening had come. The air was warm and fragrant, a caress upon the skin. A veil had been lifted. We went out through the gate in the wall.

THE FORETELLING

A Pre-*Cataclysm* Tale of Azeroth

In 2012, some friends from my World of Warcraft guild and I had the idea of writing an anthology of essays about the game we loved. The book would also include short stories and was titled What a Long Strange Trip It's Been: Wilderness Tips for World of Warcraft, *published through Immanion Press. The tale I wrote for it concerned a part of WoW history, when catastrophe hit the world of Azeroth. The places I've described no longer exist in quite the same way; they've been destroyed or altered in their virtual world.*

While this piece will obviously offer a familiar environment to readers who also play WoW, the story itself explores themes from reality – being an outsider, suffering prejudice. The lands and races, and some of the minor characters, were invented by the game developers at Blizzard Entertainment, but the main character is an invention of mine. A curio amongst my other stories, perhaps, but it still has something to say that's relevant in any world, real, imaginary or virtual.

Anahyta hadn't really thought about possessing a tail until she was living among people who didn't have one. Much as you don't think much about your eyes or your nose, you just use them, that's how Ana felt about her tail. Like most of her kind, she was accustomed to having it on show, and it wasn't until the time she used it to brush some dew from a bench outside the Temple of the Moon one morning that the appendage suddenly became visible to her in the way it was visible to others. Her Kaldorei companions looked aghast, as if she'd done something extremely crass. All it had been was a few quick flicks, a slight wriggle before sitting down. Silver-eyed Meyla was the first to laugh, a slim hand to her mouth. 'Ana, really!'

'What?' Ana really didn't know.

Meyla shook her head. 'The tail... *manoeuvre.*'

The other two began to laugh as well.

'What else can you use it for?' Meyla asked, prompting more hilarity.

Smacking you across the face, Ana thought, but decided not to voice that aloud. She had enough trouble fitting in as it was, always having to feel slightly apologetic for being different, for being Draenei. 'For polishing my horns, of course,' she replied lightly, and opened the book on her lap, pretended to read, pretended she didn't care.

When her teacher had told her she would be going to the Kaldorei city of Darnassus to train with the Sisters of Elune at the temple there, she'd known instinctively that her impatience with authority would make life difficult. The Kaldorei, these 'Children of the Stars', were always slightly condescending, inexpressively mannered and polite, but with an underlying sarcasm behind every sweet word. Ana supposed they silently congratulated themselves for their tolerance in taking on "foreign" trainees. And she was more foreign than most. It had occurred to her that her teacher had decided she needed taking down a peg or two, and where else but Darnassus could that be achieved in such a short time?

'It will be good for inter-species relations,' her teacher had said. 'It is a gesture of goodwill to learn their ways.

And you will learn also of their customs.'

Oh yes, she had done that all right! While those who were the closest to being friends – and in truth that was not very close – regarded her as an exotic curio, and therefore of benefit for display at social gatherings, they would never confide in her or want her to confide in them. She had learned the meaning of the word lonely.

Ana was convinced that most of her new companions privately thought she looked like a demon, and unfortunately, she could understand the comparison. Like them, her people had horns, tails, and hooves instead of feet. All Ana could do was grit her teeth and make light of the remarks, the jokes, the sometimes impertinent questions. Never mind her spiritual path, it was life training in itself learning how to defend and parry against the petty cruelties of words.

Meyla was clearly intent on sport that day: 'Aren't some of your spiritual leaders shamans? I thought only the Horde had *them*. Shamanism is very animalistic isn't it? Not like our sisterhood. But, of course, Tauren have horns, hooves and tails too, like your people do, so I suppose you all feel closer to animals.' Laughter. 'At least you have a normal face, not a snout. And you *are* quite *pretty*, Ana.'

These were the kinds of remarks she had to endure all the time. A few knife thrusts followed by a slight salve that made it difficult to retaliate.

Thinking about Meyla's comments annoyed Ana more as the day wore on. She could feel anger building inside her and knew from experience an outburst was sure to follow. It was best she got away for a while, before she said or did something she'd regret. Like pulling someone's over-size elven ears out at the roots, for example.

She went to visit her mentor, Priestess Alathea, in the Temple of Moon, that place of haunting melodies and soft-breathing grass underfoot.

Bowing before Alathea, Ana said, 'My lady, I have been here some weeks and wondered if you might have some task for me so that I may see more of the Kaldorei lands. I am eager to learn about your history.'

Alathea raised a brow, and for some moments Ana inwardly froze because Alathea was no fool. She was sure the priestess would see right through her and say something about her temper, how she should be patient with others. But perhaps Alathea was shrewder than she appeared. After a pause she said, 'Yes, that would be of merit. I was about to send one of my assistants to deliver a package to Onu, the Oracle Tree in Darkshore. You may do this if you wish. You will certainly learn from the journey, although of course you must take care. The path is not without its perils, despite the watchfulness of the Sentinels.'

Ana was somewhat taken aback she hadn't had to use more persuasion. 'Yes... Thank you. I would gratefully do this task.'

Alathea smiled. 'Wait here. I will fetch the package. Speak with Lelanai in the Cenarion Enclave and ask her for a saber cat to ride.'

Anahyta had been avoiding the traditional Kaldorei mounts, because the idea of riding a cat, the most intractable creature known to Azeroth, or indeed any world where their kind or similar resided, seemed daunting at least. She preferred her plodding and dependable Elekk but had left him behind at her home, The Exodar. 'I don't have much experience...' she began, but Alathea silenced her with a curt gesture.

'The bond between you and the mount is of the mind and heart,' she said. 'If you wish to immerse yourself in our ways, then this is something else you must master.'

'Yes, my lady.'

Lelanai smirked when Ana made her request. Around her, the enormous saber cats lay on the grass, groaning and licking their paws. 'Hmm, let me see,' Lelanai said, a hand to her mouth. 'This dawnsaber, Mornclaw, is a tractable sort, good with novices. Ride her around Darnassus for a while, then use a mental command to dismiss her. You can summon her again once you're in Auberdine.'

'It's that... simple?' Ana enquired. Looking at the basking cats she didn't think any of them looked remotely tractable with their huge fangs and monstrous paws.

'These cats were trained by me, they understand the commands,' Lelanai said briskly. 'Treat Mornclaw with respect and she will be kind to you.'

'How do you *train* a cat?' Ana couldn't help asking.

'Isn't it obvious? By making the relationship beneficial to the cat. I will give you a sack of treats for Mornclaw. The secret of saber training, and indeed coercing them, is that they are slaves to their bellies. If it would make you feel more confident, practice dismissing and summoning Mornclaw before you set off, but be sure to give her rewards. Once she knows you're a source of pleasures, there won't be any problem for you.'

'I will,' Ana said dubiously. 'I suppose it won't be that different to controlling my Elekk.'

Lelanai snorted. 'The experience will be totally

different. Look forward to a swifter and more comfortable ride. Plus, sabers are more intelligent. Here...' She handed Ana a large leather bag. 'Introduce yourself, give her a treat, then mount up. Watch what you do with that tail of yours. Don't want to alarm her.'

Although Mornclaw might well have been 'good with novices' she also knew how to exploit their nervousness. She refused to move unless Ana gave her extra treats, and although swift enough to depart when dismissed, was somewhat tardy in reappearing when summoned. She would stand on the path some distance from Ana, staring at her, and when Ana approached her, gave her treats and climbed tentatively onto her broad, muscular back, would then lie down until more treats were administered. When Ana first used a mental command to go faster, Mornclaw shot off so quickly Ana fell off backwards, but the cat at least had the decency to halt almost immediately and look back. Before that moment, Ana hadn't realised a cat could grin. She hoped Lelanai had given her enough treats to last the journey.

Feeling at last she had cursory control, Ana directed Mornclaw towards the portal to Rut'theran Village. 'Listen, we both have tails,' she told the saber. 'I'm more like you than they are. Be good.'

Ana could have taken the safer-seeming boat to the port of Auberdine on the main continent, but as she was on some kind of adventure, decided to overcome her reservations and hire a hippogryph for her journey across the sea. And soaring over the sparkling ocean was indeed exhilarating. Ahead Ana could see the lighthouse tower on its island close to the shore and could already perceive the mist that perpetually shrouded the mainland in that area. She had heard tales of Darkshore but had never seen it herself. When she'd visited Auberdine briefly before, en route to Darnassus to begin her training, she'd not left the docks area. Early in her training, Ana had spoken often with the Stillpine shaman Arugoo on Azuremyst Isle, and he'd had many tales to relate of his brethren in Darkshore, how a darkness had come to them and driven them mad. There were tales of how the land was corrupted, and that the Kaldorei had to be ever vigilant to keep their haven safe. Ana loved the Furbolgs and respected their ways. She could speak the Furbolg tongue fluently, which hadn't seemed to impress Alathea when she'd told her.

Landing at Auberdine, directly outside the town, Ana was surprised to find it was built mainly of wood, unlike Darnassus with its majestic structures of stone. There was a dour atmosphere to the place; the sunlight filtered through mist. The people, however, were not as stand-offish as the Darnassians, presumably because they were familiar with Draenei using their port every day, and travellers of many other races passed through on their way to far lands. From Auberdine, it was possible to take a boat to the Eastern Kingdoms or the Azuremyst Isles. *I could go anywhere*, Ana thought, then sighed, made a mental signal to summon Mornclaw, and asked a nearby Sentinel directions to the sacred Grove of the Ancients where Onu resided.

'Stay on the road,' the Sentinel told her. 'If you hear calls from the forest pay no heed. If they know your name, they bear you no good will.'

The road to the Grove was like a tunnel: the blackened branches of the trees met overhead, and the meagre sunlight that penetrated the perpetual mist was watery and dim. Sound was muted but for the soft thump of Mornclaw's feet against the hard dirt. High banks flanked the road, and the forest to either side was dark, but even so Ana was aware of silent movement and the sense of being watched. Occasionally, a deer might run across the path, but the deer here looked diseased, their pelts mangy, their eyes and noses crusted. Corruption had indeed come to Darkshore, as it had to Bloodmyst Isle. Ana could feel it in the air, take it into her lungs like a noxious scent. Was nowhere in this world free of such taint? Perhaps nowhere in creation was, Ana thought. Perhaps living beings themselves were the blight that doomed a world.

There was a sound, like a tickle in her mind, a soft susurrus. Was that the sigh of the wind through the gnarled trees, or were they words she was hearing? The indecipherable sounds, strangely, made her feel more self-righteous about her condemnation of Meyla and her kind. She could break a fragile Kaldorei in two if she so chose. How dare they mock her.

Mornclaw crossed the Wildbend River, her claws ticking against the ancient wooden bridge. Her stride did not shorten and even without a command from Ana she veered left and leapt up the roadside bank, heading into the forest, because she knew the way to the Grove. Ana's breath felt tight in her chest, her mind disorientated. She knew from experience this meant that strong energy permeated the atmosphere. Magic, of one kind or another, oozed from every porous fallen log, from the creaking trees, from the great stones of the Grove itself. And there was Onu in the midst of the stones, perhaps rooted to the forest floor.

All trees are sentient, but most are lost in their own deep thoughts, removed from the world of the quick races. Some, however, are partly quick, in that they have taken on feet of a sort, like the great Ancient Protectors of Darnassus that shake the ground as they patrol, their heads in higher air where thoughts are clearer. Onu was an Ancient of Lore, keeper of the secrets of nature and of wisdom as old as the world itself. As he had mixed with the quick, so he had taken on a face with which to communicate with them. Branches had become arms, trunk had become legs, but when he was motionless he still resembled a gigantic tree. Lanterns hung from his upper branches, symbolising the light of true knowledge, and the foliage that adorned him was the colour of autumn, perhaps to symbolise the fading nature of all things.

Mornclaw had slowed to a walk, her head lowered, ears back. Her breathing had become heavier. She was not comfortable in this place. Ana did not dismount because she feared Mornclaw would vanish and then not return if commanded to. Onu had given no sign he was aware of her presence but when she removed Alathea's package from her leather bag the Ancient emitted a deep moaning creak from within his body. 'I have a delivery for you,' Ana said, in a voice that was seemingly swallowed whole by the thick forest air.

The Ancient's immense form shuddered and then Ana could perceive his face. Eyes gazed at her, down through the layers of her being to the memories of the elders of her race. 'Little goat,' Onu rasped.

Ana was disappointed to hear these words, because they were the sort she imagined that Meyla and her friends shared between themselves, even if they never voiced them aloud in Ana's presence. When they emanated from the mouth of such an ancient wise being, it made them worse, because there was no laughter behind them.

'That's me,' Ana said. 'Once removed from demons.' She held out the package. 'Take it. I'll be on my way.'

The Ancient uttered a series of cracks and groans that sounded like laughter. 'Child, you believe yourself superior to a goat? Would a goat cry to be called Little Draenei?'

'I do not compare myself to a goat,' Ana said, 'and for most Draenei the comparison would be offensive. I can't say I care if a goat would find being called Draenei offensive, since I doubt goats have the intelligence to perceive any affront.'

'Then you know little of goats.'

'I dare say. Look, please take this package.'

'Open it,' Onu said.

Impatiently, Ana did so, tearing away the leafy wrappings around it. Within lay a crystal bowl. Ana held it up, and when the dim sunlight touched it and evoked a spark of light, a faint chime sounded, as if it came from very far away. At once a sound like a giant intake of breath shivered through Ana's mind. The air heaved with whispers, so fleeting they could not be interpreted. Mornclaw pricked up her ears, shivered. 'It's very beautiful,' Ana said. 'Shall I put it here on the ground for you?'

'No, take it to a site nearby, and learn from it.'

'But it's for you, not me.' Ana didn't imagine Alathea would be pleased if she took this gift; it was clearly a precious artefact.

'You have questions about this world, as any priestess

should, whether she is native to it or not.' Onu said. 'Our ways are not yours, and perhaps the gods of our world are dim to you. Perhaps they do not exist at all, forever beyond the collective mind of your people, a dream in the minds of other races. But what exists for all is history, and the legacies of the past. You would understand these quick souls you live among? Take this bowl to the Master's Glaive. Fill it from the waters there and look into it. Perhaps some answers will come to you. Take care, but at this time of day, few of ill intent walk abroad there.'

Sites often have fanciful names. A tree can be given the name of a woman, because its branches droop to the ground like hair. A rock can resemble a great natural seat, so of course a god of olden times must once have sat upon it. This was no different to how things had been in Ana's original home world: The imagination of sentient beings projected onto the landscape. But when Ana asked Mornclaw to pause at the top of the slope leading down to the Glaive she realised that for once there was more to the naming than simply observed coincidence. Below her, in a circular crater, lay a small still lake, its surface like pewter in the dim sunlight, surrounding an island where stone ruins tumbled across the ground, covered in moss. But dominating them all was a monument that reared from the soil: a gigantic glaive of adamantine piercing what looked like a monstrous skull. That could be no natural simulacrum.

That Darkshore was oozing with potent, slithering energies, Ana had no doubt. They had rested on her skin like mosquitoes as she'd ridden the old road to the Grove. They had fingered through her hair and breathed in her ears. But what she was looking at now could only be the source of that etheric violation: sentinel, motionless, massive. She not only felt light-headed gazing down upon it, her eyes actually ached.

Mornclaw was not as reluctant to enter the Glaive as Ana feared; perhaps the saber had been there before. Ana herself had no desire whatsoever to approach the place, but Onu had intimated it was safe in daylight, and scrying the waters there could be some rite of passage all Sisters of Elune endured as part of their training. She might as well get it over with, return to Onu, earn his approval and hopefully that of Alathea too.

Mornclaw splashed through the shallow water, head low to the ground. The air was utterly motionless in that place, as if the landscape held its breath. Ana had a sense of recent activity and wondered if perhaps creatures had fled on hearing her approach and were now watching her from their hiding-places.

In the middle of the central island was a stone altar, covered in dubious stains. *Berry juice perhaps*, Ana thought, unconvinced. The soil around the altar was muddy, indented by what looked like the tracks of deer. What she'd taken for petrified tree roots around the monument now looked disturbingly like tentacles attached to the skull. Holes in it that surely had to be empty eye sockets had a distressingly watchful quality. Now Ana had to dismount from the saber and felt entirely vulnerable doing so. 'Stay there', she told Mornclaw and sprinkled a few treats on the ground in the hope they would keep the beast's interest.

The waters of the Glaive were still, the surface marred only by the feather touch of insects that conjured circular ripples. Ana knelt down and filled the crystal bowl with fluid, which was not murky as she expected. Then she set the bowl down upon the altar and stared into it, but her mind was in no mood for scrying. She had no doubt that much could be learned from this place, but part of her balked at learning it. Instead of focusing inward, her senses yearned to stretch outwards. She could hear every small sound around her, the faint creaking of the trees that surrounded the edge of the Glaive, the almost imperceptible hum of insect wings, the distant huff of a bear. And a sound that was not a sound, like the throb of vast machinery, felt rather than heard. Ana found her gaze drawn repeatedly to the strange monument, no matter how much she tried not to look at it. Fashioned in ages past, perhaps it represented an event that had been important in its time but was now forgotten. Blood might have been spilt here, the waters running red. There would have been terrible cries as immense forces collided. Ana shuddered. Some memories it was best not to disturb. A flash of thought forked through her mind: *It wasn't always visible; it was buried. There would have been no water.* This was clear to her now. The almost perfectly circular crater wasn't natural; it was an excavation. Someone, or something, had uncovered this place, and perhaps were still doing so. She was drawn to approach the monument, reach out a hand to touch it. The surface was smooth, not cold to the touch. Perhaps it was not carved from stone at all. If this *was* a skull, how much still lay beneath the earth? And what mighty force had been capable of wielding so enormous a weapon, driving it deep into this being, forcing it into the ground? She closed her eyes, instinctively opened herself up to whatever impressions might come to her.

They came instantly

Images tumbled through her mind in tones of sepia,

red and black. Moving shapes. A face swimming close to her through the shadows, mouth agape. A silent scream. Turmoil. The sky aflame. *All is doom...*

Ana couldn't draw breath. She fell against the monument. It couldn't be stone, too warm. A carapace of some other substance. She could only cling to it, as if it was wreckage within a storm, immoveable and solid inside a maelstrom of churning elements. The waters of the lake were circling round her, invading the land, lapping furiously over her feet. Trees were ripped from the earth, screaming. Were her eyes open or closed? She could no longer tell. Neither could she determine what was inside her mind or happening in reality.

Here you are safe. Give yourself to me and I am your sanctuary. Hold fast.

All she could see was boiling colour. Was this what Onu had meant her to experience? Whose voice was it that promised sanctuary?

The question you should ask is: do I see the past or the future?

'I ask it!' Ana gasped. 'What do you show me?'

The past and the future are one. There can only ever be great returnings. Listen to me and save yourself in all times...

There was a spiralling gulf before her, where red and black flames swirled like ink. Lithe creatures swam within it like serpents or wyrms.

The madness of desire, of aspiration, of need... all are the downfall of the peoples of this world. Every leader is destined to be flawed, to be weak, to be corruptible. Every being, no matter how powerful, craves only more power, because at heart they are afraid. Show me a truly powerful leader, truly strong and incorruptible, and I will show you a leader without followers. There are no great kings or queens, only failures who fell because they were weak and full of fear. Power could not protect them, because they could not perceive that power does not equal strength. And so the wheel turns, the cycle repeats, and will do so for eternity.

The voice was beautiful, filled with sadness at the folly of creation. It was telling her that the only point in being alive was to learn how worthless life was, because sentient beings were flawed beyond redemption. They could only ruin everything they touched. Even the most glorious worlds were contaminated by those who lived upon them. Everywhere was weakness, greed, stupidity and ignorance. The only compassion came from the most ancient of beings who had long abandoned the world; the compassion to end this diseased existence.

This is the ultimate truth. Step into the void and cast off all that makes you weak.

All it would take was a single step. Ana could lean forward, tip over into spiralling abyss, let the flames consume her, become one with the supple beings within it.

The Kaldorei mock you because they fear you. They do not have strength, only the power to inflict petty wounds.

Yes! She could see that now. Foolish, inconsequential wretches! She would rise as a mighty beast from this abyss, scour the land of the insignificant and pointless creatures that scuttled over it. Free of the taint, it would be liberated, renewed, purified.

A single step.

But no! Had not her home world been ravaged and scoured? Could she collude in the same fate for this world? Sentient beings might be stupid and weak, but they were like children, helpless and without knowledge. The flaws might not be damning but simply the pangs of adolescence, as all living beings strove towards evolution. The dark whispers were wrong. There was always hope of redemption.

Fool! Would you share their fate? Then let it be so. Your mind is mine. I shall crack it like a dried nut.

'And I'll fight you with all my strength until you do!' Ana screamed, though fully expecting annihilation.

Then, a touch upon her arm. The world expanded and contracted infinitely in a moment of time. Sound rushed in and out, and then, as Ana opened her eyes, reality see-sawed back into focus: The motionless waters of the lake, her pounding heart, the endless sky glimpsed through tangled branches.

'You shouldn't touch it.'

At first, Ana could not properly see who had uttered those words. She twisted her neck painfully, for her body seemed made of stone. Then the shadows of green and brown, the colours of the forest, took on shape and she saw a dryad standing behind her, one of those capricious and enigmatic guardians of the forests who were part deer, part elf.

The dryad cocked her head to one side. 'If you touch it you might never leave, or if you do, you'll find yourself back again always. I should know. I came here to see, but I can never leave, no matter how many times I escape.'

Ana wasn't sure she'd be able to speak if she tried. Her throat felt scorched and her hands were frozen against the monument.

The dryad took hold of her arms and pulled her gently away from the stone. It felt to Ana as if she was being hauled from a sticky substance, which eventually let go of her with an audible snap. Reality shimmered before her eyes, then settled. Behind the dryad, she could see Mornclaw still nibbling on the treats she'd cast on the ground.

'The waters are safe, drink them,' said the dryad. 'They will give your voice back to you.' She took the crystal bowl from the altar and offered it to Ana, who drank cautiously.

After what she'd just experienced, she had no belief that anything was safe. But the dryad had spoken truly. The water soothed the burning in her throat and she was able to speak. She pointed at the monument without looking at it. 'What... what is this thing?'

The dryad grimaced. 'What is left of an old lord of the earth, slain many ages ago. But it cannot truly die for its whispers live on. And as long as the foolish feed it with attention, so its whispers thrive. There are many foolish creatures here.'

'I can't see anyone except us,' Ana said, but was still unable to resist glancing around herself.

The dryad sighed. 'When the sun rests, they will come. They will never stop coming.'

Ana noticed that the sun was beginning to fall into the arms of the trees above the Glaive. She should not linger here for she had no desire to discover who "they" were. 'It spoke to me,' she said. 'I saw... terrible things. Do you know their meaning?'

'There will be devastating change,' murmured the dryad, her gaze turned to the forest above. 'It won't be long now. Can you feel it?'

'I feel this is not a good place.'

'It is not good, but it is not evil either. It is just bigger than anything you could ever think of, beyond all moral compass. If you should breathe in a tiny fly and it dies in your mouth, does that make you evil?'

'I think whatever lingers here wanted me to die.'

'There are many levels of understanding. Death is but one of them.'

'I must go,' Ana said. She put the crystal bowl back in her bag and mounted Mornclaw, the dryad watching her speculatively.

'Will you guide me from this place?' the dryad asked. 'I am tired of hiding.'

'I thought you said you could never leave.'

'It is my doom to keep trying.'

'But the path is there; we can see it from here. Just follow it.'

The dryad shook her head. 'I can't. I have to be led. That is the rule.'

'Then come.'

The sunlight through the mist was now the colour of old ale, staining the forest umber and gold. As Mornclaw climbed the slope back to the road, Ana saw that two cloaked and hooded figures were standing beside the path. They were motionless, stooped; she could not see their faces. For some moments, they watched her, then just as Ana was considering directing Mornclaw to go faster, much faster, the figures melted back into the forest. Ana looked behind her; the dryad was still following. The moss in her hair looked dry and cobwebby; her green skin was papery and fragile. She seemed to be a lot older than Ana had first thought. They had reached the road. 'We are safe,' Ana said, 'Now go.'

'I thank you,' said the dryad and bounded off towards the north.

She seemed to have escaped. Was it really true she would find herself back in that cursed place so soon?

Ana did not look back. She went directly to Onu, vowing she would never return to this place.

The Ancient inspected her gravely when she stood before him once more. 'So you saw,' he said.

'I saw *something*,' Ana replied. 'If that place was once sacred, it isn't now. It's infected, like the core of an abscess. Why don't the Sentinels guard it, prevent people going there? I met a dryad who I think was mad. She said she was trapped there.'

'No Sentinel could linger there for long,' Onu said. 'I think you must understand why. Poor Therylune, the dryad you encountered, is evidence of that. You are right: she is quite mad.'

'The Kaldorei are weak,' Ana said. 'Is that it?'

'Not so much weak as wounded with racial memories,' Onu said. 'Their queen fell to temptation, many ages ago. The wound has never healed.'

'The Glaive...' Ana said. 'It's a disaster waiting to happen, isn't it?'

'One disaster,' Onu agreed.

Ana's heart juddered in her chest. 'Will you... will you be hurt?'

'That is knowledge beyond me,' Onu replied. 'The future is dark.' He shifted slightly, his heavy body emitting creaks and rasps. 'Think long on why you are here,' he said. 'Think long on how you touched the void and walked from it sane. Think of the Daughter of Cenarius you encountered, a bright soul of the woodland, and how even she in all her innocence was blighted. Then consider what the trivial insults and hurts you endure in Darnassus really mean within the great scheme.'

Ana drew in her breath. 'I see your point; I needed perspective.'

Onu groaned, heaved a great sigh. 'They will need you in the coming days,' he said. 'They will need your strength, Anahyta. Any of the daughters who touched the Old One as you did would have succumbed or perished.'

Again, Ana's heart faltered, and for a few brief moments, she glimpsed the future like the flash of a firecracker in her mind. She heard terrible cries of pain, saw the world turn black, turn inside out. Great buildings fell in a smoke of powdered stone and the waters of the misty shore churned and boiled. She saw herself tending to the fallen, issuing orders, pulling bodies from the rubble. She heard Meyla's voice, 'Ana, I can't, I can't!'

And her own voice replying, 'But you must! Take my hand. We can make it.'

Reality snapped back, and Ana released the breath she found she had been holding. Emotion filled her; she uttered a sob, put her hands to her face.

'Return to them,' Onu said gently. 'And hold compassion in your heart. Keep the scrying bowl. You might find it useful, one dark day.'

Ana could barely speak but managed to murmur. 'Thank you... I... thank you.'

'It is not just the denizen of the Glaive you must be vigilant for,' Onu said. 'That being is but one facet of the true darkness.'

'Is there no averting this future?'

Onu was silent for a moment, but for the creak of his limbs. Then he said, 'No. It is written.'

Ana was surprised to find Meyla sitting on a bench near the flight master in Rut'heran Village outside Darnassus. The Kaldorei stood up when Ana came down the worn wooden walkway towards her. From Meyla's demeanour,

Ana could tell she had been waiting there for some time.

'What is it?' Ana asked abruptly. 'Has something happened?'

'No,' Meyla snapped. 'It's just... well... it's just Alathea told me she'd sent you to Onu. He always makes new visitors go to the Glaive. It's part of our training but... You know little of our lands. I thought... I thought the request was misguided, that's all. You should have had an escort. I was... well, I was going to give you a few more minutes then come to find you, even though Alathea said I mustn't when I suggested it.'

Ana suppressed a smile. 'Meyla, am I correct in thinking you were *worried* about me?'

Meyla shrugged irritably. 'I've just felt peculiar all afternoon, ever since I heard,' she said. 'I took it to be a portent.'

'I'm unscathed,' Ana said. 'But thank you for your concern. Perhaps us goat people are more resilient than you think!'

Meyla made some blustering sounds and raised her hands as if to deny an accusation.

'It's quite all right,' Ana said. She summoned Mornclaw who appeared swiftly. 'Well, I don't know about you, but I'm ravenous. Do you fancy a morsel of supper in Dolanaar this evening? The cuisine at the inn is very good. And the sunset is so beautiful; we could sit and watch it.'

'Well... yes, yes of course.' It was clear Meyla was somewhat confused about the new turn of their acquaintance. Perhaps her concern about Ana had taken her by surprise.

'Do you think Lelanai would let me keep this saber?' Ana asked.

Meyla summoned her own mount. 'I expect so,' she said. 'I will put a word in, if you like.'

'I'd like,' Ana said. 'Come on – race you!'

Together they rode into the city.

ABOUT THE AUTHOR

Storm Constantine has written stories ever since she was a child and first went to school. Before that, she made them up in her head. She is the creator of the Wraeththu Mythos, the first trilogy of which was published in the 1980s. However, the influences and inspirations for the Wraeththu world go much further back than that and continue into the future as she plans more stories for it.

Her other full length works cross genres from science fiction, to dark fantasy, to epic fantasy, to slipstream. She has written over thirty books, including full length novels, novellas, short story collections and non-fiction titles. Her short stories, which she continues to write prolifically, appear in diverse magazines and anthologies.

Storm is the founder of Immanion Press, created initially to publish her out-of-print back catalogue, but which evolved into the thriving venture it is today. Her interests include magic and spirituality, movies, music and MMOs. She lives in the Midlands of the UK with her husband and four cats.

PUBLISHING HISTORY OF THE STORIES

The Drake Lords of Kyla – *Legends: Stories in Honour of David Gemmell*, ed. by Ian Whates, Newcon Press, 2013

Long Indeed Do We Live – *Looking Landwards*, ed. by Ian Whates, Newcon Press, 2013

A Winter Bewitchment – *Femme*, ed. by Ian Whates, Newcon Press, 2014

The Saint's Well – *Tales of the Vatican Vaults*, ed. by David Barrett, Robinson, 2015

At the Sign of the Leering Angel – Dark Discoveries Magazine *'Sinister Appetites'* edition, Winter 2015

Master of None – 2015, previously unpublished

In the Earth – *Creeping Crawlers*, ed. by Allen Ashley, 2015, *Best New Horror*, ed. by Steve Jones, Drugstore Indian Press, 2017

From the Cold Dark Sea – *Dreams from the Witch House*, ed. by Lynne Jamneck, Dark Regions Press, 2015

In Exile – *Night's Nieces* ed. by Storm Constantine, Immanion Press, 2015

The Secret Gallery – *Dark in the Day* anthology, ed. by Storm Constantine & Paul Houghton, Immanion Press, 2016

The Foretelling – *What a Long Strange Trip It's Been: Wilderness Tips for World of Warcraft*, ed. by Storm Constantine, Immanion Press, 2012 (World of Warcraft produced by Blizzard Entertainment)

*Calenture
Thin Air
*Silverheart (with Michael Moorcock)

Short Story Collections:
The Thorn Boy and Other Dreams of Dark Desire
Mythangelus
Mythophidia
Mytholumina
Mythanimus
*Splinters of Truth (NewCon Press)

Wraeththu Mythos Collections
(co-edited with Wendy Darling, including stories by the editors and other writers)
Paragenesis
Para Imminence
Para Kindred
Para Animalia
Para Spectral
Songs to Earth and Sky *(edited and with 3 stories by Storm Constantine)*

Non-Fiction
Sekhem Heka
Grimoire Dehara: Kaimana
Grimoire Dehara: Ulani (with Taylor Ellwood)
Grimoire Dehara: Nahir Nuri (with Taylor Ellwood)
*The Inward Revolution (with Deborah Benstead)
*Egyptian Birth Signs (with Graham Phillips)
*Bast and Sekhmet: Eyes of Ra (with Eloise Coquio)
Whatnots and Curios (essays and reviews)

All books listed are available as Immanion Press editions except for
those marked with *

IMMANION PRESS

Purveyors of Speculative Fiction

A Raven Bound with Lilies by Storm Constantine

The Wraeththu have captivated readers for three decades. This anthology of 15 tales collects all the published Wraeththu short stories into one volume, and also includes extra material, including the author's first explorations of these beings. The tales range from the 'creation story' *Paragenesis*, through the bloody, brutal rise of the earliest tribes, and on into a future, where strange mutations are starting to emerge from hidden corners of the earth. ISBN: 978-1-907737-80-0 £11.99, $15.50 pbk

Blood, the Phoenix and a Rose by Storm Constantine

This triptych of novellas begins with an enigma: Gavensel, who appears unearthly. He has been hidden away in Sallow Gandaloi by Melisander, an alchemist, but is this seclusion to protect Gavensel from the world or the world from him? As his story unfolds, the shadow of the dark fortress Fulminir falls over him, and memories of his past slowly return. The only way to find the truth is to go back through the layers of time, to when the blood was fresh. ISBN: 978-1-907737-75-6 £11.99, $18.99 pbk

Songs to Earth and Sky by Storm Constantine and Others

Six writers explore the seasonal festivals of the year, dreaming up new beliefs and customs, new myths, new dehara – the gods of Wraeththu. From the silent, snow-heavy forests of Megalithican mountains, through the lush summer fields of Alba Sulh, into the hot, shimmering continent of Olathe, this book explores the Wheel of the Year, bringing its powerful spirits and landscapes to vivid life. 9 new tales, including 3 from Storm herself, also *Wendy Darling, Nerine Dorman, Suzanne Gabriel, Fiona Lane* and *E. S. Wynn*. ISBN 978-1-907737-84-8 £11.99 $15.50 pbk

Madame Two Swords by Tanith Lee

An unnamed narrator, in the French city of Troy, finds an old book of the writings of the revolutionary, Lucien de Ceppays, who lived and died in the city two centuries before. She feels a strange bond to the life and thoughts of this long-dead man, and finds herself inexorably guided to meet the peculiar and unnerving Madame Two Swords, an old woman with a history, and her own enduring bonds to Lucien – as well as the book.
ISBN 978-1-907737-81-7 £11.99, $15.50 pbk

The Weird Tales of Tanith Lee

This anthology of 28 tales comprises all of Tanith's stories published in the seminal magazine *Weird Tales* during her lifetime. Some of them are previously uncollected, and appeared in print only in the magazine, so will be new to many of Tanith's fans. Her highly-respected and influential work spanned every genre, and this sumptuous collection demonstrates the range of her versatility. This collection showcases the myriad styles of the writer rightly known as the High Priestess of Fantasy.
ISBN: 978-1-907737-73-2, £11.99 $18.99

Venus Burning: Realms by Tanith Lee

Tanith Lee wrote 15 stories for the acclaimed *Realms of Fantasy* magazine. This book collects all the stories in one volume for the first time, some of which only ever appeared in the magazine so will be new to some of Tanith's fans. These tales are among her best work, in which she takes myth and fairy tale tropes and turns them on their heads. Lush and lyrical, deep and literary, Tanith Lee created fresh poignant tales from familiar archetypes. ISBN 978-1-907737-88-6, £11.99, $17.50 pbk

All these and more on our web site
Immanion Press
http://www.immanion-press.com
info@immanion-press.com

Steampunk International

An anthology showcasing the very best steampunk stories from three different countries released by three different publishers in three different languages. From the UK, **George Mann Jonathan Green** and **Derry O'Dowd;** from Finland, **Magdalena Hai Anne Leinonen,** and **J.S. Meresmaa;** and from Portugal, **Anton Stark, Diana Pinguicha,** and **Pedro Cipriano.** ISBN: 9781910935910 (hbk) £24.99 9781910935927 (pbk) £12.99

Tanith By Choice by Tanith Lee

This collection includes many of Tanith Lee's finest stories, as chosen by those who knew her. With contributions from (among others) **Storm Constantine, Craig Gidney, Stephen Jones, Sarah Singleton, Kari Sperring, Freda Warrington** and **Ian Whates,** each story is accompanied by a note from the person responsible for selecting it explaining why this tale means so much to them. ISBN: 978-1-910935-57-6 hbk, £24.99, ISBN: 978-1-910935-58-3 pbk £12.99

Visionary Tongue edited by **Storm Constantine**

Original editor Storm Constantine has revisited every issue of the ground-breaking dark fantasy magazine *Visionary Tongue* to select the very best stories across a 12-year period, more than 30 in all, including early stories from some of the UK genre scene's biggest names, including **Liz Williams** and **Justina Robson.** Available in pbk and a numbered limited-edition hbk. The limited edition includes 4 bonus stories. ISBN: 978-1-910935-60-6 pbk £12.99 ISBN: 978-1-910935-59-0 hbk £24.99

http://newconpress.co.uk/

www.ingramcontent.com/pod-product-compliance
Lightning Source LLC
Chambersburg PA
CBHW020419260626
47156CB00007B/2468